The Sea Hawk

Brenda Adcock

Yellow Rose Books

Nederland, Texas

ISBN 978-1-935053-10-1
1-935053-10-8

First Printing 2008

9 8 7 6 5 4 3 2 1

Cover design by Donna Pawlowski

Published by:

Regal Crest Enterprises, LLC
4700 Highway 365, Suite A, PMB 210
Port Arthur, Texas 77642

Find us on the World Wide Web at
http://www.regalcrest.biz

Printed in the United States of America

Acknowledgements:

This was a novel I never intended to write. The sole motivation to even attempt it was because of a promise to a friend. However, once the first word appeared on my computer screen, I was hooked. This was, without a doubt, the easiest writing I have ever done and I loved every minute. It took me years to write my first book and this one emerged fully formed and on paper within three months. It was such a joy to write and I've never had more fun.

Every novel is a collaborative effort and this one is no different. Many others made the final version possible. My eternal thanks to Teresa Cain, Gail Robinson, and Norma who endured the earliest drafts of the story. It takes gutsy women to endure the birth of a novel. Many thanks to those who assisted me with the French translations throughout the story and kept me from looking like a blithering idiot. Although I've thanked my best friend, Ron Whiteis, many times, thanks will never be enough for his contributions to my writing. He knows my mind better than almost anyone and likes me anyway. Donna Pawlowski came through with another memorable cover design. Lori Lake contributed valuable lessons in writing and, thankfully, pointed out some of my rather nasty writing habits. I told my editor to be brutal and she took me seriously. Patty Schramm did a remarkable job of pulling it into its final form and slapping me around about an annoying point of view problem, while still keeping it fun. My publisher took a chance by accepting my books and I can never thank Cathy LeNoir enough for her faith and friendship. Last, but never least in my mind and heart, I have to thank my partner, Cheryl, for her patience while I sat in front of the computer night after night when I could have been spending quality time with her.

I would be remiss not to thank the fans of lesbian literature for reading my stories. Everything writers produce is nothing without you. I hope you will enjoy reading this story as much as I enjoyed writing it.

Dedicated to

Cathy LeNoir

An old proverb says: Opportunity seldom knocks twice.
Thank you for opening the door when I knocked.

Chapter One

THE MID-MORNING SUNDAY sun promised another hot July day. Dr. Julia Blanchard slipped into her tank top rash guard and minimalist skin shorts, pulled on a buoyancy vest, and clipped an underwater work light onto it. She hoisted an air tank onto her back and fastened it snugly across her chest. She squinted against the sunlight reflecting off the calm water of the Atlantic Ocean and inhaled its salty smell. She knew she had broken the rules by returning to the site unaccompanied, but needed time alone to think. The perfect life she thought she was living was unexpectedly gone. She took a breath through the mouthpiece to check the air flow, then flipped into the water for a final short dive before returning to the Tybee Island Marina.

The fragile hull of the recently discovered shipwreck, officially known as Project 3213-D, but lovingly referred to as the *Georgia Peach* by the excavation team, rose to greet her as she made the slow forty-eight foot descent to the site. It was a magnificent sight. A ghostly apparition. Julia almost expected to hear the sound of voices rising from the remains of the vessel. Despite looking well-preserved, she knew it was fragile, held together by an underwater ecosystem of organisms making it their home. Spurred on by her curiosity about a cannon hole she noticed in the bottom of the hull on a previous dive, she swam closer. Collapsed sections of the ship's upper decks obscured a portion of the hole and she drifted into the lower deck area with as little movement as possible. Out of the corner of her eye she saw small fish skittering away and smiled to herself. Her love affair with the ocean began when she was a small child and dreamed of one day marrying Aquaman, growing gills, and living happily ever after in the peaceful calm beneath the tumultuous waves. By the time she was in high school she was no longer interested in Aquaman but wouldn't have minded meeting his sister.

She maneuvered closer to the gaping hole and flipped on her underwater light. The hole was larger than she originally thought. From the position of the wood surrounding the opening the hull appeared to be splintered outward, exactly as it would have been if the damage originated from within the ship. She was convinced the vessel was scuttled by its crew and wondered if they made it safely to shore.

Checking the air supply remaining in her tanks, Julia decided it was time to return to the surface and leave the *Peach* and its secrets for another day. She kicked her powerful legs to begin the ascent to the Atlantic Marine Institute's recovery vessel *Discovery*, a thirty-five-foot Bayliner cabin cruiser. She watched the *Peach* grow smaller and eventually disappear in the cloudy water as she rose and gave it a tiny wave. Halfway to the surface she looked up and abruptly stopped her ascent. She saw the bottom of the *Discovery* with its sonar boom attached. Next to it a slightly smaller second vessel, no more than a twenty-five-footer, rolled lazily in the water. She couldn't imagine who the hell would be so far from shore. The buoy clearly marked the location as a research area. It and the *Discovery* were both emblazoned with the Institute's logo.

She rose slowly beneath the cruiser to obscure her air bubbles. Her head broke the water just enough for her to remove her mouthpiece. She pushed short strawberry-blonde hair away from her face and could hear voices through the hull. It sounded as if someone was ransacking the interior cabin. She pressed her body close to the hull and made her way along the waterline to the front of the cruiser. Grasping the mooring ring on the bow, she glanced to her left at the second boat. It was a sleek white vessel, obviously built for speed. A man on the bridge of the smaller boat leaned over the side and scanned the water below.

"How long we gonna wait around here, man?" he called out to someone. "Just take the fuckin' thing."

"It didn't float out here by itself, you moron," a deeper voice answered from on board the *Discovery*. "They can't stay under water forever. Patience is a virtue."

"Fuck you and your patience. The Coast Guard could cruise by at any time."

A third voice whooped, "Hot damn! This electronic shit is worth a fuckin' fortune!"

"Then start the damn engine and let's get it someplace where we can strip it," the first man yelled.

"What if I told you there was only one person on this tub and it's a woman?" the second voice said. "Think that would be worth waitin' for, you horny bastard!"

Julia peeked around the bow and saw the man on the speed boat laugh as he grabbed his crotch. "I'm up for some of that!" Julia readjusted her mask and mouthpiece, checked the time remaining in her tank and slipped silently below the water. Fifteen minutes maybe. It seemed obvious that no matter what else happened, these modern-day pirates would take the *Discovery*, as well as her computer and all its precious data. She needed to get as far away from the two boats as possible unseen. But fifteen minutes or less wouldn't get her very far. She knew there were extra tanks secured to the diving platform on the stern. Getting to them was her only option. She would be safe beneath the water. When she didn't answer a hail from the harbor master on Tybee Island, or didn't return that afternoon, they would send a ship out to search for her. She would have to wait. But until the pirates tired of floating around, and left with the *Discovery*, she needed more air.

Julia glided under the hull of the *Discovery* and re-emerged on the side away from the second boat. She heard the sound of more items being tossed around inside the cabin and a quick glance revealed the back of the man on the bridge examining the cruiser's equipment. The second boat had drifted slightly forward and she carefully made her way to the dive platform, quickly reached up and flipped open the latch on the cage holding the reserve tanks. She ducked back into the water and waited a moment before bringing her eyes level with the platform again. She cursed silently to herself when she realized the reserve tanks were secured to the sides of the cage by a second strap, just out of reach. She hoped they had been refilled after Friday's dive, but her options were dwindling fast.

"Hey!" the man on the second boat called out, causing Julia to slip back into the water under the platform.

"What?" a voice on the *Discovery* replied.

"That's it, man. Let's get the hell outta Dodge. I can find some pussy on dry land."

"Okay, okay. Five more minutes. Then we're outta here. That work for you, Pinkie?"

"Yep," the man on the bridge answered. "This baby won't be as fast as ours, but she'll move."

With time running out Julia had to act soon. Placing both hands firmly on the platform deck, she pulled herself out of the water, released the straps holding two tanks, and grabbed them. A small swell caused the *Discovery* to list unexpectedly. Julia lost her grip on one of the tanks and it fell to the metal platform surface with a deafening clatter. Her eyes darted up to find a man staring at her from the doorway of the cabin.

"Well, hello there, sweetness," he grinned as he pulled a pistol from the waistband of his wrinkled tan khaki shorts. "Come on up here and let's party." Waving the gun, motioning for her to come on board, he looked away for a second and yelled, "Hey, Carlos! I got a present for you. And it's already good and wet," he laughed.

Julia glanced at her air indicator. Less than five minutes left. She backed up slightly, keeping her eyes on the man wielding the gun until she felt the back edge of the platform under the heels of her feet. Sucking in a deep breath, she jumped off the back of the *Discovery*, keeping her body as straight as possible, hoping her position and the additional weight of the reserve tank would take her deep enough, swiftly enough to get away from the men. From the change of pressure she knew she was descending rapidly. Bullets zinged through the water above her as she moved her legs to even out her descent. Saying a prayer of thanks, she slowed significantly and took a shaky breath. She was surprised when her lungs only partially filled. Below her she saw the *Peach* begin to emerge, beckoning to her. Working as fast as possible she removed the spent air tank and released the hose to her mouthpiece. Her lungs screamed for air as she worked to attach the hose to the new tank. Her hands were shaking and she struggled to control her panic. The lack of oxygen made her light-headed as she looked from the *Peach* below her to the wakes of two boats above her speeding away from the site.

Miraculously, her air hose attached and she locked it in place, greedily drawing in air. Suspended in the water she breathed slowly and steadily to regain her sense of time and space. Swinging her flippers in a slow arc, she clung to the air tank as she rose from the depths and watched the *Peach* disappear once again. *I won't be joining you today.* Reaching the surface, she removed her mouthpiece and breathed in fresh salty air. Side-stroking, she made her way to the site buoy and grabbed it. When the Coast Guard came to look for her they would know her intended location from the harbor master and could hone in on the signal from the buoy's beacon. It wasn't ideal, but would have to do until help arrived.

"HEY OSCAR," FRANKIE Alford said as she walked into the harbor master's office Sunday afternoon.

"Well, hey, yourself, Frankie. Good trip?" Oscar asked, leaning back in his swivel desk chair.

"What trip?" Frankie asked. Frankie Alford was one of two marine archaeology graduate assistants working with Julia to excavate the new site.

"Didn't you just get back from the *Peach* with Doc Blanchard?"

"I haven't been anywhere. I came in to ask where the *Discovery* is. I wanted to check the tanks and make sure she's been refueled in case we need her tomorrow."

"Well, I got a call from the Doc early yesterday morning. Said she was going to the site and had you with her."

"Have you tried to raise her on ship-to-shore?"

"Nope. Said she'd be back this afternoon. When I see her she'll be in a heap of trouble. She knows she shouldn't go out there alone."

Glancing at her wristwatch, Frankie said, "Try to raise her. It's already after five."

As soon as Oscar disappeared into the radio room, Frankie pulled her cell from its case on her belt and pushed two buttons. Resting her back against the counter, she waited as Julia's home phone rang three times before a woman's voice answered.

"This is Frankie Alford. Is Dr. Blanchard at home?"

"No," a woman answered bluntly. "And I don't give a shit if she ever comes back."

Frankie stared at her cell as the line went dead. "Damn," she muttered. She saw Oscar return and looked at him hopefully. "Anything?"

"Nothin'," he answered.

Frankie punched in more numbers on her cell and got a recording telling her the number she called was outside its service area. "Well, shit!" she said. "Call the Coast Guard, Oscar. Give them the last known location for the *Discovery* and let them know she's MIA. I'll call Damian and we'll take another boat out and head that direction," Frankie said as she brought her cell phone to her ear once again and walked toward the door.

"Can't let you go out, Frankie," Oscar said.

"Why the hell not?"

"There's a storm comin' this way. It's just enterin' the long range radar, but looks like it's movin' pretty fast. You'd never make it out there and back before it overtook you. Coast Guard chopper is our best bet."

Frankie paced around the small office while Oscar reported the situation and relayed the coordinates for the *Georgia Peach* site to the Coast Guard.

"Be sure to tell them the Institute's buoy has a beacon," Frankie said. "And there's a GPS locator on the *Discovery*."

Oscar waved a hand at Frankie and relayed the information. A moment later he hung up. "They can't send the chopper up. It's down for maintenance. They're dispatching a cutter. Should be able to handle any rough seas."

"Well, this is certainly turning into a cluster-fuck. What the hell was she thinking going out alone?" Frankie fumed as she walked to the office window and watched high dark clouds rolling toward the coast.

JULIA WATCHED THE sky, and didn't like the look of it. If help was going to come for her, she hoped it would be soon. The seas were becoming choppier and the increasing wind was beginning to form large whitecaps. As quickly as she could, she strapped on the air tank, but didn't use it. If the weather deteriorated further she would go under the water and hang onto the buoy line until the storm passed over. Good plan except that as long as she was under water a rescue chopper or ship wouldn't see her. If the storm lasted more than forty-five minutes she would run out of air and be forced to hang onto the buoy topside while the storm raged around her. Either way, she would be thoroughly screwed without enjoying it one bit. The sky was already darkening prematurely and she watched the water for large waves. Night would fall soon and she wouldn't be able to see a wall of water coming at her until it struck. She didn't think it would help much, but wrapped one arm through a metal strut on the buoy and entwined her fingers for a tighter grip. I hope you've called the Coast Guard, Oscar, she thought as she pulled her mask down to protect her eyes. She was already overdue. Her argument with Amy two days before nagged at the edges of her mind as she tried to remain calm and focus on physical survival. The cutting words between them were indelibly imprinted in her memory and refused to let go...

Julia was running late, as usual. Amy wasn't home when she arrived. After receiving no answer from Amy's cell she speed-dialed the antique shop where her partner worked.

"Hello?" a man's soft voice drawled.

"Les. Is Amy still at the shop?"

"Uh...no. She left a little early saying she was going out to celebrate her birthday with a few friends," Les answered. Amy had been working with Lester Fields at his antique store since she and Julia moved to Tybee Island four years earlier.

"Thanks, Les," Julia said. "See you soon." She closed her cell and showered and changed in record time. She was almost out the door when she remembered the birthday present she bought for Amy a few weeks earlier. She ran back into their bedroom and pulled it from its hiding place on the top shelf of their closet.

Fortunately, there were only so many places in the Savannah area Amy might go with friends for a night on the town. After checking a couple of their favorite restaurants, she entered Xanadu, the local women's club. Looking around over the heads of a lively Friday night crowd, Julia searched for the familiar redhead with green eyes that glittered like emeralds. She spotted a couple of Amy's friends seated at a table near the DJ stand, but Amy wasn't with them. Shifting her eyes to the dance floor, she caught a glimpse of red and smiled. She didn't recognize the attractive brunette her partner was dancing with. Amy loved to dance almost as much as Julia loved holding the petite woman in her arms. It would be the perfect time to surprise Amy by breaking into the dance to apologize for being late for her birthday celebration. The diamond tennis bracelet in her pocket was guaranteed to cushion the hurt of her late arrival.

As the music began to fade away and couples drifted off the dance floor, Julia stopped in her tracks. Amy was still clinging to her slender brunette dance partner as they talked intently to one another. Sweeping an arm around Amy's waist, the woman led her from the floor. Amy was wearing Julia's favorite dress, a sapphire blue silk dress that clung seductively in all the right places. As Julia watched, Amy held the woman's hand and strolled with her toward the back of the club. She followed the two women, easily remaining out of sight in the crowd. When they reached a far corner of the club, the stranger turned Amy around and pressed her against the wall, kissing her in a smoldering, passionate kiss that seemed to last an eternity. Although stunned, Julia felt as if her feet had grown roots, keeping her bound to the floor where she stood. What was she thinking? Amy needed to be rescued from the woman's clutches. When she finally took a step forward, she stopped again as Amy reached around the woman and ran her hands over her ass, pulling her closer and into an even deeper kiss. Clearly the other woman's advances were not unwanted and Amy had no desire to be rescued.

Unable to watch her lover and the brunette grope one another any longer, Julia spun around and pushed her way through the pulsing throng and left the club. She jerked her truck door open and jumped in, fighting back the tears threatening to spill down her cheeks. Her hands gripped the steering wheel tightly and she rested her forehead on her white knuckles. She didn't know what to do. She had been dumped before, but as far as she knew she had never been cheated on. Surely it was a mistake and Amy would have a logical explanation. Maybe she was drunk. Maybe the woman slipped something into her drink. Maybe she was just fucking around behind Julia's back! Slamming her hand against the steering wheel, anger quickly replaced disbelief. Julia turned the key in the ignition and slowly drove home.

She sat in the dark in her favorite chair mentally reliving the last six years with Amy and their life together. The memory of Amy's touch against her skin, the melting softness in Amy's eyes as she succumbed to her passion and desire. All of it brought burning, bitter tears to Julia's eyes. Her vision seemed to be the same as it was beneath the water while she was diving. Only now she was drowning on dry land, the air forced from her lungs by the pressure of betrayal and loss. She sat, unmoving, staring blankly at the walls around her. Sitting in the dark gave her time to think without being distracted by the objects around her. She knew they were there, of course, but didn't have to analyze the patterns in the furniture fabric or the uneven nap of the carpeting. In the dark, her senses were heightened. She heard the fronds of the palm trees in the front yard of her home rustling against one another in the soft Georgia breeze. She smelled the heat of her anger rising from her body, mingling with the familiar scent of...home. She felt her pulse change as her thoughts wandered aimlessly from one memory to another. She felt incredible loneliness welling up inside her and wanted it to go away. Leaning her head back against the soft back of her chair she finally dozed off.

The clicking sound of a key turning in the lock of the front door jolted Julia from her dreamless sleep. Shifting her eyes quickly around the room she watched the door quietly open and saw Amy's body outlined in the door frame by a feeble streetlight.

"Did you have a good time tonight?" Julia asked, the sound of her voice steady and low as it cut through the darkness.

"Jesus Christ!" Amy said, spinning around. "You scared the shit out of me, Julia. Why are you sitting there in the dark?" Amy flipped on the light in the entry and slipped out of her shoes, bending down to pick them up. Julia blinked against the sudden eruption of light.

"Waiting for you, of course," she said calmly, pushing her body up from the chair.

"When you didn't come home, I decided to go to dinner and the club with a couple of friends," Amy shrugged. "Was your dive successful?"

"Yeah." Julia shifted her weight from one foot to another and watched Amy walk toward her. She loved the seductive way Amy's hips moved when she walked. A glance at the antique clock hanging in the entryway told her it was nearly three in the morning. Amy looked as though nothing unusual had happened, as if she hadn't been screaming a new lover's name in ecstasy an hour or two earlier. She stopped in front of Julia and trailed a hand down her arm. Continuing the charade, she stepped into Julia to grace her with a kiss.

"Who is she?" Julia asked coldly, pushing her away.

"Who?"

"I saw you together, Amy. At the club. Who the fuck is she?" she seethed.

"No one. Just someone I met." Amy shrugged as she turned away.

"Was she good?"

"Good enough," Amy answered, looking at Julia over her shoulder. "And she was there, which is more than I could say for you."

"I was working!" Julia stormed.

"You're always working, Julia. Did you expect me to be waiting for you to come home from your little sea adventure, wearing an apron and stirring a pot of soup to warm you like a good little mariner's wife?"

"That's ridiculous, Amy. You know how important my work is to me." Julia fought to remain civil, waiting for Amy's logical explanation. "I called, but you didn't pick up."

"You completely forgot today is my birthday, didn't you?"

Julia didn't answer and just stared at Amy.

"Didn't you!" Amy demanded.

"And that made it all right for you to go out and fuck someone else?"

When Amy finally spoke, her voice was cold, her eyes dark. "It's not like it's the first time, Julia. It's just the first time I've been caught."

Julia opened her mouth to speak, but no sound came out. Amy's matter-of-fact admission sucked the air from her lungs. She watched silently as Amy walked toward the bedroom — their bedroom — undressing as she went. By the time Julia numbly followed her, she found a sight that should have enflamed her passions, but now repelled her.

"Why did you do it, Amy? You knew I'd be there for your birthday even if I was late. Did you want me to catch you?"

"And what if I did? It's the only way I can get you to notice me or what I'm doing!"

"You've always known the demands of my job. The excavation of the *Peach* will make my career into what we've always dreamed it would be."

"And of course that's so much more important to you than I am!" Amy's voice began to rise, challenging Julia to deny the accusation.

"At least I'm not fucking it behind your back!" Julia shouted. "How many others have there been?"

"This is bullshit!" Amy yelled back. "There are plenty of other women who would be more than glad to come home to me every night."

"Then go find one of them," Julia said. "Take what the hell you want, but I want you gone by the time I get back Sunday afternoon." She couldn't believe she found the strength to utter those words and turned away resolutely.

"Don't be ridiculous, Julia. This is my home, too," Amy snorted as she followed Julia down the hallway.

"The mortgage is in my name, babe. Don't make me call the sheriff to remove you," Julia snapped as she turned once again to leave. Pulling her truck keys from her pocket, she remembered the bracelet. Jerking it from her pocket she said, "Oh. By the way, Happy fuckin' Birthday." She tossed the gift-wrapped box to Amy, opened the front door, and stepped into the damp pre-dawn fog moving inland from the ocean not far away.

The swells of the sea around her gradually strengthened and snapped Julia from her thoughts. The wind caused the buoy to sway violently from side to side as it began to dance around in the water, occasionally driving her under water unexpectedly before she could take a breath. Her arms ached and she was certain her body would be covered with bruises from being slammed into the metal marker repeatedly. When she couldn't stand another minute of the pounding, she pressed the mouthpiece into her mouth and reached beneath the buoy to grab its anchor line. As she went beneath the churning water it was calmer, but she was forced to hold the line with both hands to keep from losing her grip as the buoy was tossed around. Surrounded by the blackness, she shivered. As night fell the surface winds were cooling the water rapidly and forcing colder water from farther east toward shore. She shivered, wishing she had worn her full diving suit. After a few minutes of catching her breath, she pulled herself back to the surface. She wasn't sure how much air remained in her tank and was afraid to go deeper seeking calmer water. She hoped the storm was nothing more than a squall line and would pass over quickly, but as the minutes ticked by it seemed to be intensifying. She was exhausted from her fight with the buoy and readjusted her hold on it several times. She called upon her anger at Amy to take her mind off the numbing cold.

"Goddamn you Amy!" she shouted against the increasing wind. "This is all your fucking fault!" Amy never understood that Julia's work was more than merely a paycheck. If they hadn't argued she wouldn't be bouncing around in the churning waters of the Atlantic Ocean like a fucking cork, fighting not to be killed by the one thing she loved.

As she hung on, wondering if help would arrive, she felt her body lifted out of the water and slammed against the buoy. She was dazed as her head struck the strut she was clinging to. Plan B, she thought. I can either give up the fight and drown or let myself be beaten to death by this goddamn buoy. The thought that her death was only a matter of time seized control of her mind and her eyes stung from the salt of her own tears. She loved the ocean and respected its awesome power, but held no desire to become fish food. Maybe she could use the last of her air to go down to the *Peach*, tying her body to it so it would be found — eventually. In the midst of her thinking, she felt the buoy pull her up and tried to adjust her grip to make it stronger. Before she could interlock her fingers the bottom fell from beneath her as the buoy slid down a wall of water. When it rose beneath her again, she was jolted by slamming into the wave and lost her hold on the strut. Biting down on the mouthpiece, she dove and tried to locate the anchor line. Her breathing came in panicky gasps rather than slow smooth breaths, using up her air supply too quickly, but she couldn't stop the terror growing inside. She slung her arms around, praying she would find her lifeline again. She kicked her legs and popped to the surface. She removed the mouthpiece, gulping in water from the sea and rain from the sky.

In what seemed like a miracle, the wind began to taper off and the swells she bobbed in became less violent. She treaded water, using her dwindling air supply as little as possible. There was nothing she could do other than wait for the sun to come up and hope she hadn't been carried out of sight of the buoy.

Chapter
Two

AS THE SUN began to make its spectacular appearance Monday morning, Julia couldn't believe she was still alive. Most of her air supply was depleted during the long night and she was exhausted. It would be hard enough to stay afloat without dragging along extra useless weight. She connected the hose from her air tank to her buoyancy vest, using the last of her air to inflate its air cells before removing the tank from her body. The sea around her had returned to its pre-storm calm, but the buoy was nowhere in sight. She had no idea how far the current of the Gulf Stream might have carried her. Trying to find one person in the thousands of square miles of the Atlantic Ocean made looking for a needle in a haystack seem like child's play. In the calm water, she flipped onto her back and took a deep breath as she pushed her dive mask onto the top of her head. She had been a world champion floater as a kid, even known to occasionally fall asleep in her parent's pool while floating on her back. The buoyancy vest would help her stay afloat, at least for a while. If she happened to hear a plane or see a ship in the distance, she could use the glass-like surface of her mask to reflect the sunlight as a signal.

She squinted into the sun, trying to find identifiable shapes in the scattered clouds and wondered if anyone was looking for her. She was still fairly certain she would die at sea, but then she hadn't thought she'd make it through the night. She figured she could survive a week without food, but would probably die of thirst even though she was surrounded by millions of gallons of water. *Where is Aquaman's sister when I need her?* She laughed out loud. *Hell, at this point I'd fuck his mother for a drink of fresh water!*

"You can have a drink after Mass," her father told her every Sunday. Then, sure enough, Talbot Blanchard stopped on the way home and bought his little girl a milk shake or a fountain drink at the A & W near their home in Richmond. Those were good days. Church would just last a little longer this time was all. She smiled. *I can wait, Daddy. I can. You'll be proud of me.* The sun made her sleepy and she sank into the embrace of the world's largest water bed.

"WHAT DO YOU mean you can't find her?" Frankie snapped. "It's Tuesday for Christsake! We gave you her last known location!"

"There wasn't a trace of her anywhere near the site, Miss Alford. We've done low level flights over the entire area," the Coast Guard officer stated. "I'm sorry, but it's extremely unlikely she could have survived Sunday's storm. Her body could have been carried miles outside the search area."

The officer's use of the word "body" struck Frankie like a slap in the face. "You can't call off the search," she said, tears pooling in her eyes.

"I'm sorry, ma'am."

"What about the GPS on the *Discovery*?" Damian asked, his arm encircling Frankie's slumping shoulders.

"We picked up a weak signal briefly, but it was far outside the search area."

"Well, perhaps she tried to get away from the storm by taking a heading away from it," Frankie sneered. "Did ya happen to think of that one and plug it into your computer algorithm?"

"The signal came from just north of St. Augustine. If she made it safely to the coast, wouldn't she have called? She could have made it back to Tybee faster. In all honesty we believe someone hijacked her cruiser. Dr. Blanchard may have been killed in the process"

Frankie rubbed her face helplessly. "So that's it then?" she finally asked. She hadn't slept much since Saturday night and was well beyond her exhaustion level.

"I'm sor—"

"I know. You're sorry, Commander. You will notify us if wreckage or anything...else is found?"

"Immediately."

"What are we gonna do now, Frankie?" Damian asked as soon as the officer left the Institute's offices.

"The same thing Julia would have done. Continue the excavation of the *Peach*," Frankie said, striding out of the office.

SHE COULDN'T REMEMBER how many sunrises had come and gone, but knew enough had passed for her to be in serious trouble. Small cracks were beginning to open on her lips and burned continuously from contact with salt water. Surrounded by billions of gallons of water, she was dehydrating from the lack of fresh water. Even swirling sea water around in her mouth to moisten it led to dry heaves. She couldn't remember the last time she had been so hungry, but lack of water would kill her long before starvation had a chance.

She tried to guess where she might be. Since the storm swept her away from the *Peach* site she had seen no landmarks to give her a clue to her location. If she had been caught by the Gulf Stream she was floating north. If the storm surge had sucked her farther away from shore, she was aimlessly floating somewhere in the Atlantic, a dot surrounded by endless miles of water. If she had lost her grip on the marker buoy sooner, the storm might have carried her closer to shore. If, if, if! None of those thoughts would save her now. She was exhausted. Her muscles ached and only her knowledge of survival skills if lost at sea was keeping her alive.

She leaned her head back and squeezed her eyes shut. Every logical thought running through her mind told her she would never survive this ordeal, and yet she couldn't make herself give up. What had it all been for? Had her hard work and dedication been worth the loss of everything, perhaps even her life? Hazy memories of her proudest moment as a marine archaeologist bobbed through her memory. Was it all worth it?

Slowly her mind drifted back to a few days earlier when she stepped onto the deck of the *Discovery*, gently rolling on the waves making their way toward the Georgia coastline near Savannah, ten miles to the west. Watching the crew of the recovery ship prepare to bring their precious cargo into the sunlight for the first time in over a hundred and fifty years filled her with anticipation. Eighteen months earlier the Georgia Marine Archaeology Institute was contacted with news of a possible new shipwreck site. Images made while Coast Guard cutters tested their sonar booms revealed an outline indicating where a ship had gone down.

She walked to the railing and peered into the blue-green depths beneath her. Her short-cropped sun-bleached hair fluttered in the mild breeze wafting off the water. She could see the once huge wooden ship in her mind's eye. The year and a half long excavation revealed, a little at a time, the remnants of a three-masted wooden ship. While nothing as impressive as chests full of gold and precious jewels were discovered, to Julia the cannons and other wreckage debris near the ship represented a priceless link to the past. *What happened to you? How many died along with you?* Only time and patience could unveil valuable clues to the origin and history of the mysterious ship.

JULIA'S EYES POPPED open as a small wave of sea water crested over her head. She coughed and wiped the water away from her eyes, scanning the horizon once again. Was it worth it? she thought. "You're damn right it was!" she said to the emptiness around her. She smiled as she remembered the rest of the best and worst day of her life. "I'd do it again without a second thought."

"You can see her in your sleep, can't you?" a voice from behind Julia said.

Without looking back, she answered. "I do dream about her. She calls to me like a lover in my sleep."

"Well, I don't know if I'd go quite that far." Frankie Alford said as she leaned against the rail beside Julia. "Scared?"

Julia smiled as she looked out over the water. "A little. This is the biggest project I've ever been responsible for. I don't want to fuck it up, Frankie."

"You're doing great. You've been inordinately careful, painfully slow and precise, annoyingly demanding and critical and I won't even start on your micro-managerial skills."

"Run out of negative adverbs for my work methods?"

"Pretty much," Frankie chuckled. She turned Julia to face her and added, "I've learned how it's supposed to be done from you, Dr. Blanchard. It's been worth taking it slow and today is the pay-off we've all been waiting for. Now get going so that damn cannon doesn't have to wait another century."

Laughing, Julia pulled the rubberized hood of her diving suit over her head and tucked in stray strands of hair while striding toward the diving platform at the rear of the ship. The day began as slightly overcast, but the sun finally won the battle, making the peaks of the small waves around the *Discovery* shimmer. Julia climbed down the four-step aluminum ladder from the main deck to the diving platform, joining the second member of the project dive team, Damian Lorenz. Like Frankie, he was a volunteer graduate student working on the marine excavation.

"Everything set?" she asked.

"Ready to rock and roll, Doc," Damian answered with a boyish grin. Despite his shaggy head of black hair and generally unkempt appearance, Damian proved to be a serious marine archaeologist with an ingrained belief that work should be fun or it shouldn't be done at all.

Julia slung an air tank onto her back and snapped the belt around her waist. She brought the mouthpiece to her mouth to test the flow of air. She sat on the lid of a storage compartment and slid her feet into her flippers. Julia then made her way to the rear edge of the platform where she knelt down and dipped her mask into the water and pulled it on, letting it sit on her forehead. She pivoted around with her back to the water and smiled up at Frankie who was leaning on the railing of the main deck and gave her a thumbs up. She pulled her mask down, adjusted it slightly and inserted her mouthpiece. With a nod toward Damian she flipped off the platform into the silent world below the *Discovery*.

Approximately five fathoms separated the final resting place of the ship and the ocean's surface. Even though the underwater world she loved was beautiful in many ways, Julia remained wary as she and Damian made their four-story descent. It always surprised her to read about the relatively shallow depths in which many shipwrecks were discovered. One well-preserved Spanish galleon was discovered in only twelve feet of water off the Texas coast. *The Peach* was thirty-six feet deeper. Over time, sediment flowing into the Atlantic from the Savannah River estuary and bottom soil carried into shore by Atlantic storm surges successfully entombed the large ship.

Sunlight filtered through the water, becoming dimmer as the depth increased. With each descent Julia was shocked when the now-exposed vessel unexpectedly came into view. One moment there was nothing. The next the graceful ribs of the inner hull rose from the murky waters like the ribs of an ancient mammoth. Perhaps it was a blessing that the Continental Shelf was sparsely populated by either vegetation or more than small schools of fish. Only occasionally would they spot a nurse shark or a barracuda, but the team's presence didn't seem to provoke them into more than mild curiosity.

The Peach wasn't her first shipwreck, but was, without a doubt, the oldest and the first for which she was chosen lead conservator. Most marine archaeologists worked a lifetime without getting the privilege to see or touch a glimpse into a distant past from the beginning. *I'll do right by you, old girl,* she thought with a smile. *Thank you.*

IN THE DAYS following Julia's disappearance, Frankie and Damian continued bringing artifacts up from the ocean floor. Damian was exhausted when he dragged himself onto the diving platform on the stern of their new cruiser. At first he resisted the idea of continuing the dives, but Frankie convinced him they owed it to Julia's memory to complete her last project. As he leaned against the hull to catch his breath, Frankie strapped on a new tank.

"You need to give this a rest for a while, Frankie," he said as he squinted up at her, sea water dripping down his face. "The *Peach* has been down there two centuries. She isn't going anywhere."

"This will be my last dive. I thought I spotted something the last time down and want to check it out before I forget where it was," Frankie said as she tightened the strap across her chest holding the tanks in place. "I've still got a couple of hours of good light left."

"Didn't you mark it?"

"I was on my ascent and just caught a glimpse of something."

"Probably another fuckin' beer can or license plate," Damian groused as he unhooked the tank strap across his chest and took a deep breath of fresh air.

Shoving the mouthpiece between her lips, Frankie flipped into the water and began one more trip to the *Peach*. She knew Julia reveled in working on the excavation, but Julia was gone. *The Peach* was nothing more than a grave site. Now it had taken yet another victim and Frankie was beginning to hate it.

She couldn't remember what her depth had been when she saw the object that caught her attention as she dropped deeper, slowly scanning the ocean floor below. Whatever she saw had been perhaps two or three yards from the main excavation site. As soon as the *Peach* loomed up from its final resting place on the bottom, Frankie stopped her descent and looked to the right, but saw nothing. Remaining at the same depth she moved slightly, looking up at the bottom of the *Discovery II.* Shafts of sunlight penetrated the water, wavering in the gentle movement of the water. She thought she was about in the same position she had been when she saw the object the first time. Turning her head back toward the seabed she saw it, caught for a second in the dim wavering light. Swimming lower, her eyes never left the spot. When she finally reached the location, she got her mask as close as she could before tentatively moving the sediment away with the tips of her fingers.

Reaching to her waist belt, Frankie switched on a small waterproofed work light to examine the object. It was metallic and even though it was round, it didn't appear to be ammunition, or an ever-present beer can. The portion not buried in sediment was heavily pitted, but seemed to be in fair condition. Using a plastic probe, Frankie followed the edge of the object and began carefully moving more sediment away until she saw what appeared to be a metal tankard of some type. *Probably pewter.* It would have been a common item aboard such an old ship. Afraid she might damage it by pulling it from the location, she continued removing it from its tomb. It was amazingly intact and she shined the work light over its surface and examined it carefully. Perhaps a clue to a crew member, she thought as she placed the drinking vessel carefully into a mesh bag attached to her work belt. Marking the spot with a bright yellow plastic flag, Frankie began her rise back to the surface. She wished Julia could have been there to see her discovery. She blinked away tears as the *Peach* disappeared below her once again.

THE DAY AFTER the storm passed, the sun had felt good against Julia's face, warming her body. Now, two days later, the summer sunlight reflecting off the water became the enemy. The muscles in her face ached from squinting against the glare to prevent blindness. The skimpy neoprene rash suit left her arms and shoulders exposed to the sun, as well as her upper legs. Even if she ducked her head in the water to cool off, the sun quickly turned it into hot water against her already burning skin. While her torso remained relatively cool in the water, her head, arms, and legs were continuously exposed. For the first day or so she managed to float effortlessly. But by the end of the second day, she could feel the tightness of her skin as it dried and burned. The cold water which accompanied the storm was gradually replaced by temperatures in the lower eighties. Even though the water was warmer, it was still less than her body temperature. She could burn to a crisp under the glaring sun while suffering from hypothermia. As the sun began its descent once again, she was shocked as she brought her hand up to wipe sea water away from her face. Blisters had begun to form on the flesh on the backs of her hands. If the blisters broke open and salt water got under her skin—she didn't want to think about how painful it could be.

Gingerly she touched her face with her finger tips. Her skin felt hot and, as tightly as the skin was pulled, she suspected her face may have begun to swell. The sun beat relentlessly down on her head and shoulders and the water around her began to noticeably heat as well. She treaded water and spun in a tight circle, looking for anything on the horizon. Anything outside the sight of land would have to be at least as large as the *Discovery*. But there was nothing.

She was a strong swimmer, but her arm and leg muscles screamed with fatigue, forcing her onto her back again. Her eyelids ached, but on her back she couldn't keep her eyes open and expose them to the blinding sunlight. Squeezing them shut eventually began to give her a headache. *I have to take my mind somewhere else. I can't keep thinking about every little ache and pain, damn it! Just suck it up!* But every part of her hurt too much to ignore.

She never saw the wave coming before it curled over her, catching her just as she exhaled and pushing her beneath the water. With little air in her lungs and precious moments slipping away, she became disoriented and couldn't locate the surface. Panicking, she flailed her arms and legs, forcing her eyes open, enduring the biting salty sting of the water that blurred her vision. She wanted to breathe the air one more time. A sliver of light pierced the water and she fought the impulse to open her mouth and take a deep breath. Using the last of her energy, she forced her arms to stroke toward the light. As her head rose above the water, she gasped for air between the nauseous gagging caused by inhaling water at the same time.

I'm sorry, Daddy. I tried to wait until church was over, but I can't. Salty tears ran down her face, adding to the water around her, as she sobbed and gave herself to the sea.

TALBOT BLANCHARD SAT with his arm around his wife Regina, looking down at her soft profile as she dabbed at her eyes with a tissue, hugging her slightly. When she looked up at him, the grief in her eyes tore at his heart. Tal, Jr. and his wife sat on the other side of Regina, holding hands and listening to a litany of speakers sharing their memories of Dr. Julia Blanchard and her work. As Talbot stared at a large picture of Julia in her dive suit, her head thrown back, laughing at something as the sunlight reflected off her short sun-bleached reddish-blonde hair, he thought how beautiful his thirty-four-year-old daughter was. The picture captured her at her best, nearing the peak of her profession. Talbot was proud of his daughter although he knew he hadn't told her so often enough. He always believed there would be time for that. He'd taught his children never to brag about themselves and their accomplishments. In a strange way it made him feel good to hear others do that. Some of the memories they heard were poignant and occasionally Julia's exploits led to laughter. It felt good to be able to laugh, at least on the outside.

The Coast Guard abandoned their search for Julia nearly one week earlier. Even though Talbot and Regina didn't want to give up hope, realistically they couldn't believe there was any way Julia could have survived alone on a vast ocean longer than a day or two. She was killed by the thing she loved, Talbot thought to himself. Although not officially declared dead, it seemed to be something they would all be forced to accept.

As the final eulogy and prayers were said at the memorial service at St. Jude's Catholic Church in Richmond, Virginia, Talbot helped his wife up and hugged her close to him. Stepping into the mid-July heat, Talbot and Regina were met by their priest and exchanged a few words with the man who had christened both of their children. Talbot knew Julia hadn't been to church for quite a while, but hoped she was in God's good care now. As they turned and made their way down the church steps, they were intercepted by an attractive red-head who had obviously been crying. Talbot recognized her immediately.

"Mr. and Mrs. Blanchard, I'm so sorry about Julia," Amy said as she wiped at her eyes.

"Thank you," Tal said stiffly. "We'll be in Savannah next week to pack Julia's things and place her house with a realtor." Although he and his wife had tolerated Amy because she was their daughter's "friend", in truth their dislike for the woman was obvious. "I'm assuming you will have your belongings out before we arrive."

"I was hoping to stay in the house. It was our home," Amy said.

"My understanding is that the house belongs solely to Julia."

"I am...or was...Julia's partner. She wouldn't want me forced out of the home we made together."

Looking coldly at Amy, Tal said, "Our daughter is dead, Miss Robie. As her family, we will make whatever decisions need to be made regarding the disposition of her property. You have one week to remove anything you believe is rightfully yours. Please make an inventory list in case we have a question about any of it." With that final statement, Tal and Regina walked solemnly to the waiting limousine.

TAL REMOVED HIS suit jacket and loosened his tie. He was more tired than he could ever remember being. A moment later the telephone in the living room rang. Regina had gone upstairs to change as soon as they returned home. Tal was worried about his wife. The bond between mother and daughter had been a particularly strong one until Julia began bringing women home. Regina, however ridiculously, blamed her own family for her daughter's orientation. Always considered the black sheep of the family, Julia's Uncle Bertie was a flamboyant gay man unabashedly unashamed of the talk his escapades caused. Bertram, as Regina preferred to call him, was a successful barrister in Great Britain. Uncle Bertie waited until his financial security was well established before beginning to lead the life he wanted to lead, complete with an extremely attractive young man Bertie referred to as his house boy.

"Hello," Tal said as he rested the receiver between his shoulder and jaw, struggling to remove his cuff links.

"Mr. Blanchard? This is Detective Long with the Savannah Metro Police Department," a disembodied voice announced through light static.

"Yes, what can I do for you, Detective?"

"I tried to reach you earlier today, sir. Your daughter's cabin cruiser has been located," Long said.

"What?" Tal nearly dropped the receiver. It took him a minute to collect both it and his abruptly scattered thoughts.

"The cruiser was found in a marina near Jacksonville. From what we can determine, the boat was pirated by a group of men the drug task force in Jacksonville suspect are part of a modern day pirating ring."

"But what about my daughter?" Tal managed to ask.

"The individuals in custody say they found the cruiser abandoned and simply took it into a safe port."

"That's bullshit and you know it!" Tal seethed.

"The harbor master on Tybee Island says that Miss Blanchard..."

"It's Dr. Blanchard," Tal interrupted, not knowing why it suddenly seemed so important that Julia's academic title be used.

"Sorry. It seems that Dr. Blanchard took the cruiser out alone and apparently went diving. It's possible the boat was stolen while she was on her dive. There was no evidence of foul play on board."

"Well, didn't they think it was a little strange that they found the clearly marked damn thing empty? Why didn't they contact the Institute? They took it and left my daughter out there alone to die!"

"We're not sure we can charge them with more than theft at this point, Mr. Blanchard. They all deny seeing anyone on or near the boat."

"Thank you for letting me know, Detective," Tal said. "Please keep me informed if you learn anything else."

"Who was that, Tal?" Regina asked as her husband replaced the receiver.

"The Savannah police. Julia's cruiser has been found in Florida," he said as he walked toward her.

"My God! She might still be alive!" Regina said, the dullness in her eyes for the past week brightening a little. "She might have made it to shore and is wandering around not knowing who she is."

Taking his wife in his arms, he took a deep breath. "The police are confident the boat was stolen while she was diving."

"They left her out there!"

"She shouldn't have gone out alone, Gina," Tal said, trying to face the stupidity of his daughter's actions. "What the hell could she have been thinking?"

"She was thinking the boat would be there when she returned to the surface. Please, don't give up on her, darling. She's an experienced diver and an incredibly strong swimmer," Regina pleaded.

"I know. I know, Gina. I just don't want you to get your hopes up too high. Promise me," Tal said as he held her face between his hands.

"I might have to eventually, darling, but I can't give up on Julia yet."

Chapter
Three

AN UNFAMILIAR SOUND roused Julia from her watery nap. She closed her eyes against the sun beating down on her and wished she had her Ray-Bans. She brought her hand to her face. It felt hot to her touch and she knew she was getting the mother of all sunburns. The best she could do was tread water periodically before resuming her floating. As she forced her legs down and moved her arms slowly to keep herself above the water, she looked around. The sound she heard was a thumping noise, but, knowing sound could travel great distances under water, she couldn't tell how far away it might be. She wished she could cover her face before it turned into a charcoal briquette. Glancing around she saw the same thing she had seen since sunrise...nothing. A few minutes later, her arms and legs grew tired and she flipped onto her back again. I can see the headlines now, she thought with a grin. Woman floats around the world.

Dozing and trying to ignore her growing sunburn, Julia was suddenly awakened by something hitting her body and the sound of voices calling out to her. Half opening one eye, she rotated it in its socket and gasped. *Oh, God! Now I'm hallucinating! Father forgive me for I have sinned.*

"Grab the rope!" voices were shouting at her. Instinctively she reached out and felt coarse fibers scratching her hand as her fingers closed tightly around them. She felt her body being dragged quickly through the water. She looked up and saw off-white sails billowing against a clear blue sky from three tall masts rising above the deck of a huge wooden ship. She knew this kind of ship—a frigate. A row of closed cannon ports extended along its side. Although she could see the sails being lowered, the ship continued cutting through the water, dragging her along. She didn't have the strength to pull her body closer to the cargo netting thrown over the railing of the main deck. As the last of her strength seeped away, she released the rope and began to sink into the water beneath her. It was over.

DYING ISN'T SO *bad,* Julia thought, taking a deep breath. For the first time in—how many days—she felt warm and dry. She lifted a hand and winced at the soreness in her arm muscles as she gently touched her sun-burned face and ran fingers through her short hair. She felt something slightly scratchy rubbing her skin when she moved. Perhaps when you died you entered Heaven or Hell unclothed. She was afraid to open her eyes, afraid she was in a horrible place.

"She's coming to, lad. Fetch the Captain," a firm British-accented voice said as Julia felt a hand come to rest against her head.

Julia blinked her eyes open and let them sweep quickly around her surroundings. The wall beside her was wooden and had been white-washed off-white. A lantern attached to the ceiling swayed gently back and forth. Finally her eyes came to rest on a man who appeared to be in his forties or fifties. A pair of glasses rested halfway down his aquiline nose and his graying hair was pulled back into a pony tail drawn together at the nape of his neck. He wore a stiff white shirt with a stand up collar buttoned all the way to his neck. A dark blue vest, also completely buttoned, with gold decorative buttons covered the shirt.

Seeing the confusion in her eyes, the man leaned slightly forward. "I am Ship's Physician Anthony Cornelius. You are in the sick bay of *HMS Viper*. What is your name, child?"

Julia blinked blankly at the man without speaking. She needed time to awaken from this dream.

Taking a different tack, Dr. Cornelius said, "*Quel est votre nom, ma chère?*"

Once again he received no response from his patient and scratched his head. "Well, that is the extent of my linguistic abilities," he muttered to himself. Standing, he motioned for Julia to sit up and prepared his stethoscope, pantomiming what he wanted her to do. "Take a deep breath, please," he said as he demonstrated breathing deeply. Julia complied, holding the blanket tightly against her chest. The doctor moved the instrument around her back before sitting again and listening to her chest.

"I shall cause you no harm, madam," he said softly as he loosened Julia's grip on the blanket and continued listening. His examination was interrupted by firm rapping against the sick bay door. Making sure he had Julia's attention, he gently pushed her shoulders. "Lie down, please." As soon as he readjusted the blanket to cover Julia's naked body, he turned and strode to the door.

Although she couldn't hear what was being said, she guessed the doctor was giving a report on her condition to someone. A moment later Cornelius walked back toward her followed by a handsome man in tight, snow-white breeches buckled at mid-calf. Equally white stockings covered the rest of his legs until they met shiny black shoes topped with gold buckles. A dark blue pullover shirt was topped by a white vest held together with hooks and eyes. Completing his uniform was a dark blue waist length jacket with white lapels and gold fringed epaulets. The jacket was short in the front and hung down in the back like the tails of a tuxedo. Although the jacket was unbuttoned, Julia noticed a row of gold buttons down each white lapel. The man carried himself with what Julia could only call a regal bearing. In the crook of his right arm he carried a black bicorn hat outlined in gold cording. It was difficult for Julia to determine his age considering the pursed mouth and Roman nose. His face was elongated and topped by long dark brown hair drawn back and tied in place at his neck.

Bowing slightly and with a look of indifference, the man spoke in clipped words. "Terrance Bentham, madam. Captain of His Majesty's Ship *Viper*."

Julia nodded briefly at the man and looked at Dr. Cornelius. "She does not respond to either English or French," the doctor reported.

"Is she a mute?"

"Possibly, but I doubt it."

"What about the unusual...undergarment she wore?" the captain asked, his eyes flicking toward Julia.

"I am unfamiliar with the substance. Apparently it was intended to protect her body from the elements for some reason."

"We shall turn her over to the authorities once we make port in Jamaica. They can decide the best course of action regarding her future. I cannot detour from our course. The Governor-General and his entourage have already been delayed long enough," the Captain said matter-of-factly.

As he turned to leave, Julia opened her mouth and looked from the captain to the physician. "My...name..." she started. Her throat burned and it was difficult for her to speak. As the two men stared at her, she shook her head. "Water, please," she managed.

The doctor filled a container and handed it to her. She gulped down the entire mug and handed it to the doctor for a refill. She had never tasted anything as sweet. When her thirst was quenched, she cleared her throat. *I can do this. After listening to Mother my entire life, surely I can manage the accent.* "My name is Julia Blanchard," she said clearly.

"You are a British subject?" the captain asked skeptically.

"Indeed," she replied, her eyes downcast. "I am in your debt for saving my life."

"Not to put too fine a point on it, my dear," the doctor said, "but how did you come to be floating in the virtual middle of the ocean? And what was that unusual undergarment you wore?"

"My ship was caught in a sudden storm and I was swept overboard. It was unbearably warm in my compartment and I was on deck in an attempt to cool myself. The undergarment is — um — a new fashion I discovered recently while traveling abroad," Julia answered, hoping the men would find it believable. She decided she could get into this charade. *Perhaps I have found my way into some kind of elaborate re-enactment.* Her mother would be proud.

"That is the biggest line of poppycock I have ever heard," the Captain said smugly.

"When do we arrive at Jamaica?" she asked. "I am anxious to return to my home and must book passage."

"That might be somewhat difficult, my dear," the doctor said. "Hostilities between the Royal Navy and the Americans have rather curtailed non-military travel by sea for the moment."

"What hostilities?" Pausing she said, "You'll have to forgive me, Doctor. I'm afraid my ordeal has affected me more than I thought. What day would this be?"

"July fifteenth," Cornelius said with a smile. "Considering what you've been through, my dear, some memory loss is perfectly understandable."

But what's the freakin' year! her brain was screaming. "You have my apologies, Captain Bentham, if my rescue has delayed your mission."

"No matter, Miss Blanchard. We shall be rendezvousing with the fleet at Jamaica before we continue on to Mobile and New Orleans. One day will not make much of a difference one way or the other. This is nothing more than an annoyance. Now that we have defeated Bonaparte I can assure you we shall make short shrift of these Americans."

She covered her mouth to suppress a yawn. "Captain, my patient should rest now," Cornelius said. "Perhaps you can speak with her again later this evening."

"Of course, Doctor." Bowing slightly toward Julia, Bentham set his hat back on his head. "I shall speak with Mrs. Kent. Perhaps either she or her maid will have suitable attire they might lend our guest."

As Julia shut her eyes and turned onto her side, she tried to remember her history and wished she had paid more attention. *Bonaparte? As in Napoleon?* Her body ached as she shifted in an attempt to find a more comfortable position. She searched her memory for a date. When was Napoleon defeated? Eighteen-something. She had to be dreaming. The harder she concentrated, the more her mind drifted. She was incredibly tired, but at least she was finally dry.

A HAND ON her shoulder jerked Julia awake. The sudden movement reminded her immediately of the pounding her body suffered during her wrestling match with the marker buoy. Slowly she brought a hand to her face and rubbed her eyes. Standing over her was a young woman in her early twenties. Her red hair was immaculately tucked under a white cap. Seeing Julia looking up at her, the woman smiled. Her skin was pale white, accented by rosy cheeks. Curtseying slightly, the woman said, "Good day, ma'am. I was asked to provide you with appropriate clothing."

"Who are you?" Julia asked, pushing up onto her elbows.

"Oh, my apologies, ma'am. My name is Kitty Longmire. I am the maid to Lady Hortense Kent, wife of the Governor-General." The woman looked at her as if she should know who the Governor-General was and of what. "The Captain has extended an invitation for you to join him and Lord and Lady Kent for supper, if you are feeling well enough, that is."

"Thank you. I am hungry," Julia replied.

"I will help you dress and show you where the officer's dining facility is located," Kitty said as she reached down to remove the blanket covering Julia.

Grabbing the blanket and holding it against her nakedness, Julia said, "I can dress myself, but thank you anyway."

Laughing lightly, Kitty said, "If you are concerned about my seeing you unclothed, my lady, I should tell you that I assisted Dr. Cornelius in disrobing you when you were brought aboard." Turning to shake out a dress and petticoat, Kitty continued. "I must admit it was a bit of an ordeal to remove whatever it was that covered you. At first I thought perhaps you had been tarred and feathered. Except, of course, there were no feathers." Holding a hand out to her, Kitty waited. "No need to worry."

Julia had never stood naked in front of another woman before unless the other woman was also unclothed in preparation for an intimate encounter. And certainly no one had helped her dress since she was in elementary school. Oh, well, what did it matter now? Everything happening to her was nothing more than part of an elaborate dream anyway, albeit a seemingly real one. She drew the blanket away and stood, glancing down at her body. She was aghast to see the dark blue and purple bruises along her ribs and thighs. No wonder she was achy.

Kitty must have seen the bruises, but didn't comment as she helped Julia dress. None of the clothing was familiar and Julia was glad Kitty was assisting her. She wasn't sure she could have figured out how to put the garments on. Three layers later, Kitty buttoned a long row of buttons up the back of the dress Julia wore. It was a simple dress, but certainly nothing she would have selected for herself. She missed her cargo pants and pullover.

Finally, with no more layers to drape over her body, Kitty stood back to look over her charge. "It is a little loose on you, but you are so slender, my lady."

"Julia, please." Without a mirror she had no idea what she looked like, but felt ridiculous as she looked down at the yards of lace and flowered, yellow material. In deference to her bruises, Kitty hadn't laced the undergarments as tightly as she might have and Julia was grateful. *How did anyone stand to wear this shit?* Turning to face Kitty, she smiled. "Well, lead me to the chow, Kitty. I could eat a horse."

Seeing the look on Kitty's face, Julia mentally slapped herself. "Sorry," she said. "A phrase I recently heard an acquaintance use. Apparently it is what the Americans say when they are extremely hungry."

"Oh. Well, it's quite colorful."

You have no idea the colorful phrases I know. Julia smiled as she followed Kitty out of the sick bay.

Chapter
Four

JULIA TOOK A seat next to Kitty in the Officer's Dining Room and glanced at the others seated at the table. Other than Kitty, Captain Bentham, and Dr. Cornelius she knew none of the others seated at the long table. She adjusted a white linen napkin in her lap and waited. Bentham cleared his throat and stood. He continued to look warily at his ship's newest passenger, making Julia uncomfortable. Her borrowed clothing did nothing to alleviate the feeling that everyone at the table was staring at her, despite Kitty's attempt to make the large dress fit her slender figure.

"Your Lordship, Lady Kent, allow me to introduce Miss Julia Blanchard, apparently a castaway whom we rescued earlier today," Bentham stated. "Miss Blanchard, may I introduce Lord Obedience Kent, the Governor-General of Jamaica and his lovely wife Lady Hortense Kent."

Bentham returned stiffly to his chair as the Kents and Julia stared at one another and nodded. She would have sworn she saw a lecherous gleam in Lord Kent's eyes as he gazed at her. He was a well-fed, portly man in his fifties and was dressed as if he might be meeting the King himself. Equally Rubenesque, Lady Kent sniffed and touched the tip of her nose with a lace handkerchief she pulled from inside the sleeve of her multi-layered dress. Julia couldn't fathom how they tolerated the heavy clothing in the oppressive mid-July heat.

Kitty leaned closer to Julia. "I'm glad you have joined us so's His Lordship will have someone new to leer at," she whispered, a smile gracing her full lips.

Julie looked at her companion. "What?"

"His Lordship fancies himself something of a ladies man," Kitty said in a charmingly lilting Irish brogue.

"Does he own a mirror?" Julia chuckled. "I may lack companionship at the moment, but I'm not quite that desperate. He and Lady Kent seem to be well-suited for one another."

Kitty laughed and covered her mouth as she coughed to hide her laughter.

"How many days before we make port, Captain Bentham?" Obedience Kent asked through a mouth stuffed with meat and potatoes. He grabbed his wine glass and filled his mouth to wash down his food.

"If we stay on the course I have set I estimate six, perhaps seven days. Certainly no longer. We have, however, made excellent progress with the assistance of favorable winds," Bentham answered.

"I am hoping we will not encounter any delays," Lady Kent said. Her voice had a falsetto quality to it that set Julia's teeth on edge.

"The *Viper* is more than capable of handling anything that may arise, Lady Kent. As soon as you and Lord Kent are safely in port we shall sail immediately northward to the bay at Mobile to rendezvous with other ships of the British fleet," Bentham said, sounding somewhat bored. As Julia looked up she saw Bentham's eyes boring into her. She was certain he hadn't believed her story about falling overboard for a Bristol minute, but there was nothing more she could do except wait to see whether he turned her over to the authorities when they reached port.

"This will be the captain's first actual military encounter," Kitty whispered. "I imagine he will be glad to be rid of us."

"He's sailing to Mobile?" Julia asked.

"Some of the junior officers have told me there are rumors the Americans have been diverted by an uprising of savages in Alabama. If true it should allow our troops to converge and strike along the coast of the Gulf of Mexico," Kitty said seriously. "We've been at sea a month and I, personally, will be glad to have solid ground beneath my feet again."

OTHER THAN SHARING meals each evening with the captain, the ship's doctor, Kitty, and the pretentious Kents, Julia tried to remain as inconspicuous as possible. She had a lot to think about. It took her days to feel less disoriented. She no longer believed she was trapped in a dream or any type of extravagant re-enactment. She was stuck somewhere in the past with no idea how she arrived there or exactly when. She felt out of place and was constantly on guard when she spoke to anyone else on board the ship.

Julia found she enjoyed the smooth rolling of the tall ship. In a good breeze, the sound of the sails flapping and the laughter and conversation of the crew as they worked were fascinating. Most of all she noticed how wonderful the salt air smelled. For the first time she could remember it wasn't mingled with the scent of diesel fuel or exhaust fumes. The low roaring of the two-hundred-and-fifty horsepower engines on the *Discovery*, while powerful sounding, would never compare to the sound of water splashing against the wooden hull of the *Viper* as it sliced quietly through the calm waters of the Caribbean.

As the sun dropped in the western skies on her sixth day aboard the *Viper*, Julia strolled along the main deck wondering what fate awaited her the next day when the *Viper* sailed into port at Jamaica.

"Ship ahoy!" the crewman in the crow's nest called out. Julia looked up and saw him pointing toward the east. Around her the deck crew scurried to ready for the approach of a potentially unfriendly vessel.

Captain Bentham appeared from his quarters beneath the wheel deck and set his bicorn firmly on his head as he strode onto the bridge of the *Viper* and took a telescope from his first mate. Julia squinted and scanned the eastern horizon, barely able to see the billowing white sails of a second ship. Leaning over the bridge railing, Captain Bentham called down to crew members on the spar deck, "Ready the carronades!" Noticing Julia, a civilian, standing on the main deck, he raised his voice. "Madam! Miss Blanchard! Please return to your quarters immediately!"

Julia made her way cautiously across the deck, trying to avoid interfering with the crewmen. As she reached the stairs leading below deck she heard Bentham continuing to issue crisp orders. "Open the starboard cannon ports!"

JULIA STEPPED INTO her cabin and slammed the door closed. She moved quickly across the small room and looked out the porthole. Regrettably her cabin was on the port side of the vessel. She was certain she had heard Bentham order the *Viper* to keep the approaching vessel to his starboard. From her porthole she saw a ship approaching them from the port side. She saw the British flag flying from the new ship's stern and smiled, marveling at how elegantly it ploughed through the blue Caribbean water.

She sat down on her cot and waited for Bentham to send word she could return to the deck. It was overly warm in her room and she unbuttoned the top two buttons of her dress to cool off even a little. Unexpectedly she heard shouting and the sounds of gunfire. She ran to the porthole and stopped, stunned to see a second ship tightly against the side of the *Viper*.

She started toward her cabin door. Maybe Kitty would know what was happening. As she reached the door, she heard the sound of a woman crying and flung it open. To her amazement a dirty looking man, shorter than she, turned and grinned when he saw her. He was in obvious need of serious dental care. If it hadn't been for the pistol aimed in her direction, she might have thought nothing of it. Without thinking, she took a step back into her cabin and attempted to slam the heavy wooden door closed. His body prevented her from accomplishing the feat and she jumped back from the door, glancing around for something she could use as a weapon, eliciting a chuckle from the man. From his appearance it was hard to determine his age, but Julia guessed him to be in his thirties.

Waving his pistol from her to the door, the man said, "*Madamoiselle. S'il vous plaît.*"

"*Qu'ect-ce que vous voulez?*" Julia asked, demanding to know what was happening and hoping her college French was sufficient.

The man seemed surprised to hear her speak to him in French, but reached out and grabbed her by the arm, dragging her toward the door. Forced into the narrow passageway, she saw Lady Kent crying uncontrollably and looking as if she might swoon. Joining Kitty, Julia whispered, "What's happening?"

"Pirates," Kitty whispered in return.

"What?" Julia said loudly, no longer concerned with whispering. "You've got to be shi... I mean, you must be kidding me!" A moment later a hand shoved her forward and she ran into Lord Kent's corpulent back.

The four passengers were herded toward the steps leading up to the main deck. Light in the passageway was dim and when a hand pulled Julia onto the deck, she squinted against the sun on the horizon. To her right she saw Captain Bentham involved in a heated discussion with a bored looking man in tan pants and black shirt. The man cast a disinterested glance in the passengers' direction. To Julia's left stood a group of about a dozen men, all shabbily dressed and unshaven. She hadn't seen them aboard the *Viper* before, but it was obvious they were not members of the party now standing on the vessel.

In the midst of Bentham's argument, Julia saw movement from the corner of her eye and felt her mouth drop open when she looked toward the railing along the port side of the deck. A woman with short black hair combed forward onto her face from the crown, looking rather like portraits Julia had seen of Napoleon Bonaparte, stepped over the railing onto the deck of the *Viper*. She was tall, dressed in a dazzling white shirt with flowing sleeves over form-fitting black pants. Calf-high black boots completed her attire and the effect was one of elegant panther-like sleekness. A sheathed cutlass hung from her wide belt and a pistol was anchored in the waist of her pants. The woman glanced around at the people assembled on the deck and leaned back against the railing, crossing her arms over her chest to watch the proceedings.

As the man in black and tan continued his conversation with Captain Bentham, the woman looked bored and smiled crookedly as she scanned the people around her. When her eyes came to Julia, they paused for the briefest of moments before continuing their movement. The lightness of the amber eyes meeting hers stunned Julia and caused her to look away. The woman appeared to be almost a head taller than Julia's own five-six and, although she couldn't tell much about her otherwise, Julia was willing to bet good money there was a perfect body beneath the clothing. Blushing at her thoughts, she cleared her throat quietly.

"You have attacked a ship of the Royal Navy on the high seas without provocation while you flew the British standard," Julia heard Bentham say loudly.

"Please forgive us, *mon Capitaine*," the man in tan said with a shrug, accompanied by a smile. "We cheated."

Julia tried to suppress a laugh at the absurdity of the Captain's attitude. She covered her mouth and looked around, finding light amber eyes on her again.

SIMONE MOREAU WAITED for Henri Archambault, her second in command, to finish his discussion with the ignorant and pompous British captain. It gave her time to assess the situation. She couldn't believe how easily the Captain had fallen for her ruse. Despite a few cuts and bruises, the crews of both ships had come away virtually unscathed. Now she found herself with another vessel, a group of men who were apparently prisoners, and four passengers, one of whom was incredibly attractive. Despite her beauty, if this one was like other British women of her acquaintance, she was certain to be cold and totally devoid of passion.

Growing bored with the pointless discussion with the ship's captain, Simone pushed away from the railing and strode toward the prisoners. She suspected who they might be, but wanted to confirm her suspicions.

"Who is your leader?" she asked in careful French-accented English.

A middle-aged man dressed in filthy torn clothing and sporting at least two weeks of beard growth pushed his way through the small group and stopped in front of Simone. "I believe that would be me, madam, although I have no rank."

"You are captured American sailors, are you not?"

"That's correct. I believe we are being taken to Jamaica for detainment."

"No longer, *mon ami*," Simone said as she patted him on the shoulder.

Turning away from the sailors, Simone walked toward Bentham and Archambault. As she passed the blonde with short hair she stopped and turned to look at her, taking her in from head to toe, her eyes pausing briefly at the revealing cleavage. She noticed the woman's hands clench while her body stiffened under the close scrutiny. When their eyes met, Simone saw quiet defiance in them. Without speaking, she raised her hand and trailed it down the woman's face.

"Take your filthy hands off her," Bentham demanded as he

stepped toward them. A brief smile crossed Simone's lips as she swung her arm, backhanding the British officer hard enough to knock him down. As he fell to the deck, the man in black and tan drew his cutlass and pressed it to Bentham's throat.

"No, don't!" Julia shouted.

Simone glanced over her shoulder at the blonde, looking at her darkly as she held up a hand to stay the other man's actions. "He is someone special to you?" she asked casually.

"He is a human being."

Simone laughed as two crewmen picked the captain up from the deck.

Henri Archambault stood next to Simone. "What are you going to do with the Americans?"

"Give them the ship. Lower the long boats, put the British crew and passengers on them and let them go. Collect anything of value and have it taken to *Le Faucon*."

"All the passengers?" he asked. Simone looked at Julia again without answering. "She is a beautiful woman, *Faucon*," Archambault said in French.

"Beauty on the outside means nothing without knowing what lies beneath, Henri," Simone responded in kind.

Julia quickly became annoyed. "I speak French. Please do not talk about me as if I am not here," she said.

"*Pardonnez moi*," Simone said with a slight bow. "Take this one to my ship. Put the others in the boats with provisions for one day."

"You can't do that," Julia protested, recalling her own fight for survival a few days earlier. "It will take more than one day to reach a safe port. Lord and Lady Kent are older and ill-equipped to survive long at sea."

"One day's provisions," Simone reiterated.

"I will do whatever you want if you give them two day's provisions."

Stepping closer, Simone said, "You are in no position to bargain, *Mademoiselle*." Her eyes bore into Julia's. Pulling the blonde roughly to her, she said huskily, "You have no idea what I might want from you." Simone quickly took Julia's lips as if they were her possessions and just as quickly released her, laughing as she turned to walk away. "Take them to the boats," she ordered amid the laughter of her men.

"I insist on accompanying Miss Blanchard," the flaming haired woman next to Julia demanded.

"No, Kitty. Go with the others," Julia said defiantly, still recovering from the unexpected, but breathtaking kiss.

"No, my lady," Kitty said, placing her hands on her hips. "I will not leave you alone in the hands of this...this riff-raff."

Simone motioned with her head and a rough-looking crewman grabbed Kitty by the arm and began to drag her away. She struggled against him and eventually managed to slap his face with enough force to split his lip. Angry, he released her and struck her, knocking her to the deck. He wiped the blood from his mouth and stepped toward her to strike her again. Simone drew her pistol and pointed it at him. "Marcel!"

Stopping, his hand raised, he glared at Simone. Ignoring the threat aimed at him, he spun around to seek revenge against the impudent redhead. He brought his hand up to deliver the second blow, but was stopped when Simone shoved him away from Kitty with her boot.

Seeing the look on Simone's face, Marcel smiled weakly, "But *Faucon*–"

Julia jumped at the thunderous report of Simone's pistol. The impact struck Marcel in the chest killing him instantly. The blue-gray haze of spent gunpowder drifted up and around Simone's head. Julia's hand flew to her mouth and she turned away. Calmly replacing the pistol in her waistband, Simone turned in a slow circle looking for further signs of disobedience from members of her crew.

"My orders *will not* be disobeyed!" Simone said, her voice strong and clear. "Archambault! Finish searching this ship and dispose of that," she ordered, nodding to the bloody figure next to Kitty. "We leave."

Two nervous-looking men stepped forward, each grabbing one of Marcel's arms. They dragged the lifeless form toward the ship's railing while Simone offered Kitty her hand. "My apologies, *Mademoiselle*. Are you a servant?"

"I am Lady Kent's maid," Kitty said, straightening her clothing.

"I could kill you as well and end this disagreement now," Simone said with a smile.

"Then do it," Kitty dared as she faced Simone.

"No, Kitty!" Julia said, grabbing the maid's arm and pulling her back.

"She is a brave woman," Simone said to Julia. She pointed to a handsome young man standing nearby.

"Anton, escort these two to *Le Faucon*. Lock them in the hold until we are under way," she ordered as she strode away.

Simone glanced back at the two women as they moved across the deck.

"We cannot take those women with us, *Faucon*," Archambault said as he joined her.

"Why not?" she asked, appreciatively watching the blonde with the unusually short hair.

"It will create trouble for us unnecessarily," he frowned. "The men have not been in port for too long."

"You cannot be serious, Henri," Simone said with a deep throaty laugh. "Tell the crew the women are under my personal protection,"

Simone said. "If anyone touches them, they shall answer to me."

"Does that include you as well, *Faucon*?"

Simone moved closer to Archambault. Her eyes narrowed. "Do not presume that because you are my second in command you have the right to question what I do, Archambault," Simone retorted.

"The British will be hunting for us because of these women," Henri reasoned.

"We will release them as soon as we reach a port where we can drop them off without any danger to us," Simone said with an unconcerned shrug.

Unhappy, Henri grunted as he walked away. "Lower the long boats!" he ordered.

Chapter
Five

"I CANNOT BELIEVE you practically forced that woman to take you," Julia fumed as she paced in the small room. "She could have murdered you as well as that poor man."

"It seemed a more prudent choice than floating around in a very small boat with a very large woman such as Lady Kent." Kitty chuckled. "Besides, Anton is quite an attractive gentleman, is he not?"

"You should remember that he is a pirate, not a gentleman," Julia reminded her. "What was it he called his sister?"

"*Faucon*, or something like that. What does it mean?"

Julia walked to a small porthole in the cabin and peered out. "It means falcon or hawk. A bird of prey." And just as lethal as the woman herself. Night was falling rapidly, shooting the sky overhead with gray and pink clouds. Julia looked around and saw a candle and matches on a small corner table. She struck a match and smelled the strong odor of sulfur assault her nose as the small flame from the flickering candle illuminated the damp, musty smelling room they were locked in. Julia hated small places. She wasn't claustrophobic, but hated her inability to move around freely and investigate her surroundings.

"Where do you think we are going?" Kitty asked as she stretched out on a cot.

"Who the hell knows?" Julia mumbled. "Wherever pirates go, I suppose." It was her second encounter with pirates and so far this one didn't seem to be much of an improvement over the first one.

Julia and Kitty heard footsteps coming down the ladder into the hold not long after darkness engulfed the ship. Both sat up quickly on their cots and waited, glancing back and forth between the door and one another. It wasn't until a middle-aged man unlocked and swung the door open that Julia realized she was holding her breath.

"*Suivez moi*," he ordered, motioning to them to follow him.

Silently Julia climbed out of the hold followed by Kitty, refusing the man's hand when he offered it to assist her onto the deck. The night sky looked as vast as the ocean, and seemingly shot through with thousands of twinkling diamonds resting on an endless black velvet cushion. Julia took a deep breath of the sea air to rejuvenate after the time spent in the warm and stuffy hold. The man motioned for them to continue following him past a number of men who looked appreciatively at the two women. Stopping in front of a door beneath the wheel deck, the man rapped it firmly.

"*Entrez*," a woman's voice responded. The man opened the door and stood aside as Julia and Kitty tentatively entered the captain's quarters. The wooden walls and floors gleamed like burnished copper from the lanterns illuminating the cabin. The woman they called *Faucon* was seated at a desk writing when they entered and turned briefly to glance at them. "*Merci*, Francois. You may go."

Julia glanced around the room, surprised at its warmth. A sturdy piece of furniture resembling a modern-day platform bed stood against the starboard wall beneath an open porthole, allowing the cooler evening breeze into the room. *No doubt to cool the captain following a passionate interlude.* Julia was shocked when the thought entered her mind and was sure she was blushing. On either side of the desk were a bookcase and a chest of drawers. A large table spread with maps and charts occupied the space in the middle of the room. A bottle of wine and crystal goblets were arranged on a tray on one side of the table. A porcelain bathtub took up a portion of the portside wall. If she hadn't already been impressed by the height and slender figure of the ship's captain before, Julia was now. She closed the journal she was writing in and pushed away from the desk. Light golden eyes took in Julia and Kitty as she strode to the table in the middle of the room and opened the bottle. "Wine?" she asked quietly.

While both women were thirsty, Julia declined, much to Kitty's chagrin. Pouring two glasses of wine the woman handed one to Kitty, who looked at the glass longingly and then back at Julia, who frowned disapprovingly.

"Does she speak for you, *Mademoiselle*?" the woman asked in accented English.

"Well, I...," Kitty began.

"Are you her servant?"

"I am a maid, ma'am."

"There are no servants on my ship," the captain said as she set the glass down within Kitty's reach and shifted her eyes to Julia.

"Allow me to introduce myself. I have shown a regrettable lack of manners. I am Simone Moreau and you are guests, albeit reluctant ones, on my vessel, *Le Faucon de Mer*. What is your name?" Simone asked, looking at Julia over her wine glass as she took a sip.

"Doc...um...Julia Blanchard," Julia answered, deciding it would only lead to more questions if she used her educational title. "This is my friend, Kitty Longmire. When will we be released?"

"Soon. Please be seated," Simone said softly as she lowered her long body onto a wooden chair at the table.

"We will stand, thank you," Julia said stiffly. There was

something disconcerting about the woman and Julia felt self-conscious under her steady gaze.

"The British are a stubborn lot, are they not?" Simone said to Kitty, smiling slightly. "But you are not British, unless I am mistaken."

"Irish," Kitty said.

"If anything happens to Lord and Lady Kent I will see that you are hunted down and convicted like the common criminal you are," Julia blurted out.

Chuckling, Simone said, "Certainly something has already happened to your friends, but as you can see, I am still free. The true reason I asked to see you was to apologize for my earlier behavior. It was a necessary action to demonstrate my authority to my crew. I meant no offense by my actions."

"I am sorry, Miss Moreau, but I cannot accept your apology," Julia replied. The kiss had been a surprise, but not the crushingly brutal attack she might have imagined. In fact, she found it to be amazingly soft and gentle. Under much different circumstances, Julia would have sought more.

"A captain must keep her crew happy to assure their loyalty. If they believe I am interested in you as a conquest, they would not dare to bother you. However, if it would make you happy I can still give you and *Mademoiselle* Longmire to them. They are good men, but alas, they are just men."

"Like that poor man you murdered this afternoon?" Julia sneered.

"He failed to obey my order," Simone said. Turning to Kitty she asked, "Would you have preferred I allow Marcel to strike you a second time?"

Kitty brought a hand up to touch the still-tender skin of her cheek. "No, but there must have been a more humane way."

Setting her glass on the table, Simone stood and took a step closer to the two women. "Perhaps I should take a lesson from your British friends. I could have tied him to a mast, stripped his shirt off, and bloodied his back with thirty lashes. Marcel is dead because he failed to control his emotions. He could have lingered for weeks in excruciating pain only to eventually die of infection. But I can understand how you might consider such a lashing more humane."

Julia could see the dark anger building in Simone's eyes as she spoke. The captain snapped her head sharply in Julia's direction. "Is that what you would have preferred?"

Before Julia could respond, their discussion was interrupted as the cabin door opened. A boy of around ten with deeply tanned skin entered the cabin. He flashed a wide, white toothy smile as he walked toward Simone and set a platter on the table in front of her. Simone smiled warmly at the boy, who went to her and kissed her lightly on the lips. "*Merci*, Joaquin, *mon petit chou*," Simone said as she hugged him. Julia couldn't conceal a smile at the endearment as she watched

Simone's arms encircle the child.

"You are welcome, *mon Faucon*," Joaquin grinned.

A moment later, a stunning woman with skin the color of mocha coffee and shiny black hair falling in waves over her shoulders entered Simone's cabin. She was dressed in a simple dark green skirt and light yellow peasant blouse, the scooped neckline revealing ample cleavage. A silver, hand-tooled belt encircled her waist. Pushing her way between the two women rather than go around them, she moved next to Simone. She leaned down and kissed her, sliding her hand seductively across the captain's shoulders. Julia felt a niggling wave of jealousy creep along her spine at the intimacy between the two women. When the kiss ended, the woman looked pointedly at Julia, letting her know Simone Moreau belonged to someone and was off limits. Seeing the woman's face clearly for the first time, Julia was convinced she was in the midst of an elaborate hallucination or dream. Otherwise, there was no reason Halle Berry would be making an appearance. She squeezed her eyes tightly shut and shook her head slightly. Only the captain's voice drew her back to her current reality.

"Joaquin, please ask Anton to join us in a few minutes, *s'il te plait*," Simone said. The boy smiled and nodded, bowing toward Julia and Kitty slightly as he prepared to leave.

"Please, take some food," Simone offered as her eyes drifted down the length of Julia's body. "It will do no one good if you attempt to starve yourselves until we reach a port where I shall set you free to rejoin your friends."

SIMONE SAT DOWN once again at her desk to complete her nightly journal entry. Each day she carefully noted everything of interest that happened on board *Le Faucon de Mer* for no other reason than to keep track of her time. The brigantine had been her home for nearly seventeen years, since the day she and Anton fled their home on Montserrat and were duped by its captain, Louis Rochat. The old pirate took their money and then stole three years of Simone's life before she found the strength to steal his ship. She learned everything she could about the sea and how to read it before cutting his throat and claiming *Le Faucon* and its crew as her own. Her hatred of the British remade her into a driven woman, intent on revenge for the loss of her family's home on the tiny former French island in the Caribbean, and the loss of her own innocence. She became a murderer to survive.

As she dipped her pen into the inkwell to continue writing, warm arms slid down her shoulders and loosely enclosed her. "You look tired, my falcon," Esperanza whispered.

"I am growing weary of the constant movement from place to place," Simone said as she wrote. Esperanza and her son had been with her since the day she rescued them from a loathsome man in New Orleans who believed he owned them as he would have owned livestock. Simone watched as he beat the defiant Esperanza and followed them. His fatal mistake was in believing the tall, dark-haired woman was attracted to him. When her dagger slid effortlessly between his ribs, she watched impassively as life faded from his eyes. Although she and Esperanza became lovers not long afterward, she knew her affections were initially given out of gratitude. In the four years they had been together Simone had enjoyed the physical satisfaction Esperanza gave her. But while her lover's feelings had grown almost to the point of possessiveness, Simone knew she was not in love with the woman who willingly shared her bed.

"Perhaps we should rest at Martinique for a while," Esperanza suggested. "You love it there with your horses."

"Yes, I do miss them." Simone smiled thinking of the powerful Arabians flying across the sandy beaches and green meadows of her adopted island. Frowning, she said, "But I must take the two English women safely to a neutral port."

Kissing down the side of Simone's neck, Esperanza said, "You could set them free on one of the islands as we pass by."

"Perhaps," Simone sighed, relishing the feelings awakening within her. Closing her eyes, she breathed in the scent of Esperanza, her spicy fragrance serving as an aphrodisiac. It was an earthy smell and she filled her lungs with it, driving the scent of the ocean out of her mind for at least a few moments. Simone turned in her chair and swept the laughing woman into her lap, teasing her lips before gazing into liquid brown eyes. Their faces close, they breathed in one another's heated breath before Simone bought them together in a slow, exploring kiss. As Esperanza's long fingers tangled in her short thick hair the captain knew she would not be able to resist the feel of her lover's body touching hers.

"You are a shameless temptress, *ma chère*," Simone said as her mouth traveled lower onto Esperanza's tempting chest, her hands running smoothly up her lover's sides.

"Just as you are a shameless conqueror, *mi amor*," Esperanza breathed, pressing her body closer to Simone.

"See to Joaquin, then come to bed," Simone said. "I must give the course heading to Gaston."

A SOUND PENETRATED her sleep. Julia opened her eyes and rolled onto her side in search of a more comfortable position. She was still sore from her close encounters with the buoy. She had slept in more uncomfortable quarters many times and the gentle rolling of the sea should have rocked her to sleep within minutes, but she was wide awake. Was this all really a dream? If it wasn't, was she stuck forever in the past? Everything she knew and understood wouldn't exist for nearly two hundred years. She smiled to herself thinking that if she already knew what would happen in the future, she could make a fortune and live as a wealthy woman. She was obviously stuck in a time around the period of the War of 1812. If Napoleon had already been defeated at Waterloo, the war was surely near its end. What happened after that? When nothing came to mind, she decided that must have been the day she dozed off in Mr. Logan's European history class.

In the darkness, she heard Kitty's soft even snoring. She liked the young woman and even though she could never tell her the truth about herself, Kitty was someone she didn't mind being around. It could have been worse. It could have been Lady Kent. The idea made her smile. Her thoughts were interrupted by a hand pressing roughly over her mouth. Julia grabbed at the hand but was stopped by a low threatening voice. "If you struggle, I will slit your pretty white throat." The lethal sounding threat was enough to make Julia lower her hands and lie completely still. The voice, now close to her ear said, "I see the way *Faucon* looks at you, Englishwoman. She is mine and you are nothing more than a temporary distraction." Ordinarily Julia would have found the lilting Caribbean accent attractive, but there was a cold edge to it that kept her frozen in place. "I would not hesitate to kill in order to protect her. Do you understand this?" Julia managed to nod and the hand immediately released her. She watched the silhouette of a woman's body disappear through the door into the passageway.

Julia sat up and ran her hands back and forth through her hair. Well, if I wasn't awake before, I sure as hell am now. She slipped into her shoes and felt her way to the cabin door, surprised to find it unlocked. After one or two wrong turns in the dimly lit passageways, she located the steps leading onto the main deck. She didn't know what time it was and it didn't really matter. She walked to the railing and leaned against it on her forearms, inhaling the cool sea air. She felt a burning need to do something, to do anything. She wasn't accustomed to doing absolutely nothing. There was a purpose to her life, a direction, a goal. Now she could no longer do the work she loved, with no idea what the future might hold for her in this time before cars, planes and trains, before telephones, before computers. She smiled to herself as she considered having to actually hand write her letters. God, what an awful thought. Her life depended on the use of a computer thereby allowing her handwriting skills to deteriorate over the years.

Her musings were interrupted by the sound of soft music. She turned her head from side to side, attempting to determine the source of the music. As she moved away from the railing, she let her sense of hearing guide her toward the soft dulcet sounds. It was lovely and quite haunting. Soulful, yet filled with a sense of longing and sadness. Moving quietly, Julia realized the music came from above her near the stern. Two steps up the ladder from the main deck, she froze when she saw the fluttering sleeves of a dazzling white shirt. The light of a three-quarter moon provided enough illumination for Julia to see the captain leaning back on a bench on the deck, some type of stringed instrument lying across her thighs. Julia remembered seeing a similar instrument on a weekend trip with Amy. Although the instrument looked somewhat different, it was very similar to the mountain dulcimers Julia saw and heard at an Appalachian museum. She thought then the music the simple four-stringed instrument made was beautiful.

Simone Moreau is an unusual woman, Julia thought as she settled on a step leading to the wheel deck and listened. She was apparently a woman of some culture. Then what the hell was she doing sailing around the Caribbean in another time? *Just my luck. I finally meet an interesting woman, even if it is in a dream, and she is not only out of my league, but has a jealous bulldog bodyguard to boot. Figures.* She didn't know how long she listened to Simone play when the music stopped and faded away. She heard movement followed by voices on the wheel deck and quickly moved into the shadows beneath the ladder, waiting until Simone strolled down the steps and walked to her cabin, pausing only to look up at the stars for a moment. Julia wondered if she was making a wish.

SIMONE STEPPED INTO the cabin and made her way to her desk. The soft glow of a single candle that had melted into itself provided enough light for her to slide the dulcimer on top of her book case. She sat on a long trunk at the foot of her bed to unlace her boots and slip the soft leather from her feet. She felt the bedcovers behind her shift and smiled as Esperanza's warm lips nuzzled down her neck. Simone loosened the fabric ties of her shirt and allowed Esperanza to pull the shirt up and over her head. She looked over her shoulder and smiled back at Esperanza, watching her slender, full-breasted form recline against the pillows at the head of the bed. She knew Esperanza was taking her body in as she stood and removed her pants and stockings. Crawling onto the bed, she moved over the woman's caramel skin and lowered her body, her head coming to rest between Esperanza's breasts. As she felt long fingers stroke her hair and back, Simone closed her eyes. She slowly fanned her fingers over the warm skin beneath her. She didn't need to look at Esperanza. She knew her body as well as she knew her own.

Finally relaxed, she ran her hands under Esperanza and held her as she rolled onto her back, catching a dark nipple between her teeth and teasing it with the tip of her tongue. When she released it,

Esperanza took Simone's mouth with hers hungrily. She was *Faucon's* woman and would never permit anyone to come between them.

CAREFULLY SLIPPING HER arm from beneath Esperanza's sleeping body Simone slid out of the bed and found her shirt. As it dropped over her head, she walked to a bench under an open porthole and sat down, her back leaning against the bulkhead. She watched Esperanza sleep for a few moments before looking at the moonlight glistening off the Caribbean waters. More and more often she was growing discontented with her life. She longed to settle down. She commanded the obedience of her crew and they had been successful in plundering many treasures from the British and Spanish ships they encountered. Certainly Esperanza satisfied her body, but not her soul and she knew the woman's feelings for her were deeper than her own.

Frowning as she stared out the cabin window, Simone became lost in memories of much worse times. She missed Montserrat, but knew she could never return there. Her father's imprisonment by the British as a provocateur and his unexpected death only served to leave her mother an embittered woman who soon followed her husband to the grave. Simone, only eighteen, took her ten-year-old brother and fled Montserrat, only to fall into the clutches of Louis Rochat and his men. Unaware of the old man's reputation, it took most of the money her parents left to pay Rochat for transportation to Martinique where they hoped to live with relatives.

The result was three years of servitude on board *Le Faucon de Mer* with threats of harm to her brother and beatings and rape by the crew members hanging over her. Her life revolved around the whims of an ageing and unpredictable man. The relationship between Simone and Louis was a precarious one at best. She was a young woman forced to share an old man's bed in order to survive. Fortunately, he spent a great deal of time drinking and celebrating with his crew and often fell into his bed half-conscious...but not always. Glancing at the sleeping form in her bed, she sometimes wondered whether Esperanza was using her the way she used Rochat. Although Rochat abused her on occasion, it demonstrated his control in the eyes of his crew. While she, unlike Rochat, would never force Esperanza to do anything against her will, she knew the woman harbored dreams of freedom. Simone observed everything Rochat did and, when she could, finagled information from him about tactics. She learned the lessons well, eventually using them against Rochat and taking riches from British and Spanish ships to build a new home on Martinique. Now she longed to return to the island. Even taking her revenge against the British no longer satisfied her.

Tired at last, Simone drew her body up and removed her shirt to slip back into her bed, seeking the warmth of the body that would always welcome her return. As she slipped her hand across Esperanza's abdomen and closed her eyes, the vision of short reddish-blonde hair and hazel eyes flashed through her mind.

Chapter
Six

THE SUN WAS shining through the cabin window when Julia's eyes popped open the following morning. She had slept like the dead and finally felt rested once again. Sea air always did that to her. She would have killed for a nice warm bath and wished she had different clothing, or at least less of it. As she sat up and stretched, she glanced at Kitty's cot and found it empty. She walked to the cabin window and looked out at calm seas. It would be a beautiful day. A pitcher of water sat on a small table near the window and she splashed some on her face, drying her hands and face on the hem of her dress.

Julia spun around as the cabin door creaked open. Kitty's smiling face peeked around the door. Seeing Julia awake, the young woman stepped into the cabin carrying a bundle in her arms. "Good morning," she chirped.

"Good morning, Kitty. I was just going to look for you," Julia said, running her fingers through her hair in an attempt to give it some semblance of order.

"The captain sent these clothes for you," Kitty said as she set the bundle on Julia's cot. "They are nothing fancy, but much lighter than the clothes we have."

Julia scanned the simple skirt and blouse Kitty wore and nodded. "She must be a mind reader. I was trying to think of a way to alter this one."

"When you have changed, the captain has invited us to dine with her in her cabin. She has given us free rein of the ship," Kitty smiled.

"Not like we'd have any place to go if we left it," Julia groused. Remembering her visitor from the night before, she added, "Why don't you join her and just bring me something?"

As soon as Kitty left the cabin, Julia tore part of her petticoat and used it to wash her body before dressing. The clothing Simone sent was soft and supple and Julia luxuriated in the way it felt against her skin. It was almost as soft as her old knit pullover. She missed her cargo pants and deck shoes.

The first sound striking her ears as she stepped on deck less than an hour later was the snapping sound of the sails under a steady breeze. She was pleased to discover there were pockets on either side of the ankle length tan skirt she wore and sank her hands into them while she strolled along the deck, nodding to an occasional seaman. She didn't know much about the actual workings of the old sailing ship, but found it all fascinating. Men scampered up the sail rigging as if it was nothing more than a ladder. If she had been wearing her usual clothing, she might have given it a try herself. As she neared the bow, she stepped onto a raised platform and walked to the foremost portion of the ship. She looked out over the vast water the ship was cutting through and saw nothing but miles and miles of water. She leaned over the railing to get a closer look at the figurehead adorning the ship's bow. The carved head and body of an eagle, its wings swept dramatically back, its beak open to capture its prey, protruded from beneath the bowsprit. An occasional breeze added to the forward movement of the ship and whipped though Julia's hair as she took in the water world around her. It reminded her of riding in Amy's convertible with the top down.

"Is *beau*, no, *Mademoiselle*?" a voice asked.

She cast a glance over her shoulder and saw the boy who had been in Simone's cabin the night before. Smiling at him, she said, "*Oui, c'est très beau.*"

Her response and smile brought a wide grin to the boy's face and he stepped up next to her, resting his chin on his forearms as he joined her at the rail. They watched the sea flow beneath them silently for several minutes. Suddenly standing erect and leaning over the railing, the boy pointed down toward the water. "*Dauphins!*"

Julia laughed, "Yes, dolphins." She and the boy moved from one side to the other and delighted in watching the antics of their escorts. Eventually, the dolphins dove beneath the water in front of the ship and disappeared.

Turning to Julia, the boy bowed slightly, "*Je suis Joaquin.*"

With a smile, Julia curtseyed. "It is a pleasure to meet you, Joaquin. I am Julia." Seeing the expression on his face, she said, "*Je m'appelle Julia.*"

"My English she no so good," Joaquin said. Reaching into the pocket of his baggy breeches, he pulled out a napkin and handed it to Julia. "*Faucon* say you eat."

Taking the small bundle, Julia uncovered a generous chunk of dark bread, a small wedge of cheese, and an apple cut into slices. Suddenly she was hungry and popped an apple slice into her mouth. Motioning with her head, she draped her arm around Joaquin's shoulder and the two left the bow of the ship, speaking a mixture of French and English. As they walked and laughed, Julia noticed the tall figure standing on the wheel deck, hands clasped behind her back, wind ruffling her short dark hair and white shirt.

"*Faucon* say we go home," Joaquin said.

"Where is home, Joaquin?" Julia asked, returning her attention to the boy.

"Martinique. Seven or eight days by good wind."

Nodding, Julia continued eating.

Simone had been watching Julia since she stepped on deck and wandered to the ship's bow. The English woman seemed to be lost, but Simone was pleased when she engaged easily in conversation with Joaquin. It would do him well to improve his English skills. The boy was fluent in French and Spanish already and Simone knew he was quite inquisitive and bright. He was only five when he and Esperanza boarded *Le Faucon*, but already knew as much about the ship as some of her crew. It did her heart good to see him laugh at whatever Julia was saying. The English woman seemed at ease with the boy and Simone couldn't help but notice how her smile changed her face and demeanor.

It would be good to see Martinique again, Simone thought. It had been nearly a year since *Le Faucon* had returned. She missed her horses and she knew her crew missed their families. If she were smart she would put into Martinique and remain there. She was tired of her life as a privateer and the British blockade of the American ports made shipping more unpredictable. She didn't need an excuse to attack British vessels, but she was finding less and less satisfaction with it as the years passed.

THAT EVENING JULIA once again declined an invitation to dine in the captain's cabin. Kitty's budding friendship with Simone's brother, Anton, occupied the redhead's evenings. Even after such a short period of time, she was obviously smitten with the young man. Like his sister, he was dark and handsome, but Kitty claimed he had a much softer side as well. A knock at the cabin door brought Julia back from a lazy nap. When she opened the door she found a tray in the passageway and gratefully ate everything on it. The sun was falling below the horizon when Julia made her way back on deck. This was her favorite part of the day. Even on Tybee Island she often sat on the dunes and simply watched the sun slowly disappear. She didn't think anything was quite as beautiful as the lingering rays of the sun shimmering across the top of the ocean. There were times she half expected to look into the water and see the sun blinking up at her through the waves.

"*Mademoiselle* Julia!" Joaquin called.

Looking around, Julia spotted the boy standing on the wheel deck, waving to her. She smiled and returned the wave.

"Come! We play!" he called out.

Julia made her way across the deck and to the stairs leading onto the wheel deck. She saw Simone sitting at the rear of the deck, the dulcimer lying across her lap, and paused. Joaquin ran to Julia and offered her his hand. She smiled as she took it and allowed him to escort her to the bench encircling the deck. Simone looked up at their approach and then returned to tuning her instrument. As Julia sat, Simone asked, without looking at her, "Do you play an instrument, *Mademoiselle* Blanchard?"

"The piano," Julia said. "A little guitar."

Picking up an instrument, Simone handed it to Julia. "The mandolin is similar, but with a somewhat higher pitch." Picking up a second mandolin, Simone handed it to Joaquin. "Joaquin can assist you, if you have an interest."

Joaquin patiently showed Julia a few fingerings on the instrument. Simone noticed the Englishwoman didn't seem offended taking instruction from a child. She laughed easily at herself as she tried, but didn't quite make the right chords. Even with the elementary five or six notes Julia more or less conquered, Simone and Joaquin were able to come up with a few equally simple songs.

"Is that a mountain dulcimer?" Julia asked, indicating the instrument across Simone's thighs.

"Yes. You know of it?" Simone asked.

"I've...uh...seen others similar to it."

Touching the instrument tenderly, Simone said, "I met once an old man on one of my voyages who taught me to play. He made this one for me as a surprise the next time I returned."

"Then you should treasure it. You play beautifully." Julia smiled.

Simone seemed embarrassed and cleared her throat. Julia changed the subject. "Joaquin tells me we are going to Martinique."

"Yes. My crew and I are tired and it will do us good to return home, if only for a few days," Simone said.

"How is it that you managed to become a pirate?" Julia asked casually as she plucked at the strings of the mandolin.

"No!" Joaquin said, standing and glaring at Julia. "*Faucon* is not pirate! You insult her!"

Looking startled, Julia saw the anger on the boy's face, "Joaquin, I didn't..."

He turned away from Julia and bowed curtly to Simone. "*S'il vous plait, puis-je m'en aller?*"

"*Certainement,*" Simone answered quietly as she drew him into a hug and whispered to him softly.

"I meant no offense to him...or you. I am so sorry," Julia said as she watched the boy stalk away.

"No matter. He is but a child and easily offended," Simone said, putting the instruments away. "I have watched you with Joaquin. You are good with him. He will soon forget the perceived insult. He is correct, however. Only the British consider me a pirate. The Columbians have issued letters of marque for my ships."

"Which makes you a privateer," Julia said calmly. "A legal pirate."

"You test your luck, *Madamoiselle* Blanchard." Simone smiled. "Which makes you either very brave or very stupid."

"I've been told that many times." *But mostly in the future.*

"Although you have turned down my previous invitations, I would be honored if you joined me for dinner tomorrow evening," Simone offered.

"I doubt that would be a good idea, Captain, but I appreciate the invitation," Julia said, shivering slightly at the memory of a menacing voice in her ear.

"I could command your presence and have you brought to my cabin."

"But you won't."

"How do you know that?"

"It is not who you are."

With a smile, Simone said, "You do not know me at all, my dear." Julia Blanchard intrigued her. She was obviously well-educated, but afraid of something.

"If you will excuse me, Captain, I should find Joaquin and offer him my apologies," Julia said as she stood.

JULIA SPENT THE following week tutoring Joaquin to improve his English skills and she thought he was making remarkable progress. He was extremely intelligent and more than a little inquisitive. In return, he showed her parts of the ship and patiently explained the function of each. Julia, despite her profession, never found the opportunity to do much sailing and then only on small weekend craft. She preferred the feel of powerful motors beneath her feet to skim over the surface of the water. She understood the two or three sails on small sailboats, but the number and size of the sails on *Le Faucon de Mer* amazed her. To watch the crew work the sails so smoothly was awe-inspiring, like a ballet in the air above her.

Julia grew up outgoing and friendly, too friendly according to her father. As a child she would walk up to total strangers and hug them as if they were long lost relatives. In particular, her father took great joy in telling anyone interested of the time he took Julia with him to purchase a used car. Julia was no more than five, but immediately threw her small arms around the legs of the used car salesman who approached them. Her mother was never amused and worried constantly that Julia would be easy prey for anyone with less than honest intentions. Her tendency to wander away from her mother when they went shopping nearly drove the woman to use a collar and leash to keep tabs on her inquisitive and adventurous daughter.

Now, strolling the deck of a ship such as *Le Faucon de Mer*, Julia felt safe. There was nowhere to go and she might as well learn as much about the workings of the old ship as she could, just in case she ever had the chance to tell anyone about this adventure. The top deck carried ten eight-pound cannons, but Joaquin explained that the biggest cannons were two decks below and offered to show them to her, an offer she couldn't possibly refuse.

The cannon deck was amazingly well-kept with no debris lying around to obstruct them as they walked through it. Several men worked at repairing one or two of the cannons or their carriages and nodded at Joaquin as he led Julia through the area. Busily taking in everything around her, hoping she would remember it all, Julia glanced behind her and tripped on a heavy rope attached to one of the cannons. Before she hit the deck, a strong hand caught her, preventing the fall. Looking up, she saw the face of a smiling man who might have been in his mid-twenties. His face was roughened by the weather, but his smile was friendly.

"*Merci,*" Julia said as she straightened herself. "Sometimes I am quite clumsy."

"The rope should not have been left in the walkway," he answered with a slight shrug.

Extending her hand, Julia introduced herself. "My name is Julia Blanchard."

Staring at her hand for a moment, the man wiped rough grimy hands down the sides of his pants and glanced at them quickly before accepting her hand. Bobbing his head in unison with the handshake, he said, "Jean-Claude."

"What are you doing to this cannon, Jean-Claude?" Julia asked when he finally released her hand.

"One of the wheels sticks. It is difficult to pull into the gun port. And there is a problem with the breach. It is pretty, but not of much use in a fight unless we roll it over the enemy's toes."

"What type of cannon is it?"

"This one was a gift to the former captain," Jean-Claude said with a chuckle. "Otherwise we would have dumped it in the ocean long ago."

Julia stepped over to the cannon and looked at it closely. "Is it French made?" The historian-scientist in her began to kick in as she ran her hand over the cool smooth surface of the cannon. Her fingers felt a raised section on the opposite side close to the breach and she peered over the cannon. A shiny brass plate slightly smaller than a three-by-five index card was attached to the body of the cannon. *Le Faucon de Mer* was clearly engraved into the brass plate. Looking at Jean-Claude and Joaquin, she managed, "You say it was a gift?"

Joaquin frowned. "The cannon was a gift to Captain Rochat."

"Who is Captain Rochat?" Julia asked, her fingers lingering on the nameplate.

"He was the ship's captain *Faucon* paid to help her and her brother escape from the British," Joaquin explained. His face became solemn as he continued. "He tortured her and forced her to become his paramour instead."

"Old Louis died almost fifteen years ago," Jean-Claude added. "It was then *Faucon* took control of the ship."

"Was he captured?" Julia asked.

"*Faucon* she killed him. She does not discuss it," Joaquin replied quietly. "She keeps the cannon to never forget that time in her life."

Julia glanced down at the brass plate once more.

AFTER SEVERAL HOURS exploring the decks and holds of the ship, Julia was beginning to grow tired. It was that damned sea air added to the warm, musty smell of the lower decks. Joaquin walked with her toward her cabin. When they reached the steps leading to the main deck, she stopped.

"I can find my way from here, Joaquin. Thank you for a wonderful tour of the ship," she said as she stroked his coarse hair.

"*Faucon* asked me to invite you to dinner this evening, Julia. She thought perhaps if I made the invitation you might agree to join us," Joaquin said.

She couldn't bring herself to look at the boy. "Thank you for the invitation, Joaquin, but I think I will take a nap. I will eat later."

Turning to climb the ladder, he stopped and looked back at Julia. "Why is it that you not like *Faucon*? She treats you with great respect."

"I do like the captain, Joaquin. But I have many things on my mind. I miss my family and am anxious to return to my home. Please give the captain my apologies."

Joaquin frowned, but didn't ask further questions as Julia watched him climb up the ladder. She would enjoy nothing more than spending time with Simone Moreau, but knew Esperanza would be there as well. She had no desire for another late night visit.

TWILIGHT WAS FADING away toward darkness as Julia made her way along the dim passageway from her cabin toward the ladder leading to the main deck. After a peaceful nap, lulled to sleep by the gentle rocking motion of the ship, she was starving when she awoke. Kitty was nowhere to be found and Julia suspected she was with Anton again. Kitty was a spirited young woman and Julia hoped Anton was up to the task she was certain the young maid had in mind. She was smiling at her thoughts as she walked toward the ladder. A dim square of light shone onto the floor of the passageway. After Joaquin's guided tour she hoped she would be able to locate the galley and find a snack.

As she reached for the railing of the ladder, she was roughly grabbed from behind and pulled into a darkened recess in the passageway. "What the hell..." she began before a calloused hand clamped tightly over her mouth. Another arm encircled her waist. This time she knew she wasn't dealing with Esperanza. She struggled against her attacker and scratched at his hands. Away from the sparse light filtering into the passageway through the opening to the main deck, she was thrust against a wall. The hand didn't move from her mouth as a body pressed tightly against her, holding her in place while the second hand began groping her body and pulling her skirt up. She cringed as a rough hand scraped up her outer thigh. The skirt began bunching near her waist and she felt the arousal of her attacker pressing against her. *This cannot be happening!* She squeezed her eyes closed and tried to breathe normally to gather her thoughts as the man continued to fumble with her clothing.

She managed to work the palms of her hands flat against the wall and willed all of her strength into her arms, shoving her body backward. The man seemed surprised at her strength and released her for a second. She turned toward him, prepared to defend herself any way she could. "Jean-Claude!" she hissed before he pushed her back against the wall and covered her mouth again, intent on what he wanted from her. She pushed against him, but he wrapped a long arm around her to pin her arms. Now in the dim light she saw the leer on his face as he pressed against her again.

As she began to turn her head to escape the smell of his heavy breath, she saw the smile vanish from his face and felt his grasp on her weaken. Her eyes round, she saw a surprised look in his eyes as he took a step back. Then she watched as his body collapsed to the floor of the passageway. Breathing hard she saw a tall figure standing where Jean-Claude had been moments before. The figure shifted slightly and Simone's face, still partially cloaked in shadow, came into view. An arm reached out and guided Julia away from the body lying on the floor between them. Pulling herself into the safety of Simone's body, Julia wrapped her arms around the solid figure and breathed deeply to calm her racing heart. The deeper she breathed, the more her lungs filled with Simone's scent, musky and as cleansing as the sea air itself. A hand tentatively stroked through Julia's hair before making its way around her shoulders. Julia clung to her unable, or unwilling, to break the contact between them for several moments.

"Are you injured?" Simone finally asked. She wanted to bury her face in Julia's hair. Now that the distance between them was gone, the smell of the smaller woman imprinted itself in her mind.

"No," Julia answered, her face pressed against Simone's shoulder. Turning her head to glance at the body, she said, "I just met him a few hours ago."

"You are a beautiful woman. For some men nothing more is necessary."

Julia looked up at Simone and started to say something as their eyes met, but couldn't. Stepping away from her, Simone said, "Come. Joaquin insisted I save some food for you."

Escorting Julia onto the main deck, Simone stopped and looked around. "Henri! There is trash in the passageway. See that it is removed," she ordered.

Archambault nodded as Simone guided the English woman toward her cabin. Signaling two crewmen to follow him, he made his way toward the ladder leading into the second deck.

Inside her cabin, Simone pulled a chair away from the table and motioned Julia to be seated. She pushed a plate full of bread, cheeses, and fruit in front of her, poured two glasses of a rich burgundy and took a seat across the table from her guest.

"You have my apologies for the behavior of my crewman, *Mademoiselle*," Simone said as she brought the glass to her lips.

Julia picked up the wine glass and gulped down half its contents before lowering the glass. "Thank you, Captain," she said as she wiped the back of her hand across her mouth. "However, although I am hungry, I'm not sure my stomach would tolerate food right now."

"You cannot allow the actions of a fool to prevent you from eating. The cheese is quite mild, I assure you."

"Where is your friend?" Julia asked as she glanced around the cabin, nibbling at a small wedge of cheese.

"Which friend is that?"

"I don't know her name."

"Ah. Esperanza. She is making Joaquin ready for bed. She will return later."

"She's a striking woman," Julia said in an attempt at small talk.

"Yes, she is."

"Is she...are you and she..." Julia couldn't find a graceful way to ask what she wanted to know.

"Is Esperanza my lover? Is that what you wish to ask?" Simone smiled benignly.

Julia felt her body stiffen. "Your personal life certainly is none of my business, Captain."

"Esperanza is my...companion. I care for her and Joaquin very much."

"And Joaquin is her son?"

"*Oui.* I wish to thank you again for spending time with the boy. He rarely has the opportunity to meet someone new and has learned much from you in the short time you have been with us."

"Is his father a member of your crew?"

Laughing lightly, Simone shook her head. "I know nothing of his father except I am quite certain Esperanza killed him."

Simone seemed amused by the startled look on Julia's face. "Esperanza was the property of a plantation owner on one of the islands. Joaquin is the son of the plantation owner's brother. When I brought them to live aboard *Le Faucon de Mer*, Joaquin was nearly five-years-old already. Esperanza is of mixed blood, as is her son. But that is enough to make them slaves in your country and many other places. It is an abominable institution. The only good thing the British have ever done is to outlaw it."

"She does not seem to spend much time with her son." Occasionally observing Joaquin and his mother interact from a distance Julia wasn't able to see much affection between them.

"He is the product of an unwanted liaison. She provides for him."

"He seems much closer to you," Julia commented.

"He is the son I will never have. He is aware of the circumstances of his creation."

"It all seems rather depressing."

"Life is what it is, *Mademoiselle*. No one can predict what the future holds for each of us. We make our way through what we call life the best way we can. More than that we cannot dream of."

"Why do you do this? Sail around with no purpose, attacking other ships?"

"I have a purpose, but it is mine alone. If others choose to follow me that is their choice."

"You could have decided to put me on one of the long boats with the others."

"That is true." Julia watched as Simone held her glass up to the light and observed the color and clearness of her wine.

"Why didn't you?"

Cocking her head slightly, Simone shrugged. "I cannot say. It was an irrational decision made on the spur of the moment."

"Well," Julia smiled, "we all make irrational decisions from time to time."

Their conversation was interrupted as the cabin door opened and Esperanza stepped inside. Glancing from Simone to Julia, she asked, "Am I interrupting?"

"Of course not, my dear." Simone smiled at the woman and motioned her closer. Esperanza bent down and kissed Simone lightly. "*Mademoiselle* Blanchard had an unpleasant experience and I offered her something to eat."

Julia felt self-conscious in the presence of the two women and stood. "If you will excuse me, Captain. I am a little tired." A glance at Esperanza caused Julia to hope she could find some way to lock the door to her small cabin.

Rising and hugging Esperanza, Simone said, "I shall return in a moment, *cheri*." Crossing the cabin in long strides, Simone opened the door for Julia.

"It is not necessary for you to escort me to my cabin, Captain."

"It would be my honor, *Mademoiselle*." As Julia passed by her, Simone's hand came to rest on the small of her back.

Simone stopped before they reached the ladder to the second deck. Looking around briefly until she saw her second in command, she asked, "Has the problem been taken care of?"

"The trash has been removed, *Faucon*," he replied.

"Thank you, Henri." Pressing lightly on Julia's back, Simone went down the ladder and took Julia's hand to assist her in the darkness. The passageway showed no sign that a man died there less than an hour before. As Julia reached her cabin she stopped and spun around, almost running into Simone. "I...I am sorry that my presence has led to the death of your crewman."

"He made a decision and it turned out poorly for him. You were not to blame." Unexpectedly Simone bent slightly and kissed Julia on both cheeks. "Rest well, *Mademoiselle*."

"Thank you," Julia barely managed to say as Simone reached around her and opened the door to the cabin, brushing lightly against her. Julia's breathing stopped as Simone's face passed close to hers and their eyes met. As soon as she entered the room and closed the door behind her, Julia leaned back against it. Simone's rich bay rum scent still lingering in her mind, her cheeks burning where Simone's lips touched her. *Shit!* In another time and place she would have gladly invited the sultry woman to join her in the cabin. Or perhaps in my bed, she thought and then blushed at the idea.

Chapter
Seven

A LITTLE MORE than a week passed before *Le Faucon* sailed around the southern point of the island of Martinique and made anchor in a cove on the eastern shore of the island. A cheer went up from the crewmen and Julia watched as Joaquin stood in front of Simone while she piloted the ship into a small cove. The captain ordered the anchor dropped when the crew lowered the last sails. Seeing Julia observing them, Joaquin waved and said something to Simone, who nodded and smiled at Julia. Joaquin ran down the steps and came to a breathless stop in front of Julia. She heard Simone issue orders to make the long boats ready. Moments later, Esperanza mounted the steps to stand beside Simone, wrapping an arm around her waist and pointing to something on shore.

"Look!" Joaquin said as he jumped onto the bottom rail surrounding the deck.

Julia shielded her eyes from the sun and wished again she had her Ray-Bans. "What is it, Joaquin?"

"*Les chevaux,*" he smiled up at her.

Julia watched a small group of men lead six magnificent horses onto the sandy beach. The animals appeared to be high spirited, prancing in the sand along the shoreline as if they, too, were excited by the sight of the returning ship. Julia was startled as Simone brushed past her and climbed over the railing. She dropped into one of the long boats and waited to help Esperanza and Joaquin aboard the boat. Looking up, she motioned to Julia to climb down. She looked hesitantly at Kitty.

"Go on, Julia," Kitty smiled. "I will be on the next boat with Anton."

Julia looked at the Irish woman curiously. The maid had disappeared several times during the voyage to Martinique and Julia had seen her walking on deck with Anton many evenings. Swinging a leg over the railing, Julia clung tightly to the netting and made her way toward the boat below. Near the bottom, strong hands on her waist lifted her down the final two or three feet. As soon as she sat, two crewmen began rowing away from the brig. Julia would be glad to finally feel firm ground beneath her once again. When the long boat was nearly to shore, Simone left it, dropping into water nearly to her waist and with powerful steps pushed through the water. As the crewmen jumped from the boat to pull it on shore, Julia watched the captain stride to the horses and embrace each one affectionately. Laughing, she grabbed the mane of a dark chestnut and pulled herself onto its broad back. The horse reared and danced around. Julia smiled at the sheer joy on the usually taciturn woman's face. Bringing the large animal under control, she turned it toward the boats. Kicking it soundly in the side, the horse leaped forward and began to close the distance. "Joaquin!" she called out.

The boy turned and saw Simone and the horse rapidly approaching and ran farther onto the beach into their path. Julia reached out to stop him, but Esperanza grabbed her arm. "No," she said calmly. Joaquin turned his body sideways and held up his right arm. Simone guided the horse, still running, near the boy and at the last moment reached down with her left arm and easily swung him behind her on the horse. They raced down the beach through the surf. It was a spectacular sight. There was no doubt in Julia's mind the bond between the privateer and the boy was a strong one, based on unquestioning trust.

Within an hour everyone except a few crew members was ashore. Simone made relief assignments to allow everyone an equal amount of time off the ship. Members of Simone's household staff loaded horse drawn carts while everyone else followed. Joaquin claimed a horse immediately and shared it with Esperanza while Anton rode with Kitty sitting comfortably in front of him. As Julia brushed sand from her hands, a shadow fell over her and she looked up to see Simone extending a hand down to her. With a wary glance at Esperanza, a gesture not missed by Simone, Julia hesitated to take the hand.

"You may walk if you are too stubborn to accept my offer," Simone said.

Julia climbed onto the prow of the long boat and waited for Simone to guide her horse closer. Taking her hand, Simone scooted back slightly and pulled her onto the horse's back in front of her. As she settled herself, Julia's arm brushed lightly against Simone's breasts. She could feel the nipples react and a blush made its way up her neck. "I'm sorry," she barely managed.

"Why should you be sorry if I am not?" Simone rasped in a low voice, her mouth close to Julia's ear. The blush spread quickly to Julia's cheeks. Holding Julia securely, Simone laughed and urged her mount forward at a leisurely pace.

The island was lush and green. Colorful red and yellow birds flew through the trees and small waterfalls fell from walls of flowering vines to make their way down the hillsides toward the ocean. Julia relaxed against Simone as they climbed away from the beach. Periodically Simone shifted her weight, bringing her body into closer contact with Julia's. Simone drew her horse to a stop as they topped the hill overlooking the cove. She took in the view of the ocean while they waited for the others to catch up.

"It is magnificent," Julia breathed. At their leisurely pace she didn't realize how high they were climbing. *Le Faucon de Mer* looked much smaller and the changing color of the water as it extended away from shore was a panoply of blues and greens.

"This is my favorite view. It is nearly as beautiful as the water surrounding Montserrat."

"Montserrat? Joaquin told me that was your family's home."

"*Oui*. When my family was driven from the island by the British, I came here."

"Is that why you hate the British so?" Julia asked, turning toward Simone. Her face was much closer to Simone's than she anticipated and she swallowed hard as she watched Simone's lips quirk into a slight smile.

Simone was enjoying the feel of Julia's body close to hers and wished the trip to her home was longer. Now the woman's incessant questions brought temptation too close to resist. Light amber eyes dilated somewhat as they took in the inviting fullness of Julia's lips so close to hers. It would be so easy to lean forward only a very few inches and feel their softness once again. Quickly looking away, Simone broke the moment by turning the horse back onto its path, shifting her body farther back. She thought she heard Julia release a sigh of relief as well.

Julia joined the other members of their party for dinner that evening. She felt much more secure having dinner with Simone in a formal dining room than in the captain's cabin. Simone's cousin, Jean-Pierre, the caretaker of her property and horses, joined them. Julia enjoyed the lively talk and laughter, forgetting she and Kitty remained prisoners even though they were never treated as such.

Midway through a multiple course meal, a housekeeper escorted Henri Archambault to the door of the dining room. Simone excused herself from the table and engaged in a quiet conversation with her first mate. Returning to the table, she said, "My apologies, but I must leave. Enjoy the remainder of your meal. I shall return shortly."

Julia watched Simone drain her wine glass and stride away, accompanied by Anton and Archambault.

SIMONE LED ARCHAMBAULT and Anton across the hilly low-lying area from *Le Repos* toward the small village of Sainte Anne on the western shore of Martinique. Unlike the more shallow cove near her home, Sainte Anne lay on a deep water port an easy four mile ride from *Le Repos*. It was not uncommon for ships to seek rest in the village.

"Did DuChamp say why it is so urgent to see me?" Simone asked Archambault.

"He did nothing more than ask if you were on the island, *Faucon*."

Simone frowned. She had heard the name August DuChamp once or twice in her travels, but knew little about the man other than he was the son of former slaves who had found his freedom at sea.

The last remnants of the Caribbean sun were disappearing behind palm trees along the western coast when Simone brought her horse to a stop in front of the Boar's Head Tavern. She looked around the village as she stepped down from her saddle and tied the reins to a post in front of the tavern. She stepped onto the wooden decking in front of the small building and waited for her companions before entering. Lanterns hanging from overhead beams threw a golden yellow light over the tables and benches. Several men stood nonchalantly at the bar, undisturbed by the entrance of Simone's small party.

In the far corner she spotted a black man gnawing on a large hunk of meat. He grabbed a tall tankard and gulped its contents to wash his food down, wiping his mouth afterward with the back of his hand. The closer Simone drew to the man the more weathered lines she saw etching his rough face. She strode across the tavern directly to his table, followed by Archambault and Anton.

"You have a message for me, *Monsieur*?" she asked as she straddled the bench seat on the other side of the table.

"Your reputation for directness precedes you, *Faucon*. Laffite wants a parlay," DuChamp said bluntly.

"I do not take orders from Jean Laffite," Simone smirked, motioning to one of the serving women to bring drinks for her and her party.

Leaning across the table and lowering his voice so as not to be overheard, DuChamp said, "Barataria is destroyed."

"And why would this unfortunate event be of concern to me?" Simone asked, her tone nonchalant.

"The British are planning an invasion at New Orleans. Laffite believes troops will be brought to the city from Jamaica. He wants you. Or rather, he humbly requests your assistance in defending the city."

"It was the British who destroyed his headquarters at Barataria?" Simone asked as she took a tankard from a tavern worker.

"No, the Americans, due to an ill-advised suggestion."

"Then, you will have to pardon me, *Monsieur*, if I do not understand why Laffite would have any interest in assisting the Americans. It would seem obvious they have no wish for his assistance against the British."

"You would have to ask him concerning his motives, but I am certain it would involve some type of profit," DuChamp smiled.

"When?"

"Within a week. Laffite's ships took refuge at Bayou LaFourche. He set sail for Isla de Margarita a few days after he dispatched me to find you."

"Isla de Margarita is a very long way to travel for a meeting. He must sail past the British at Jamaica to reach his destination."

"Laffite does not confide his plans to me, *Faucon*. I am nothing more than a messenger. I leave here in two days time and sail to rendezvous with him at sea." DuChamp glanced around the tavern and pushed himself up from the table. "Now if you will excuse me, I believe an evening of rest and relaxation awaits me. I hope to see you again in about a week." Bowing to Simone, DuChamp rearranged his clothing in a failed attempt to make himself more presentable and ambled across the tavern toward a buxom young woman with a thick mane of black hair and a willing smile.

Archambault and Anton took seats across the table from Simone.

"What do you think?" Archambault asked.

"I think this is none of our concern," Simone answered as she took a deep drink from her tankard.

"You know Laffite would not propose a plan unless it involves a profit," the first mate said.

"We have enough, Henri. The men are tired. As am I. We have been at sea so long I have almost forgotten how to walk without listing to one side or the other from habit."

Anton chuckled and nodded his head in agreement. "We could remain on Martinique until either the Americans or the British win their little war and then ally with the winner."

Looking intently at Simone, Archambault said, "Louis Rochat would not have allowed such an opportunity to slip by."

As he lifted his tankard to take a drink, Simone sprang from her seat and slapped the drink from his hand. Silence descended over the tavern as she grabbed his shirt and pulled his face closer to hers. "You know *nothing* of Rochat," she hissed. "If you mention his name to me again, I will kill you myself." She shoved him back onto his seat and stalked out of the tavern.

Simone swung onto the back of her horse, turning her mount away from the tavern and back toward *Le Repos du Faucon*. Archambault served with Rochat, having come on board the year after she was taken and knew nothing more about her relationship with the drunken old man other than she shared his cabin. When she killed Rochat and took *Le Faucon de Mer*, no one was more surprised than Archambault when she chose him to be her first mate. A woman with her own ship was truly a rarity. She learned much from Rochat, but needed an older man as her second in command until she was certain her crew trusted her. Although she did not trust Henri completely, he served her well in the years they had been together. As long as she was successful in keeping coins in their pockets and rum in their bellies, her crew remained loyal to her. There were times she was sure they even feared her. Despite the control she exercised, she considered her time limited.

As she guided her horse along the sandy shore of the island, Simone knew she was rapidly tiring of the continual movement of her ships. Although she agreed to keep Anton aboard as a member of her crew, she knew their life was not what she wanted for her brother. He should marry and settle down and raise fat, happy children in peace. Her greatest fear was not her own capture and probable death, but that of her brother. She had already lived longer than she would have thought possible. As the waves came into shore, Simone wanted nothing more than to stay at *Le Repos* and do what its name suggested. Rest, raise her horses, and die in her own bed.

And what of Esperanza and Joaquin? There were times Esperanza seemed filled with loathing for her own son. Simone believed Joaquin would one day grow into a fine man, overcoming the circumstance of his birth. There were times Simone believed her lover simply came to her bed to repay a debt rather than out of any true emotion, just as there were times Simone wasn't sure she could fully trust the woman who shared her bed.

The longer Simone walked her horse along the beach, the blacker her thoughts became. Her once simple world was becoming more complex. It was no more than a three day sail to Isla de Margarita and it was a beautiful island. Perhaps she should hear what Laffite had to say. If the British were defeated they might abandon the Caribbean entirely. Almost as if it knew the way home without her guidance, the stallion turned away from the beach and began the climb toward *Le Repos.*

JULIA WAS AMAZED at the simple beauty of Simone's home. Surely she had taken enough booty to live in opulence, but chose instead to live no more than comfortably and simply. Julia had been to Martinique on dives many times. Now, surrounded by its former unspoiled natural beauty, she felt like she was seeing it for the first time. A beautiful, undisturbed haven. The red-roofed, distinctly Caribbean home was graced by a large front porch and nestled in a grove of tropical trees. To protect it from the seasonal tropical storms and occasional hurricane, each window was adorned with heavy tan shutters. With nowhere else to go, Julia took a leisurely stroll through the brick-lined gardens surrounding the house.

"Would you wish to see *Faucon*'s children?" Joaquin's voice asked as it broke into Julia's thoughts. "They are very beautiful."

"I didn't see any children at dinner," Julia said.

"Too big for dining room," Joaquin smiled. "Come."

Julia followed Joaquin along a path and was surprised when they entered a long low building with a red roof matching the one on Simone's home. Joaquin struck a match and a lantern illuminated a clean stable housing twelve stalls. Joaquin carried the lantern down the hay-covered floor and began pointing out each animal.

"What kind of horses are they?" Julia asked.

"Arabian. *Faucon* says they are the most beautiful of all horses," Joaquin answered. "They are the fleetest of foot." He stopped in front of a stall and made a clicking sound with his tongue. A moment later a large dark brown head with soulful eyes appeared over the stall door. Joaquin hung the lantern next to the stall and reached into his pocket, pulling out a chunk of something and held it out to the animal. Soft, velvet lips stroked his hand as the horse gently took the offering and chewed contentedly.

"What is that?" Julia asked.

"Sugar cane," he said as he took another piece from his pocket and handed it to her. "They like it."

Julia extended her hand and laughed as the huge animal's soft lips tickled her palm.

"This is Hercules. Someday he will be mine," Joaquin said as he reached up and stroked the side of the horse's head. "Perhaps, if you lucky, *Faucon* let you choose a horse also."

Julia rested her hand on Joaquin's shoulder. "Taking care of a beautiful animal such as this is a big responsibility, you know," she said. "Despite their size and strength they depend on someone like you to take care of their needs."

"Like big baby, yes?" Joaquin grinned up at Julia.

"Yes." Julia laughed again and ruffled his hair.

Simone stepped out of the darkness, leading her horse. "You know horses, *Mademoiselle*?"

Startled, Julia blushed when she saw Simone approaching. Her form-fitting tan pants accentuated a honed lower body. An off-white peasant blouse under a sleeveless maroon tunic fell softly over her upper body. *I was definitely born in the wrong century.* Clearing her throat, she said, "Not well. My parents owned horses when I was much younger."

"Perhaps you would like to go riding with Joaquin while we are here," Simone said. "I have one or two horses that do not require an expert rider."

"I know how to ride," Julia responded a little indignantly. Looking down at her dress she said, "However, I have never ridden in a dress and certainly not side saddle."

"Ah, I see. If you decide to join the boy I will see that proper clothing is found," Simone said. Turning to Joaquin she said, "Would you see that Napoleon is taken care of, *s'il vous plaît*?"

Joaquin beamed as he took the offered reins and led Simone's horse toward its stall. Simone stood next to Julia and stroked

Hercules's neck. Julia watched the quiet woman next to her and shifted from one foot to the other nervously. She wanted to say something just to hear Simone's voice again, but had no idea what to say. "You have beautiful horses," she finally managed.

"*Merci*. They are very good animals, but occasionally temperamental," Simone said as her hand ran along Hercules' neck. "They are like people in many ways. Proud, encouraged by praise. Quite intelligent, but do not tolerate abuse." Looking at Julia, she added softly, "They must be cared for and touched with only a gentle hand."

Julia, mesmerized by the sultry softness of Simone's voice, wished desperately she could tear her eyes away from Simone, but she couldn't.

"We will be leaving here within a few days time," Simone said, her fingers running through the Arabian's mane. Finally her eyes met Julia's, lingering a moment before she spoke. "For obvious reasons I cannot take you to a British port. I will take you and *Mademoiselle* Longmire to another port where you will be able to find passage."

"I am not British," Julia said quickly. "I mean, my mother is, but my father is an American."

"My apologies. I simply assumed from your presence on the British ship..."

"They rescued me at sea. I...uh...fell overboard from the vessel I was traveling on."

As Simone frowned and stared at her, Julia explained. "We were caught in a storm unexpectedly and I was swept off deck," she added, hoping her story sounded plausible. There was something unnerving about the way Simone looked at her, but Julia couldn't force herself to break the eye contact. She was certain Simone would never believe the real story. Hell, she didn't believe it herself.

Several uncomfortable minutes later Joaquin rejoined them. "Napoleon is brushed and fed, *mon Faucon*."

Simone smiled down at the boy and wrapped an arm around his slender shoulders. "Then perhaps we should return to the house and get some rest."

When they entered the main house it was quiet. Joaquin looked around the downstairs rooms quickly. "Everyone has retired," he reported.

"It has been a long day," Simone said. "A good night's sleep would do us all good. We will ride in the morning. I have business to attend to midday."

Simone and Julia followed Joaquin to his room at the top of the stairs and kissed him good-night.

"I shall have clothing made available for your ride tomorrow," she said.

"Thank you, Captain," Julia nodded. "I shall look forward to it."

Unexpectedly, Simone took Julia's hand, turned it over, and brought the palm to her lips in a soft kiss. "Sleep well, *Mademoiselle*," she said.

"You as well," Julia said with a smile. Her eyes caught movement at the far end of the hallway. She saw a shadow pass by the partially opened doorway of the room she was certain belonged to Simone. *Esperanza.* She quickly backed into her own room and closed the door as Simone proceeded down the hallway.

BEFORE RETIRING, JULIA was able to finally take a proper bath and wash her hair. A cool breeze flowing through her bedroom window lulled her to sleep immediately. When she awoke the following morning she found appropriate riding clothes lying on a chair inside her room. She dressed quickly, surprised the clothing seemed to fit fairly well and wondered if the clothing belonged to Simone. She left the main house and turned toward the stable, but was stopped in her tracks when she saw Kitty and Anton exchanging a breathtaking kiss in the side garden. She knew Kitty was attracted to the handsome young man. It appeared he was equally attracted to the outspoken Irish red-head.

Maybe this is Never-Never Land, Julia thought, and all their wishes would come true. She almost laughed out loud as she approached the stable. She decided to enjoy whatever time warp she was now living in and waved when she saw Joaquin at the far end of the paddock. As she walked along the outside of the stables and neared the entrance to the stall area, loud voices stopped her.

"Do you think I do not see the way you look at her, Simone?"

"How do you think I am looking at her, Esperanza?" Simone's voice asked. "She is my prisoner for the moment and nothing more."

"Your eyes tell me something different. You desire her."

"Would you fault me for noticing a beautiful woman? I have not been unfaithful to you, but you do not own me. You do not have the right to presume to tell me what I should or should not do!"

"I owe you a great debt, Simone, but will not be cast aside due to your lust for this English woman."

"I have never demanded your favor, Esperanza, and I never will. You came to me of your own free will."

"And you were more than glad to take what I offered."

"You, too, are a beautiful woman. Would you have been less offended if I rejected you? The English woman will be gone soon. Until then you will treat her with the same respect you would any of my guests."

"Don't turn away from me, Simone," Esperanza said.

"I promised Joaquin we would take the horses out before I leave today."

"And this third horse? Is it for the new object of your desire?"

Julia flinched when she heard the sharp sound of a slap. She turned to walk away, but hadn't gotten more than a few steps when Joaquin called out to her. As she glanced back toward him, her eyes met the dark amber of Simone's eyes and she saw the angry red mark on her cheek. Simone held the reins of a beautiful chestnut out to her and Julia retraced her steps and took them with a nod. Simone didn't speak as she pulled herself into the saddle and waited for Julia. Adjusting herself in the saddle, she caught a glimpse of Esperanza in the shadows of the stable entrance.

THE REMAINDER OF the time spent at *Le Repos* was relatively peaceful. Once or twice Julia spotted Simone and Esperanza involved in a heated discussion and wondered if they were still arguing over her. Whenever possible Julia avoided the two women, spending the majority of her time with Joaquin. She was uncomfortable with the way Simone looked at her, but anticipated those times with a guilty pleasure nonetheless. On the other hand, the way Esperanza looked at her made her wish she were wearing a Kevlar vest to protect her from the daggers the woman's eyes threw her way. Despite her attraction to Simone, she was not a home wrecker and refused to become one now, even if it was another century, and quite probably nothing more than a dream.

Simone insisted Joaquin study every day and Julia was more than glad to serve as his temporary instructor, always careful not to bring anything from the future into their discussions. They collected shells along the island's beaches and Julia identified each species for him, explaining that she grew up on the Virginia coast and received her knowledge from her father. In truth, Talbot Blanchard hated the ocean and never understood his youngest child's career choices, let alone her sexual ones.

Chapter
Eight

LOW HANGING CLOUDS of fog rose from the floor of the thick tropical forest surrounding *Le Repos* as Simone made her way into the stable area. Her time away from the sea was passing much too quickly. She had already announced to the captains of her ships that they would be leaving Martinique and sailing westward within a few days. As she reached Napoleon's stall she looked into the animal's large, gentle brown eyes and stroked his neck. Riding Napoleon always calmed her and she needed the time to think. Or perhaps just an hour or so not to think at all. Just enjoy time alone without distractions.

Simone should have enjoyed the time spent at her home on Martinique, but her time there was marred by too many external events. She knew she was partially to blame for the discontent. If she hadn't arrogantly felt the need to kiss Julia Blanchard the day she seized the *Viper* and then compounded her blunder by taking the woman as her prisoner, she could have avoided Esperanza's jealousy. A smile made its way across her lips as she threw a saddle over Napoleon's broad back. The English woman was attractive. But Simone did not foresee either the feelings the brief kiss created within her or the subtle acceptance she felt from Julia. Unwilling to admit her actions were deliberate, Simone knew they had needlessly, and perhaps recklessly, forced her in close proximity to her captive on more than one occasion.

During the week *Le Faucon de Mer* was anchored off shore on Martinique, two additional ships joined her, one a newly captured British sloop, the *Northumberland*. Simone met with the men appointed as captains of her ships twice before she announced they would be leaving Martinique and sailing westward. Her time on Martinique would soon come to an end and she hadn't yet named one of her crew to captain the *Northumberland*. As she mounted Napoleon and settled comfortably on the saddle, she knew she should choose Henri Archambault, but something was keeping her from it. There was only one person she believed she could trust with the new ship. Archambault would be upset, but he wouldn't argue with her decision. He would get the next ship as soon as they took one. She ducked her head as she lightly tapped Napoleon's sides and moved toward an enclosure near the paddock area.

JULIA STEPPED ONTO the porch of *Le Repos* and breathed the warm, moist air deeply into her lungs. She had slept well and lazed in the comfortable bed for nearly an hour before finally getting dressed. The sun was barely at the top of the trees and the early morning dew which accumulated on the greenery and gardens surrounding the house still clung to the vegetation, awaiting the sun to evaporate it. As she left the porch and strolled through the gardens, inhaling the scent of the blossoms around her, she caught sight of a horse and rider leaving the stables. She watched Simone, sitting astride her favorite horse, adjusting the stirrups while the horse ambled slowly away. Julia walked partway down the brick path leading from the main house to the stables to a rough-hewn bench. She took a seat, admired how elegant Simone looked as she patted the horse's neck. She would have sworn Simone was talking to the animal when they moved toward an enclosed ring. Simone leaned down from the saddle, opened the gate to the enclosure and guided the horse inside. She sat erect in the saddle for a moment in the center of the ring, then nudged Napoleon forward. A gentle trot changed into a skipping step, replaced moments later by a side step. The horse's hooves kicked up small puffs of dirt as he moved effortlessly around the paddock. Simone seemed to be motionless and simply along for the ride.

While she watched, Julia tried to reconcile the woman she was seeing now with the woman who was the captain of a ship whose purpose was to attack and plunder other vessels. She was a soft-spoken woman, vibrantly sensual, yet a woman who didn't hesitate to kill. In reality, the elegant lifestyle Simone led was funded by her success as a thief. She had murdered a man to attain her position, if what Joaquin said was the truth. It all seemed incongruous with the woman Julia now observed. Simone was polite and courteous, unsettlingly charming, but certainly did not appear to be a vicious killer. Yet Julia had seen her murder two men before her very eyes without a second thought. She ran a hand through her hair and stared at Simone. She couldn't deny her growing attraction. There was something inherently dangerous about the captain, yet she was inexplicably drawn to her.

AS SOON AS she stepped on board *Le Faucon*, Simone felt at home. She wanted to check the ship's stores and ammunition before they set sail again. The journey to Isla de Margarita was no more than three or four days, even with less than favorable winds. Most of her crew had already returned and were busily making preparations to set sail on her order. They were all sound seamen and most had been with her since she took control of the ship. Satisfied that everything was progressing adequately, she entered her cabin and began going over charts of the area they would be sailing into. A knock at her cabin door distracted her for a moment.

"*Entrez,*" she said. Henri stepped into the cabin and she smiled when she saw him. "We will be departing in two days," she said.

"Everything will be ready," Henri said.

"Please tell Carlos he will be sailing on the *Northumberland* as her navigator," she instructed.

"He is a good choice."

Simone leaned back in her chair and looked at her first mate. "Anton will be her captain," she stated.

"Anton!" Henri said before he could stop himself. "He doesn't yet have the experience to captain a ship such as the *Northumberland*."

Simone stood and moved to stand in front of Henri and placed a hand on his shoulder. "I know you are disappointed Henri, but he needs this experience. The trip to Margarita will be his test. In all likelihood it will be an uneventful journey and give the crew an opportunity to know him better. He has been on board the sloop all week making preparations."

"But..."

"The next ship will be yours, Archambault. You have my word. I need you to remain here on *Le Faucon* with me for now." The look on her face told Archambault further argument would be futile.

"As you wish, *mon Capitaine,*" he snarled. "But you are making a mistake."

"Perhaps," she shrugged. "But the decision is mine to make and my responsibility if something goes wrong." She took her seat at the desk again, adding, "Continue the preparations for leaving."

LATE THE FOLLOWING afternoon, Simone took one last ride and bid her beloved Napoleon farewell. She went over the financial matters for *Le Repos* with her cousin and caretaker. By evening she was satisfied all of her affairs were in order. She stepped into the garden behind the main house, stopping for a moment to light a small cigar Joaquin gave her a few days earlier. He claimed to have won it in a contest with some other boys on the island, but Simone suspected he stole it. Considering how she paid for her own way in life, she didn't press him to be more truthful. By mid-morning the next day *Le Faucon* and her other three stolen vessels would be leaving their home once again. During her years at sea she had done everything she set out to do without the satisfaction she once felt. It didn't, and wouldn't, bring her mother and father back to her. It wouldn't allow her to reclaim the property on Montserrat stolen from her family which eventually turned her into a criminal. And now she found herself inexplicably drawn to an exasperating English woman whose eyes and lips seemed to promise much while her behavior remained annoyingly ambiguous.

Sitting on a bench in the garden, she leaned against a tree and pulled a leg up onto the bench. Thinking it might be her last peaceful evening for a long time, she closed her eyes and tried to memorize the smell of the flowers and air around her. In the stillness she heard the sound of laughter and let her eyelids slip open far enough to look around. The laughter came from the stable behind her. Joaquin. But his was not the only laughter she heard. Pushing her body up from the bench, she puffed on the small cigar. A few minutes later she saw Joaquin dash from the stable, looking behind him at a taller figure running after him, holding her dress up to keep it from dragging the ground. Simone smiled as Julia caught Joaquin and tortured him with tickles. She hadn't heard him giggle that way since he was much younger. Julia was good with Joaquin, spending hours with him during the layover on Martinique, while seeming to avoid more contact with Simone than necessary.

When Julia finally showed mercy on the boy, he took her hand as they walked toward the main house. They were nearly past Simone when Joaquin stopped and sniffed the air.

"*Faucon?*" he said as he looked around him. As she drew on the cigar, he released Julia's hand and scampered to Simone who hugged him to her waist.

"You should be asleep, *mon chou*. We leave tomorrow and I shall need your assistance," she smiled down at him.

"I had to say goodbye to Hercules," he said, looking up at her. "I will be ready."

Leaning down, Simone kissed Joaquin on both cheeks. "Sleep well, little man."

"*Bonne nuit*," he said. He paused and spoke briefly with Julia and accepted a good night kiss from her as well. Simone watched Joaquin walk to the house, acutely aware of Julia's presence. No matter how much she tried, she was involuntarily drawn to her. Simone walked to within a few feet from her. There was something she wanted to say, but no words came to her.

Julia nodded and said, "Good evening, Captain."

"*Mademoiselle*," Simone's voice stopped her.

"Yes, Captain."

"Tomorrow, as you know," Simone began, avoiding direct eye contact with Julia, "we will be leaving."

"I shall be ready."

"I am certain you will be glad to leave here and return to your home."

"Actually," Julia said quietly, "it is lovely here."

Clearing her throat, Simone said, "You and *Mademoiselle*

Longmire will be on board the *Northumberland* with my brother tomorrow."

"What?" Julia said, her eyes shooting up to Simone's face. "But I..."

"You will be safer on the *Northumberland*. The accommodations will be quite comfortable for you."

Seeming to search for a response, Julia finally said, "But what about Joaquin? His lessons? Surely you do not..."

"I do not wish more trouble on board my ship than necessary. I have other matters to occupy my mind," Simone interrupted, her eyes finally meeting Julia's. Even in the moonlight, her eyes took Simone's breath away.

"I would not be in your way, Captain," Julia said.

The pull of Julia's eyes was as steady and certain as the pull of the moon on the tides and Simone took a step back. "Anton will be expecting you. Good evening, *Mademoiselle*," she managed to say despite her distraction.

Simone watched the figure walk away from her and said softly, "Julia, please." She thought she detected a momentary pause in Julia's steps, but waited until she was certain Julia had entered the house before following and making her way to her room.

Chapter
Nine

WHILE THE *DISCOVERY II* piloted back into the harbor at Tybee Island, Frankie Alford changed into her comfortable khaki cargo shorts and a summer-weight knit pullover. Her well-worn deck shoes provided her with good traction over the cruiser's wet deck as she leaned over the railing to loop a mooring line around a pylon.

As soon as they tagged and logged the artifacts from the day's dive she would turn her attention to the one project she had been avoiding and dreading most. The cannon raised before Julia's disappearance. The chemical process of stabilizing the metal from its long immersion in salt water was completed. The directors of the Institute were anxious to see the newest prize.

Damian joined Frankie in her Jeep. "We gonna start tonight?" he asked as she adjusted her seatbelt.

"Yeah. I can't put it off any longer. The *Peach* has waited long enough to tell her story. We've got a lot data to compile. When we get back, I'll log in the items we brought in today. I want you to develop the pictures of the ship I took. I think I noticed something unusual."

"Like what?"

"Look at the pictures and tell me what you see."

Wheeling the Jeep into her usual parking space, Frankie followed Damian up the stairs to the Institute's front doors. She tossed a film canister to him. "How long?"

"Maybe an hour. Maybe less if the dryer cooperates. See you in your office," he said as he trotted down the hallway.

FRANKIE CARRIED HER computer case into her office and set it on her desk, scooting her chair closer as she brought the laptop to life. This was the boring part of her work, but it still had to be done. She plugged the computer in and walked down the hall to a break room, praying there was still coffee available.

Successful in procuring a mug of barely tolerable brown liquid, she scooted her office chair closer to the desk as she wiggled the mouse for her laptop. Based on measurements the team had taken of the shipwreck and the approximate position of its masts, they extrapolated the size and dimensions of the *Peach* and pieced together the location of several bulkheads in the lowest part of the ship. Using their combined historical and scientific expertise, the estimated length of the ship had been approximately one hundred to one hundred and twenty feet. If they had been correct in their assumption, the ship originally contained four decks, the possible height from waterline to main deck would have been nearly thirty feet. More of the ship than they first believed had survived as it came to rest in a soft section of the shallow Continental Shelf.

Based on her calculations, Julia had believed the ship could have been a British brigandine from the War of 1812 period. British ships had been active along the American Atlantic southern seaboard, intercepting American shipping as well as that of the Americans' French allies during the blockades of Georgia and South Carolina seaports beginning in late 1812.

"These are some great shots, Frankie," Damian announced as he entered her office.

"Have you looked at them all?"

"Of course," he answered, sounding slightly insulted.

"What do you think caused her to go down?"

Damian dragged a chair next to Frankie's desk and sat down next to her. Shuffling through the photos again, he puffed his cheeks out and exhaled. "Well, I think we can rule out a hurricane."

"What makes you say that?" Frankie asked as she typed figures into her computer program.

"Well, look at this freakin' hole in the side! It had to have been during a battle or skirmish." Bringing a picture closer to his eyes, he pointed to a dark splotch and said, "Looks like it took a direct hit...about here."

"Really?" Frankie questioned as she tapped a key on the laptop and leaned back. "Think three dimensionally."

"What?"

"Mentally see the ship upright and floating. Do you see it?"

"I'm working on it, but I always did for shit on those spatial tests."

"Maybe this will help," she said as she turned the laptop toward him.

Glancing at the computer simulation and back at the photograph, he said, "But that's not possible. Is it?"

"The only way I can think of for that hole to be where it is would be if the crew deliberately scuttled her." Leaning forward, Frankie stared at the computer monitor. "It couldn't have been an explosion in the magazine or the debris would have been blown to hell and back and not nearly as defined. And since the ship predates torpedoes, the only explanation is that this hole below the waterline came from within the ship itself. We'll have to examine the wood around the area and hope it still shows the directionality of the blast."

"Sabotage?"

"Possibly, but we might never know for sure."

"Well, that's more than a little frustrating," Damian said as he tossed the pictures on Frankie's desk.

"I'd almost be willing to bet it took more than one cannon shot to sink this bad girl. Pretty big ship for her day. Could have carried, what, maybe a crew of around eighty?"

"But it could have been manned by as few as a dozen good sailors. Could have been scuttled to prevent it from falling into enemy hands if they were undermanned."

"Maybe," Frankie said. "Probably gonna end up another one of those annoying maritime mysteries, like the Bermuda Triangle." Her eyes began misting over. "I wish Julia could be here to see this." Damian ran his hand over Frankie's shoulders while they watched a computer animation of the *Peach* turn on the computer screen.

FRANKIE SAT AT her desk, staring once again at the computerized picture of the *Peach*. The longer she gazed at the animation, the more clearly she could envision what the large ship might have looked like. She shut the computer down and made her way to the lab two floors below her office.

The eighty-thousand-gallon receiving tank had been prepared days before the dive team began bringing up artifacts from the *Peach*. Its salt water content matched that of the Atlantic Ocean off the Georgia coast and was kept at a temperature matching that at the ship's depth. Seeing it through the clear new container, Julia had been so proud the day the encrusted cannon had been raised to the surface. Now Frankie couldn't drag her eyes away from it. It was beautiful. The cannon rested mere inches from her fingers. She reached out and touched the glass of the tank as lab technicians prepared to hoist it onto a work bench.

A bright fluorescent work light hung over the table. Frankie pulled on rubber gloves and guided the dripping cannon into a waiting cradle. The electrolyte reduction process had loosened large chunks of the encrustation. The remaining cleaning would be done by hand, a long and tedious procedure. She ran her fingers over the metal and felt a portion of the crust near the breach loosen slightly. She moved around the table and saw a small uncovered area that looked like a brass or copper plate. She withdrew a small plastic probe from a pocket of her cargo pants and slipped the tip of the instrument under the loose section. She twisted it slightly, grinning like the village idiot when a small piece of embedded sediment fell away. She brushed the small, newly uncovered area and swung a magnifying glass over the pitted surface. Letters etched into the plate were still difficult to read, but Frankie hoped it would eventually reveal the maker or brand name for that particular cannon. Armed with that information she might be able to trace it to the name of the ship carrying it. She spent the next two hours working on the plate, typing entries into her field notes and activity log.

Chapter
Ten

SIMONE WAS SADDENED to leave her island home, but the excitement of setting sail always seemed to dispel that sadness. She went to her ship before daybreak and now stood on the main deck of *Le Faucon* watching the long boat carrying Julia and Kitty toward the *Northumberland*. Reaching down she offered a hand to Esperanza and lifted her onto the deck before pulling Joaquin up to join them. Esperanza cast a glance at the *Northumberland* anchored nearby, making sure she had Julia's eye as she slid an arm possessively around Simone's waist.

Julia watched Esperanza and her son board *Le Faucon*, and what she saw seemed like a cohesive family unit. She knew she could easily submit to her attraction to Simone, but also knew she couldn't do anything to hurt Joaquin. She didn't understand the forces that brought her to this time and place and thought, if she were very lucky, it would all wind up being a dream from which she would eventually awaken. Simone was nothing more than a fantasy, a temptation, an internal manifestation of her own desires. A hand meeting hers brought her back to her current reality as she stepped onto the deck of the *Northumberland*.

FOR THE NEXT three and a half calm days, Julia did little more than think. Gradually her thoughts turned back to the *Georgia Peach*. Sadness swept through her as she stood near the deck railing and observed Simone's ships plying through the open waters. She missed her life. Even without Amy there was so much she looked forward to. None of her skills prepared her to live in this time. She missed flush toilets, documentaries on television and long drives into the Georgia countryside. She laughed out loud at her thoughts, followed immediately by the overwhelming knowledge she might never see or do those things again.

"Are you all right, *Mademoiselle*?" a male voice asked from behind her. Julia looked over her shoulder and saw Anton.

"Yes. I was just thinking about my home," Julia answered, turning and leaning against the railing.

"You will return there soon, *Mademoiselle*," Anton smiled. "Simone may travel to the American coastline once we leave Isla de Margarita."

"How long a trip is that by ship?"

Rubbing his jaw, Anton said, "It is quite a long journey. We must sail past the British strongholds in Jamaica and the Cayman Islands. Perhaps a month if the winds are with us."

Another month, Julia thought as she stared down at the water. "Do you enjoy this life, Anton?" she asked.

"It has been profitable, but soon Simone and I will be leaving it behind us."

"Why?"

"Simone only wishes to be with her Arabians now. She is at an age that marks the decline of her life."

Julia laughed. "She is still a young woman."

"My sister will soon pass her thirty-fifth year," Anton said, looking at her incredulously.

Only a year older than I am. Thinking back, she had no idea what the life expectancy might have been in the early 1800s. "And what about you? What are your plans before you become an old man?" she asked.

Blushing slightly he continued, "I hope one day to take a wife and have many fat, healthy sons. This would be no life for them."

"No daughters?" Julia smiled.

"No more than one," Anton chuckled. "Women are such fickle, but delightful creatures. I do not know if I could tolerate more than one."

"Will your sister keep Esperanza with her if she gives up this life?"

"Esperanza would stay, but Simone does not keep her. She is a free woman and my sister is an honorable woman." Anton seemed offended by Julia's question.

"I did not mean to suggest otherwise. I know the Captain is quite attached to Joaquin."

"He is like a son to her, that is true." Looking down, as if weighing his thoughts, Anton said, "Esperanza fills a need. Other than that I cannot comment as to the nature of their relationship."

"I did not mean to pry," Julia said, pushing away from the rail. "Where is Kitty?"

Blushing furiously, Anton said, "Ah, yes. Last I saw her she was still sleeping."

Patting Anton on the arm as she passed by him, Julia smiled. "You are a fortunate man, *mon Capitaine*."

SIMONE SAT AT her desk, writing the day's entry in her journal. The days had been long and she was restless, walking along the deck of *Le Faucon* and needlessly rechecking the ship's supplies. The only distraction was her explanation to Joaquin about the importance of even the smallest details involved in commanding a ship such as *Le Faucon*. She and the boy spent their evenings playing their instruments and laughing at their mistakes. Often they were joined by Esperanza, who sat patiently and listened to their concerts. Simone was finding it more and more difficult to engage in intimate moments with her companion. She was comfortable with Esperanza, but knew she was not in love with her, no matter how much she wished she could force herself to be.

She hadn't said anything to anyone except Anton, but was determined that once her business with Laffite was completed, she would leave her life at sea behind. The ship she promised to Archambault would be *Le Faucon*, her flagship. He had more than earned the honor. Even though he questioned her decisions periodically, she trusted his loyalty as much as that of any crew member. She glanced up from her writing when the door to her private cabin opened.

Esperanza closed the door and walked to where Simone was seated. Running slender hands across Simone's shoulders she leaned down and kissed her.

"To what do I owe the honor?" Simone asked, her face still close to Esperanza's smiling lips.

"You work much too hard, *mon amour*," Esperanza said in a low, inviting voice as she drifted her hand down Simone's chest.

Stopping the hand before it stroked her breasts, Simone replied, "There is much to do." She knew Esperanza could arouse her body easily, but taking her to her bed would not alleviate her passions.

"Are you punishing me by withholding your favor, Simone?"

"Of course not. I am anxious about the meeting with Laffite. Nothing more."

Esperanza breathed deeply as she stood and rested her hand along Simone's shoulder. "Even when placing her on another ship away from you, you cannot remove the English woman from your thoughts."

"She has nothing to do with this, Esperanza," Simone said sharply as she stood. As close as her body was to the caramel-skinned woman, Simone would have taken her as a matter of course under normal circumstances.

"If you desire her, then take her and be done with it, Simone." Esperanza's eyes burned with anger. "Once you have satisfied yourself, you will return to my bed and I will forgive your temporary weakness."

Grabbing the woman's wrists, Simone jerked her closer. "Perhaps I will rid myself of the both of you and find someone more willing and less jealous for no reason."

Speaking softly, Esperanza said, "I see it in your eyes. The falcon has seen her prey and will strike when the time is right, filling the hunger in her belly."

The door to the cabin burst open. Simone pulled Esperanza behind her as she withdrew her musket from her waistband. Joaquin stopped immediately in his tracks and stared at the weapon pointed at him, eyes wide.

Lowering the musket quickly, Simone let out the breath she had been holding. "What is it, Joaquin?" she asked as calmly as she could manage as she returned the weapon to her waist.

"Land, *mon Faucon*! We arrive at Isla de Margarita within the hour," Joaquin answered.

"The other ships?"

"The signal has been sent."

"Excellent," Simone smiled as she crossed the room. "Tell Archambault we will stay aboard tonight and go ashore in the morning, will you?"

"Of course, *Faucon*," Joaquin said and left.

When she was sure Joaquin was gone, Simone returned her attention to Esperanza. "I do not wish to speak of these matters again. Do you understand me, Esperanza?" There was no anger in Simone's voice as she spoke. "A difficult time may await us when we leave here and I cannot have this distraction for the safety of my ship and my crew. That will always include you and Joaquin. The English woman will be gone soon, so please retract your claws." The tone in Simone's voice was one of resignation.

Esperanza nodded and walked past Simone to leave the cabin.

A DOZEN CREWMEN from the four ships scoured the island for any sign of intrusion before they sent word the others could come safely ashore. Laffite and his ships had not yet arrived and Simone ordered shelters constructed while they waited. She would allow Laffite three days to appear. She looked at her charts carefully. If Laffite did not arrive she would sail back toward Martinique and leave Julia at a port in the Grenadines. She could have dropped her there on the way to Isla de Margarita. Perhaps she should have and been done with it. But she couldn't bring herself to remove the woman from her life just yet.

By mid-afternoon, with the exception of a standby crew left aboard each ship, all crew members and passengers were on the island, the ships anchored just off its western shore. Simone spent the next two days in her personal tent. Food was brought to her and she rarely left except late in the evening, when she walked the white sandy shoreline and scanned the horizon, deep in thought.

She was awakened the morning of the third day when Esperanza slipped into her tent. Ships were seen approaching the island. Within minutes, Simone observed the movement of five ships that appeared to be turning in the general direction of Margarita. Alerting her crews to remain vigilant, Simone took her telescope and climbed to the top of the rise behind their encampment. She smiled when the ships were close enough for her to identify Laffite's flag ship. As the first vessel entered the cove, it dropped its top sails and began to pilot into a position away from her ships.

An hour later Simone crossed the beach and greeted a dapper looking man with a long nose and shoulder-length, wavy black hair. Removing his plumed cavalier hat he bowed slightly and took her hand, kissing it. Simone smiled at the gesture, but knew Laffite was a gentleman of the old school, if nothing else. He was a tall, slender man dressed in black. Gold buttons and trim broke his monochromatic clothing. As the other ships joined the first of Laffite's flotilla and launched long boats, Simone and Laffite strode up the small rise overlooking the beach toward her tent.

"IT IS GOOD to see you again, Simone," Laffite said as he followed her into the privacy of her tent.

"If you had been one day longer, I would not have been here to greet you," Simone said, sitting leisurely on a chair and propping her feet up.

"The wind was not as cooperative as I had hoped," Laffite said, taking a seat nearby. "And of course, there was the British problem."

"How many British ships did you see?"

"Only a few and naturally our ships are much swifter than those albatrosses they claim as sea vessels," Laffite grinned. "I see you have added one to your little group."

"Yes, the *Northumberland*. Raul was able to persuade her captain to relinquish her not long ago. Drink?"

"Please. Your recent exploits have preceded you. In fact, I have heard that a certain Captain Bentham would like to renew his acquaintance with *Le Faucon*."

"That is not likely," Simone laughed, remembering the arrogance of the British captain, which was nearly as great as her own. "So," she said as she handed him a glass of wine and leaned back, "why did you send DuChamp to request this meeting, Jean?"

"He told you of Barataria?"

"*Oui.*"

"A month before the destruction of my headquarters, a British naval officer visited Barataria and proposed an alliance against the Americans. The British are planning to launch an attack and seize New Orleans."

"And what was your response?"

"That I would consider it, of course. I actually have no intention of assisting those pompous asses in taking my city. I sent a message to the Louisiana governor apprising him of the proposal and offering my services against the British."

"And their response was to launch an attack against you and destroy your home? Perhaps you should reconsider the British offer," Simone chuckled.

"Never!" Laffite said as he rose and began pacing the small area in front of Simone. He abruptly stopped his pacing and gazed down at her, his expression serious. "Our days are numbered, Simone. You know that as well as I do. I have come to ask you to bring your ships to New Orleans and help repel the British attack."

Laughing loudly, Simone set her glass down and stood to face Laffite. "Why would I consider such a ridiculous invitation, Jean? I say stand off and see who the victor will be. We risk nothing."

"I am preparing to relocate farther to the west. By allying with the Americans we would be granted amnesty for anything we have done in the past and be allowed to continue privateering against the British, all with the blessing of the Americans. That, along with the Letters of Marque issued by the Republic of Cartagena would make Spanish ships an easy prey as well."

"You, more than anyone, should know the Americans can be trusted no more than the British. God, man! Look what they did to you."

Waving his hand dismissively at her, he continued. "They burned Barataria, yes, but they were not able to seize a single iota of my supplies. I have sent a courier to the leader of the American troops, General Jackson. His soldiers and volunteers will need the flints and powder I can offer. In return, all we have to do is use our ships to prevent the British from landing more troops near New Orleans."

"I still see no advantage in this endeavor."

Laffite rubbed his face and looked at Simone. "Despite the attack on my headquarters and the idiocy of Governor Claiborne, I believe in the ideals of liberty and equality the Americans stand for. If New Orleans falls, then all of French Louisiana will be under the control of the British."

"Do not speak to me of liberty and equality, Laffite. You, a man who has profited from the sale of slaves hundreds of times. One of your lackeys attempted to beat Esperanza into submission and sell her and her son to another pathetic excuse for a man."

"But you killed him, doing me a favor in the long run." Laffite shrugged. Reaching out, he held her by the upper arm. "Join me, Simone, and send ships packed with British troops to the bottom of the Gulf."

"I will call my other captains together and you may speak to them, if you wish. If you can sell this load of manure to them I will not stop them. You are asking a great deal for nothing more than a piece of paper."

"I am offering the chance to sail without the fear of being stopped and arrested."

"We will see, Jean. We will see. When do you set sail again?"

"I will give my men two days to rest from their long voyage."

"You shall have my final decision by then."

"Thank you, Simone."

THE SUN WAS rapidly falling below the horizon, sending red and orange and yellow rays into the sky. Simone sat outside her tent and watched the celebration beginning on the beach below. Laffite would present a strong argument for her ships to join with his to repel the British, but she doubted her crew would agree to fight for some abstract idea rather than more concrete riches. The best they could hope for was the acquisition of more ships and the paper gratitude of the Americans. If the Americans lost, they would have risked their lives for absolutely no reward.

"*Faucon!*" Joaquin's voice called out. A moment later she smiled as Joaquin ran over the rise leading to her tent. He was panting when he stopped in front of her. "Are you coming to the celebration? The food is wonderful!"

"I will be there shortly, *mon petit*." The sound of music drifted up toward her and she smiled. It had been a long time since she and her men had had cause for festivities. "Bring the instruments!" Joaquin called out as he left. "There are concertinas, ocarinas, and other instruments. You promised to teach me to dance!"

She remembered her promise, but there had never been an opportunity to honor the request. Carrying the mandolin and dulcimer, her eyes lit up when she saw the men twirling around a large fire on the beach. It was a good night for laughing, drinking and dancing.

JULIA WATCHED THE Nineteenth Century version of a beach party from a distance. Although there was an absence of bikinis and a volleyball net, the scene didn't appear to be all that different. She stopped to remove her shoes when she reached the edge of the beach. She wiggled her toes, enjoying the feel of the sand that still held the warmth of the sun between them. Her eyes scanned the revelers until she found Kitty seated next to Anton several feet back from the heat of the bonfire.

"Is this seat taken?" she asked, wondering if Kitty would rather have some time alone with Anton.

Kitty grabbed Julia's hand and pulled her down beside her. "Isn't this wonderful!" she exclaimed.

The two women pointed to different members of the crews and laughed at their antics. Rum was dispensed freely and certainly lowered the inhibitions of the men as they reveled in the music and dancing. Julia was dragged into a dance more than once. She had never been much of a dancer. It wasn't that she didn't like the music or feel its beat inside. She thought she looked ridiculous when she danced. Right at that moment it didn't matter since the consumption of rum made it impossible for anyone to be critical. It seemed that falling down in the middle of a fast dance was an expected event.

Across the fire ring, she watched as Simone joined the celebration and was happy to see her again. It seemed to Julia that the captain had been avoiding her while they waited for Laffite's arrival. She smiled when Simone and Joaquin took out their instruments and joined in the music. Simone looked more relaxed than usual and the sound of her laughter was sweeter to Julia's ears than the music around her. Julia suspected Simone would be quite an enjoyable woman to know if taken away from her life on the sea and placed in a safe and comfortable setting. Especially if the intimidating Esperanza wasn't continually hanging on her.

Julia smiled when she saw Simone take Joaquin's hand and walk with him to an area not crowded with drunken crewmen. Julia observed them as Simone spoke to the boy briefly. Placing his hands in the proper position, more or less, she slowly took him through the simple steps of a slow dance, smiling down at him as his face became a mask of concentration. Several times he stopped to regain the beat of the music. Simone was the epitome of patience, periodically offering words of encouragement and praise. By the second dance, he would be the hit of the dance floor among the ten-year-old set, Julia thought.

Well after dark, as Julia chatted with Kitty and Anton, their conversation stopped when there was a change in the music. The sound of drums, guitars, and concertinas began a pulsating, sultry tune. Kitty caught Julia's attention and pointed to the far side of the fire. Julia's mouth fell open as she watched Esperanza dancing alone, her body moving erotically with the driving pulse of the music. *What the hell is she doing?* Julia thought. She blinked, but couldn't take her eyes off Esperanza's undulations, her body becoming an offering. The movements were more than suggestive. They were a prelude to sex. It was the most sexually inviting dance Julia had ever seen. She scanned the others sitting around the fire. Esperanza had everyone's undivided attention, but it quickly became obvious the dance was intended for only one person. Simone's eyes followed Esperanza appreciatively and a knowing smile teased the corners of her mouth. By the time the music ended, even Julia was considering jumping Esperanza's body. Glancing at Kitty for a moment, she noticed the Irish woman was blushing even though she, too, was unable to look away. Esperanza's chest rose and fell as she extended a hand down to Simone. Taking it, Simone stood and drew Esperanza to her, kissing her lightly. They exchanged a few words before Simone returned to her seat.

"God!" Kitty breathed. "How did her body do that? Her hips must surely be double-jointed!"

"You may dance for me in such a way anytime you wish, my dear," Anton chuckled.

"I...I...," Kitty attempted as her cheeks reddened, bringing laughter from both Julia and Anton as the redhead fanned her face with her hand.

In the midst of their laughter Joaquin sat down next to Julia and folded his legs in front of him. Smiling up at her as she brought her arm around his shoulders and hugged him affectionately, he handed her a tankard. "What is this?" she asked as she took it.

"Rum, of course," he laughed. "It is mixed with a fruit of some kind."

"Have you been drinking rum, Joaquin?" Julia frowned.

"No. *Faucon* says I am yet too young," he said.

"Well, in this case, *Faucon* is right," Julia said.

Leaning closer to her, he whispered conspiratorially, "But I took a very small sip."

Julia couldn't suppress a laugh at the unrepressed mischief in the boy's dark eyes as she brought the drink to her lips. She could hold her liquor well and was surprised by how sweet the drink was. "This is very good, Joaquin. Thank you," she said as she took another deep drink.

By the time Julia finished her drink she felt much more relaxed. She closed her eyes and listened to the music and smiled. When she opened her eyes a few moments later everything around her seemed sharper, clearer. She shook her head and wondered what kind of fruit was mixed with the rum. Her skin prickled and she felt suddenly quite warm. Maybe she couldn't hold her liquor as well as she thought she could. *Perhaps rum in this time period is stronger than the rum I'm accustomed to.*

The musicians began a slow pounding rhythm that seemed to match the beating of Julia's heart. She began to feel too warm and untied the fabric around the neck of her blouse to cool off. Across the fire circle, Simone was engaged in an animated conversation with Laffite, who was seated next to her. Julia couldn't force her eyes away from Simone's smile and rose to her feet. Walking slowly around the edge of the celebrants, the sand warm beneath her bare feet, she stopped in front of Simone. She was inexplicably overcome with the desire to please her. Her body began swaying in its own provocative dance to the driving pulse of the music. She looked down at Simone's face, her beautiful face, framed by hair the color of midnight, golden eyes taking her in. Holding a hand out, Julia beckoned Simone to join her. Julia never took her eyes off the captain's beautiful face as she rose, seemingly moving in slow motion. When Simone stood, Julia circled her, bringing their bodies closer. She felt the heat radiating from Simone's body, inhaled her changing scent as her body reacted to Julia's dance. Running her hands through her short hair, Julia felt completely uninhibited while still knowing this was something she would never ordinarily do, not even in her most erotic dreams.

Turning her back to Simone, Julia pressed against her, hips swaying seductively with the music. Simone placed her hands lightly on Julia's shoulders and slowly drifted them down her arms. Julia wanted more of her touch. She wanted Simone. Reaching behind her, she pulled Simone as close as possible. Hot breath grazed her ear and neck as she raised a hand over her head, drawing Simone's head down. She felt the skin of her neck ignite as Simone's lips made contact. Spinning to reverse their positions, Julia pressed her body against Simone's back and slipped her hands around her waist and teased her way up Simone's sides and over her chest. Feeling firm breasts beneath her hands inflamed Julia's passion and desire to the point of painfulness.

The music faded away and Simone turned to face Julia, both of them aroused and breathing heavily. Julia brought her hand up and stroked the side of Simone's face with her fingertips. Then she pulled her hand away and stared at it. Simone tilted Julia's chin up, their mouths close enough for their breath to intermingle. A frown flickered across Simone's face when she saw the desire in Julia's eyes. As Julia clung to her, Simone scooped her into her arms and carried her up the rise toward her tent, followed by the stares and knowing smiles of her crew.

SIMONE WAS FURIOUS realizing what had caused Julia's sudden affectionate behavior. She would deal with Esperanza the following morning. She gently laid Julia on the cot in her tent and watched the rise and fall of her breasts. It would be so simple to succumb to the offering before her. Esperanza was right. She did want Julia. She wanted to feel the lushness of her body against her own, its softness beneath her fingers. But not in this manner. She turned her eyes away, unable to look at the enticing woman any longer. A warm hand grabbed hers.

"Simone," Julia breathed. "My body burns for you. Please."

Simone smiled down at Julia. "You have a fever. It will be gone soon. You must rest now."

Julia sat up, swung her feet off the cot and stood. She stared into Simone's eyes as she moved closer, her hand stroking over the captain's chest. "I know you want me," she said, her voice husky with desire. "My God, you are so beautiful," she continued, her fingers making their way along Simone's waist.

"I cannot deny my feelings, but..."

"Then why do you hesitate? Do you not find me desirable?" Julia lower lip stuck out in a teasing pout.

Simone felt herself weakening as Julia drew her closer. She wanted to feel Julia's touch. She ached with desire as she took Julia's face between her hands and kissed her cheeks. It would be so easy to have what she couldn't get out of her mind.

"Captain Moreau?" Kitty's voice said from outside the tent.

Simone gently drew away from Julia. "You are not yourself, *Mademoiselle*. Please lie down." She took in a ragged breath and turned away.

She was certain her face was flushed as she pushed the flap of the tent open. "*Mademoiselle* Longmire," she acknowledged, her voice hoarse. "*Mademoiselle* Blanchard is not herself. May I ask you to see to her? I am returning to my ship for the evening. We leave soon."

"Captain," Kitty said as Simone stepped by her to leave.

"Yes, *Mademoiselle*," Simone answered without turning around.

"I...I am aware of your sexual proclivities, but I can assure you Miss Blanchard does not share them." Simone turned to stare at her. From the look on her face Kitty must have known she had overstepped her boundaries and was prepared for the repercussions that could follow. Simone admired the redhead's loyalty and concern for her friend.

With a simple nod Simone cleared her throat and said, "I can assure you nothing inappropriate occurred between *Mademoiselle* Blanchard and myself. Please see that she is made comfortable for the remainder of the evening." With nothing further to say, Simone strode away from the tent.

Chapter
Eleven

JULIA OPENED HER eyes and immediately squeezed them shut as they were assaulted by light. She tried to sit up, but the pounding in her head caused her to drop back onto a pillow. She rolled her body away from the offensive light and opened her eyes into the smallest slits possible. *Where the hell am I?* She rubbed her eyes and looked around without raising her head. She knew she wasn't in her cabin on board the *Northumberland*. Tentatively she raised her body onto her elbows. She was in a tent. She saw her clothes draped neatly over a nearby chair and sucked in a breath as she pulled the cover up far enough to look at her body. She was completely naked. Lying on her back she covered her eyes with her arm and tried desperately to remember how she came to be in the tent. Realizing where she was, she jumped up as if there was a snake in the bed with her, ignoring the continual throbbing in her head. She was reaching for her clothes when she heard angry voices outside the tent. Quickly returning to the bed, she covered her entire body.

"What the hell were you thinking?" she heard Simone ask. "You could have killed her!"

"Consider her my gift to you," a woman's familiar voice retorted. "You wanted her and I gave her to you."

"You know well enough I would never take a woman in such a manner."

"Perhaps I should have put some of my potion in your drink as well."

"If I ever suspect such a thing, your time with me will be at an end, Esperanza."

"You wanted to bed her, Simone. Now you will have her out of your system. You have taken her and she will remember nothing."

Julia squeezed her eyes tightly and felt hot liquid travel down the side of her face. She was drugged and taken to bed by Simone. Was she given the nineteenth century equivalent of a date rape drug? The thought of it made her stomach churn. She didn't feel any of the usual after-effects of lovemaking and wondered if it was as good as it was in her fantasies. Had Simone enjoyed the one-sided tryst? How could she have?

When Julia no longer heard the voices, she slipped out of bed and began dressing. She managed to get as far as her petticoat when the flap of the tent opened, causing Julia to attempt to cover her body with her arms.

"Good morning," Kitty said cheerfully with a broad smile which faded rapidly when she saw Julia's pale face and red-rimmed eyes. Going to her side, Kitty wrapped an arm around Julia's waist as she sat on the edge of the bed and buried her head in her hands. "I suspect you have quite a headache," she said softly.

"How could she?" Julia asked as she brought her tear-stained face up and looked at Kitty.

"Because she is a mean bitch, if you'll pardon my language," Kitty said as she held Julia.

"But she has always been so kind to me."

"She has hated you since the *Viper* was taken. I think she is jealous of you."

Raising her head Julia asked, "Why would the Captain possibly be jealous of me?"

"Not the Captain," Kitty said. "Esperanza. She put something into your drink last night which made you rather–um–rather, well, affectionate."

"Just so the Captain could bring me in here and fuc...have her way with me," Julia said bitterly.

"Perhaps. But the Captain did not do anything, although I confess I was concerned about her intentions and followed her as she carried you here."

"I was buck naked when I woke up this morning so something must have happened!"

"The Captain brought you here and asked me to undress you. Whatever Esperanza put into your drink made you feverish and, I must say, I thought the Captain looked somewhat flushed as well. I am certain, although I cannot understand it, that she lies with Esperanza as a man lies with a woman. I told her I was equally certain you did not engage in such perverse liaisons," Kitty said with a frown. "That you are not that kind of woman."

"But..." Julia began. But I am exactly that kind of woman, Julia thought, not knowing whether she should feel relieved or disappointed.

"The Captain retired to *Le Faucon* last night and met with her other captains. Anton and the others returned to shore quite late, but she remained on board alone, not returning until less than an hour ago. She was still as angry as a hornet."

Julia nodded numbly as Kitty rose and smiled at her. "She sent me to wake you before she returned to her ship. We will be setting sail in a few hours. Come with me and we will find you some breakfast. You must be starving by now."

Straightening her clothing and hair as best she could, Julia followed Kitty from the tent. There was no sign of Simone as Julia nibbled at a hard biscuit and a piece of jerky. Anton poured her a cup of rich black coffee and squatted next to her as she ate.

"You are feeling better, *Mademoiselle*?" he asked.

"Yes. Thank you, Anton," Julia nodded as she watched men loading the long boats in preparation for departure. Everyone must have seen Simone take her to her tent the night before. Julia felt self-conscious and was certain they were all staring at her.

"Your belongings have been transferred from the *Northumberland* to *Le Faucon*," he said, doodling in the dirt with a slender stick. When she didn't respond, he glanced up at her. "We leave today for New Orleans. It is a long journey and my sister wishes for Joaquin to continue his studies."

"I would rather stay on board the *Northumberland* with you and Kitty. But I assume that choice is not mine to make," Julia frowned.

"I will relay your request to *Faucon* if you wish."

Standing and rubbing her hands together briskly, Julia shook her head. "No. But please convey to the Captain that I do not wish to have her lover anywhere near me."

"Esperanza will be punished, I assure you, *Mademoiselle*. She has left *Faucon* little choice."

"What do you mean by punished? Banished from the Captain's bed?" Julia smirked.

"For what she did to you, my sister can no longer trust her. It is nothing for you to be concerned with. It is Simone's decision. She will carry out the punishment herself."

Turning to face him as he stood, Julia asked, "Where are they?"

Glancing at the ships lolling in the cove, Anton nodded toward them. "Aboard *Le Faucon*. Esperanza will be sent to another vessel afterward."

Julia felt panic as the meager breakfast began to rise up in her throat. "Take me there! I must speak to the Captain."

"I cannot. *Faucon* has ordered —"

"I don't give a damn what she ordered," Julia said as she grabbed his shirt. "Take me to the ship immediately!"

"Prepare your things, *Mademoiselle*. We will be leaving soon," Anton said coldly, pulling her hands from his shirt.

"Shit!" Julia muttered to herself as she looked around. Running as quickly as she could, she intercepted a long boat being pushed away from the shore.

"Which ship are you going to?" she asked in English and French.

"*Le Faucon*," one of the men answered, looking at her appreciatively.

"Take me to the ship immediately!" Stepping onto the boat, she said, "And set a world record rowing pace." When the men looked at her dumbly, she raised her voice. *"Vite! Vite!"*

IT SEEMED AN eternity passed before Julia made her way onto the deck of *Le Faucon*, cursing the clothing she was wearing. She would have given anything for her old cargo pants to allow her more freedom of movement. Crewmen were untying the ship's sails and storing materials being brought aboard. She grabbed the arm of a passing older man. *"Faucon.* Where is she?" When the man didn't answer, she shook him. "Where is *Faucon*?"

Quietly he answered, "Below." Then he pulled his arm away and went quickly to the railing to help bring material from the long boat on board.

Julia ran across the deck and made her way to the ladder leading down toward the hold, searching quickly as she moved farther down into the ship. When she couldn't go any lower, she stopped to catch her breath and heard the sickening snap of a whip and a muffled cry. *No!* She moved toward the sound until she reached the farthest end of the hold. She stopped, not wanting to believe the scene in front of her. Esperanza's hands were tied around the stern capstan. Three bleeding angry lashes striped her exposed back and her body shook. Simone stood a few feet behind her, preparing a small whip to strike again.

"No!" Julia screamed. She dashed toward Esperanza and stood between her and Simone. "How can you do this?" she seethed, turning to face Simone. "It's barbaric!"

"If you do not wish to take her place, you will return to the deck immediately," Simone said coldly.

"Why are you doing this? Because of last night? Surely it cannot warrant this," Julia pleaded. "Nothing happened. I am fine."

"Leave!" Simone ordered. Julia had never heard Simone sound so menacing. Suddenly, she could believe the woman was capable of much worse than killing.

Standing her ground, Julia stared into Simone's eyes. "No," she said, her voice low.

Simone drew her arm back and swung the whip forward. Julia hoped Simone would stop the whip before it struck, but it lashed across her upper arm, cutting through the thin material of her blouse and drawing blood. Julia's hand flew up and covered the stinging cut. She sucked in a breath and squeezed her eyes shut. A tear trickled down her cheek as she opened her eyes again and stared resolutely at Simone.

"Go," Esperanza whispered. "Do not shame her."

"I am the cause of this and will not see you suffer for it," Julia responded, dropping her bloodied hand and lifting her head slightly, challenging Simone to strike her again, hoping the blow wouldn't come.

Simone glared at Julia for a moment before turning and stalking away. Letting out a breath she didn't realize she was holding, Julia moved to the far side of the capstan and worked the thick rope around Esperanza's wrists loose. As Esperanza rubbed her wrists and began drawing her dress up over her body, Julia gingerly touched the cut on her arm. "How can you possibly love such a woman?" she asked as she winced.

"What I did was wrong," Esperanza answered quietly. "Simone cannot maintain control of her crew if she allows even the smallest violation of our code to go unpunished. I was willing to accept my punishment without judging her."

"But Joaquin. He would hate her for harming you. Doesn't she realize that?"

"Of course, but I left her no choice."

"There is always a choice," Julia said softly. Turning to leave the hold and its damp musty smell now intruded upon by the smell of blood and sweat, she was stopped by Esperanza's voice.

"Simone is fighting against her own desires. She wants you."

Looking at the woman over her shoulder, Julia said flatly, "But *I* don't want her."

Julia considered demanding to be returned to the *Northumberland*, but decided against it. She helped Esperanza leave the bowels of the ship, pretending her injuries were much greater than they actually were. Julia couldn't believe the lengths Esperanza was willing to go to in order to maintain Simone's control among her crew members. If she was capable of beating the woman who shared her bed, anything she might do to them was too horrible to comprehend. Julia saw the look of gratitude in the woman's eyes as the long boat began moving away from *Le Faucon* and toward the waiting sloop. She knew she and Esperanza would never speak of the incident again. As she watched the boat leave, Joaquin came up and leaned against the railing next to her.

"What happened to your arm?" he asked.

"I slipped and cut it. It was a stupid accident," Julia lied, unable to look into the boy's eyes.

"Have you been to New Orleans before?"

"Yes, a long time ago," Julia said. She and Amy spent a romantic weekend in the Bayou City during the Mardi Gras celebration not long after they met. She smiled at the memory even though she felt certain the New Orleans she was now traveling to would look nothing like the one she remembered.

"Joaquin!" a strong voice called out.

Turning away from the railing, he saw Simone motioning for him to join her on the wheel deck. He smiled up at Julia. "*Faucon* is letting me pilot out of the cove."

"Good," Julia smiled. "When we are underway we will resume

your lessons." She watched the boy run across the deck and climb onto
the bridge, and wondered if he was told why his mother had been sent
away. Taking his place behind the large wheel, Joaquin stood in front
of Simone who rested her hands on his shoulders as she leaned down
to speak to him. The stinging cut on her upper arm brought Julia back
from her thoughts about the woman she had been so attracted to as
she left the deck to attend to her injury.

Chapter
Twelve

WHILE THE FLOTILLA of nine ships of assorted original ownership sailed away from Isla la Margarita, Julia rearranged her meager belongings in her cabin. It would feel strange not to hear Kitty's soft snoring each night. She was told the trip to New Orleans would consume nearly a month and wasn't sure she could avoid Simone for that length of time. But she fully intended to try. Once they arrived in the Bayou City, the Big Easy, the city where one day the motto would become *Laissez les bon temps rouler*, she would be free of the conflicting feelings roiling inside her.

For several days Julia spent her time alone with her thoughts or tutoring Joaquin, carefully avoiding contact with Simone. Her arm would heal, but she was certain it would leave a scar. It was early November and the winds were calm, although cool.

Julia and Joaquin sat on deck discussing political events, a subject that mystified the boy. Julia attempted to explain the differences between the monarchies of Great Britain and France and the democracy of the United States. He asked good questions and she searched her memory to recall who the President of the United States was in 1814. Eventually she changed their studies to English, a subject she felt a little more confident about. As she looked over his shoulder watching him practice writing, a shadow fell over his journal. Squinting against the sun behind the figure, she recognized the tall figure at once. "Captain," she said.

"*Mademoiselle*, may I have a word with you privately?" Simone asked in a subdued voice.

"Of course. Joaquin, complete the line you are writing and we will be finished for the day," she instructed as she stood up and followed Simone onto the wheel deck.

Resting her hands on the railing, Simone watched the ships behind her for a moment. Without looking at Julia, she said, "When we arrive at Bayou LaFourche we will accompany Laffite to a plantation on the German Coast. A few days later I shall escort you and *Mademoiselle* Longmire to the Cabildo in New Orleans to be placed safely in the hands of the Americans."

"Thank you, Captain."

Glancing at the woman beside her, Simone continued, "I also wish to convey my apologies for my behavior at Isla de Margarita. While it is true I was angry, it was no excuse for my actions. Is your wound healing satisfactorily?"

"Yes, it is fine. I am sure Esperanza is recovering as well." Julia saw a glimpse of hurt flicker across Simone's eyes and regretted reminding her of the incident.

"I am sure she is. She and Joaquin will be accompanying us to New Orleans. The boy will want to wish you a safe journey back to your home."

"It has been an interesting voyage, Captain. I want you to know I have appreciated your hospitality," Julia said.

With a laugh, Simone turned to face Julia. "You remain my prisoner, *Mademoiselle*. I would hardly consider that hospitable."

"I–I wish we could have met under different circumstances. You are an...interesting woman."

"Perhaps we shall meet again one day," Simone smiled. "Joaquin will miss you. I appreciate the manner in which you have treated him."

Looking down at the main deck, Julia smiled. "He is a wonderful boy and shall one day be a fine man."

"I hope you are right." There was sadness in Simone's eyes as she glanced at the boy as well. "It would be my wish that he live a long and peaceful life."

"Is there anything else, Captain?" Julia asked.

"No," Simone said, returning her gaze to the sea around them. "It has been a pleasure to know you, Julia."

Julia turned to walk away before she realized it was the first time Simone had used her first name. She liked the way it sounded, with a touch of the captain's French accent, even though somehow it sounded as if it was goodbye.

FOR FIFTEEN DAYS the ships made their way north toward the southern American coast. Although Simone saw Julia from time to time, she avoided her whenever possible. A cautious mood seemed to descend over the crew and they remained vigilant as the ships approached the waters near Jamaica. Simone kept two crewmen aloft during the daylight hours searching the horizon for signs of British ships. If an attack on New Orleans was planned, the British could be expected to patrol the Gulf of Mexico between Jamaica and the American coastline with regularity. Signals were passed among the ships while Laffite and Simone made sure they were positioned to fight if necessary.

The closer they came to Jamaica, the longer Simone spent pouring over her maps and charts. She hoped Anton would not have to be involved in a battle, uncertain of how prepared he was. She taught him much, but knew there was a vast difference between knowledge and application. There were many who let panic set in only to lose everything. She would take *Le Faucon* to the bottom of the sea if it meant she could protect him. She and Laffite formulated a plan for the middle portion of their journey and now she watched calmly as Laffite's ships began moving away from her group. Laffite commanded more heavily armed ships which would have to react quickly in the event her ships engaged the British.

Tired of attempting to second-guess what the British might be up to, Simone rubbed her eyes with the heels of her hands and stretched as she rose from the table strewn with her papers. The next two or three days would leave her with little time for sleep and she needed to prepare herself mentally. Leaving her cabin, which was becoming a prison of loneliness, she strolled along the main deck, stopping occasionally to speak to the members of her crew who were passing the time patching sails or checking and cleaning their assigned cannons. She tried to keep her voice light and unconcerned as they chatted. These men were her family and she hoped their eventual reward would be worth the risks they were being asked to take. Her decision to help Laffite in a cause she cared little about promised nothing in return for their effort other than the dubious gratitude of a government which didn't want their assistance. Laffite argued convincingly of the riches that could be theirs if they helped the Americans. She chose to stay away from Laffite's discussion with her captains, not wanting to influence their decision in any way. Now that he had been successful in convincing them to join with the Americans, even temporarily, Simone would do what she could to make the venture a successful one.

By the time she reached the bow she felt calmer. The sea was a beautiful place on days such as these. Despite the knowledge it could turn on them, constantly warning them of its silent power, Simone knew there would be times she would miss it.

"Excuse me, Captain," she heard from behind her. Turning around, she saw Julia offering her a piece of fruit. "Joaquin told me you haven't eaten all day."

Taking the food, Simone smiled. "I sometimes forget to eat when I am occupied with my own thoughts. *Merci.*"

"Are you worried about a British attack?"

"We are as close to Jamaica and the British fleet as we will be the remainder of our journey. Laffite saw a few ships during his voyage to Margarita. It pays to be vigilant in the face of one's enemy."

Julia cleared her throat and looked at the water passing beneath them. "I love the ocean," she said. "I have since I was a child."

"Where is your home? You said you were an American, despite your accent."

"I live in Georgia. A small place called Tybee Island. I have a home there."

"And that is where your family has settled?"

"No. My parents live in Virginia."

"Do you live there alone?" Simone asked as she stepped down from the bow.

She thought she saw a flicker of sadness in Julia's eyes as she answered, "Yes."

As they strolled back along the deck, Simone seemed to be in deep thought, glancing periodically at the ocean around them and checking the position of her other ships.

"Are you concerned about Anton if we should encounter other ships?" Julia asked.

"He is still young and untested. Perhaps I should have let Archambault take command of the *Northumberland*," Simone said. "Do you have siblings, *Mademoiselle*?"

"A brother, two years older than I," Julia answered.

"*Faucon!*" a voice high above them called out.

Simone looked up and saw the crewman pointing toward the eastern horizon. Quickly she ran to the wheel deck and picked up her telescope, scanning the horizon until she saw three sets of sails turning in their direction. Moving to the half rail of the deck she called out, "The British! Make ready all cannons!"

Julia watched as members of the crew began rolling the deck cannons toward the rail. Elevating the barrels slightly, each cannon crew of four men moved quickly and quietly about their business. Archambault walked purposefully from one cannon to the next, making sure each was prepared to engage the enemy.

"Signal the other ships!" Simone ordered. "Turn into the approaching ships!"

As the sails snapped in a steady breeze, Julia felt the ship turning.

"Archambault! Raise all cannon ports!" Simone dashed down the steps to the main deck. Taking Julia by the arm, she led her toward the stairs leading to the lower decks. "Go to Joaquin. He will know the safest place to go. Do not return until I send for you."

"But, Captain —"

"I do not have time to argue or debate with you, *Mademoiselle*. Please do as I have asked." Seeing the look of concern in Julia's eye, Simone said, "We will be fine, but I cannot worry about either you or Joaquin. Please keep him, as well as yourself, safe until this is ended."

Nodding, Julia went down the stairs, dodging crew members rushing to their assigned posts. She knocked on the door to Joaquin's room, but entered before he could open it. The boy knelt on his bed, peering out the porthole.

"The Captain has asked me to remain here with you until it is safe on deck," she said as she walked across the small room.

"Come," he said with a smile. "We can watch from this porthole."
"Shouldn't we keep it closed?"
"Do not be concerned, Julia. *Faucon* has good plan."

SIMONE WATCHED FROM the wheel deck as the distance between *Le Faucon de Mer* and the British ships narrowed. *Not quite yet.* She had gone over her plan many times, but knew no plan was perfect. The one thing in her favor was the predictability of British captains. By turning directly into their path she was projecting the hostile intent of her ships. She quickly glanced at her remaining three ships and smiled. They were perfectly aligned behind her and beginning to alter their course to draw to a right angle to the approaching British vessels. As soon as Laffite rejoined them the British would be outnumbered three to one. Good odds even against trained seamen aboard the larger enemy ships.

Le Faucon cut swiftly through the water, her billowing sails propelling her forward. A volley of cannon fire from one of the British ships splashed harmlessly into the water ahead of her vessel. They were still out of effective range of the British cannons as the British maneuvered into a line facing Simone's vessel. Timing and speed would be critical if her plan were to work.

"Get down!" she ordered as they drew even closer to the three ships. "On my order drop the mainsails and fire cannons in staggered volleys!"

The helmsman turned the ship's wheel to guide *Le Faucon* between two of the British ships. Simone raised her arm, all eyes of the deck crew awaiting her signal, anxious for the fighting to begin.

As much as Simone wanted to leave the sea, she couldn't deny the excitement a battle held for her. "Prepare your weapons! Chain shot to the masts!" Judging her speed and distance she counted to five. "Lower the sails! All cannons fire!" she ordered, dropping her arm. Half of the deck cannons and those below deck fired, followed a few seconds later by a volley from the remaining half while allowing the first group to reload and continue the firing. Return fire from the British ships struck *Le Faucon*, but the British, under full sail moved quickly past. Chain shot struck two masts of one of the ships and crippled it. Simone ran to the railing of the wheel deck.

"Hoist the sails! Bring us around quickly!!" she ordered. "Prepare to board! No prisoners!" As her ship turned to reapproach the stricken ship she saw her other vessels open fire with withering volleys against the two remaining British vessels. In the distance five sets of sails moved to join them from the west. "Ready the cannons and fire at will!" she commanded as they approached the British ship. "Grappling hooks!"

The first cannons aboard *Le Faucon* opened fire directly on the hull of the crippled British ship, firing in sequence to disable the British cannons. Grappling hooks flew through the air and attached to the ship. As soon as the ships were close together Simone's crewmen swung or jumped aboard the British vessel, engaging in hand-to-hand combat with soldiers and sailors of the British fleet.

Simone ran down the steps of the wheel deck, stopping atop the main deck railing to fire her musket, killing a red-coated British soldier. Drawing her cutlass she jumped onto the deck of the British ship and joined her men, slashing her way across the deck. There was nothing to plunder. There was only the assurance that fewer British soldiers would live to fight another day. Faced with a more determined fighting force many of the soldiers chose to jump overboard. As the sound of the fighting diminished, Simone and Archambault made their way around the main deck assuring themselves there were no survivors.

"You are injured," Archambault said, pointing to a red plume spreading along Simone's sleeve.

"It is a scratch. Send some men below to ferret out anyone attempting to hide."

"If they find someone?"

Simone squinted and watched the two remaining British ships, both on fire. "Kill them," she said calmly, striding across the deck toward her own ship. "I will check *Le Faucon* to see how badly she is damaged."

JULIA COVERED HER ears as she tried to protect Joaquin. The sound of the cannon fire was deafening. She lost track of time and had no idea how long the firing continued. They heard the sound of splintering wood and she was certain the ship was struck by cannon fire more than once. The firing ended abruptly, followed by the shouts and screams of men and the sound of pistol fire and metal striking metal. Unexpectedly, an eerie quiet fell over the ship, followed by sporadic gunfire and the smell of something burning. Julia wasn't sure what to do when Joaquin broke from her arms and ran to the porthole.

"What is happening?" Julia asked. "Have we been boarded?"

"Never," Joaquin said. "*Faucon* would sink the ship before allowing it to be captured."

Well, that's reassuring. The waiting made her nervous. She was startled when the cabin door banged open and jumped to her feet to pull Joaquin behind her.

"*Faucon!*" Joaquin said when the captain entered the cabin. Dark sooty smudges marked her face and shirt as the boy ran to her.

She picked him up and swung him around, laughing. "Were you worried, little one?"

"Of course not," he answered, looking indignant. "*Mademoiselle*

Julia was worried, but not I."

"You are very brave, Joaquin. Thank you for protecting Julia," Simone said as she set him down and flashed a smile at Julia. "You may go on deck now, if you wish."

Joaquin left his cabin and ran toward the ladder. "Are you all right?" Simone asked as Julia sat down abruptly on Joaquin's bunk.

"Was anyone injured?" Julia asked, trying to calm the adrenaline still coursing through her body.

"Some of my men have been injured, yes," Simone answered solemnly. "We must leave this area quickly and I must tend to my crew," she said as she turned to leave the cabin.

Grasping Simone's arm Julia said, "I can help, Captain. I have some training in caring for injured people." She saw the captain wince and looked at her more closely, finally seeing blood seeping through her shirt sleeve. "You've been hurt!" Her eyes flew to Simone's.

"It is nothing more than a scratch. It will—"

"It will get infected if we don't clean and bandage it. Sit on the bed," Julia ordered. She pulled the hem of her dress up and tore a strip of cloth from the petticoat beneath. Dipping the cloth in a basin of water near Joaquin's bed, Julia turned her attention to Simone's arm, carefully pushing the sleeve up. She washed away the blood running down Simone's arm and cleaned the wound. "After we see to your injured crewmen I'll replace this with a better bandage." She wrapped and tied the cloth over the cut on Simone's arm.

Simone stood and strode toward the cabin door. "Your assistance will be most appreciated," she said as Julia joined her.

Julia paused at the cabin door. She wanted to wrap her arms around Simone and feel her strength, but couldn't. Stepping past the captain she made her way down the hallway and up the ladder. The sight on the main deck stopped her momentarily. She knew the ship received rounds from the British ships, but wasn't prepared for what she saw. She looked onto the deck of the British ship beside them and turned away quickly, covering her mouth.

"Cut us away! Simone ordered as the last of her men stepped onto the deck. "Hoist the sails!"

Julia brought her eyes up to meet Simone's. "Are they all dead?"

"We have no room for prisoners," Simone answered.

Debris littered the deck and the pungent smell of gunpowder still hung in the air. Large holes in the railing indicated where the British cannon balls had struck *Le Faucon*. Julia was careful where she stepped as crew members scurried around already working to repair the damage. As the ship moved through the water to rejoin the other ships Julia looked over her shoulder at the British vessels. Two were on fire and the third was motionless in the water, her masts no longer rising from her deck. She watched sailors from the burning ships swim toward the lone survivor and turned away. A hand on her back brought her attention once more to the deck of *Le Faucon de Mer*. The ship was damaged and injured men were being tended to by other crewmen. "How many are dead?" she asked, almost to herself.

"Four," Simone's voice answered quietly.

"*Faucon!*" a voice called out.

"Please excuse me," Simone said. She quickly walked across the main deck and up the steps to the quarterdeck. Julia looked around her and knelt next to the nearest injured crew member. She checked his injuries and even though he was bleeding profusely from a head wound, it was not life threatening. She saw Joaquin and called to him to join her.

As he knelt beside her, she asked, "Can you bring me clean cloth and water?"

He nodded and stood to leave, but she stopped him. "Is there rum on board?"

"Of course," he answered.

"Then I shall need that as well."

Simone watched as Julia instructed the men in moving her injured crewmen to one area of the main deck and began moving from man to man administering to their wounds. One after another, she cleaned the wounds and used the rum to disinfect the injuries before wrapping them. While there were several men with deep cuts to their head or limbs, most would recover in due course. However, there were three who had sustained more serious injuries.

When she was sure the ship was safely away from the scene of the battle, Simone made her way to the main deck to assist Julia. She recognized the crewman Julia was tending when she arrived. She dropped to her knees and ran her hand across the man's forehead. "How are you, Pierre?"

The man, an older crewman, blinked and tried to give Simone a smile, but it came out as a grimace. Julia tied a tourniquet around his arm above his elbow and wrapped a bandage around the deep gash on his forearm. Keeping her voice low she said, "He's lost a substantial amount of blood and both bones in his lower arm are shattered." Looking at Simone she added, "I cannot save his arm and it cannot remain this way until we reach New Orleans. It must be removed or he will die from the infection that is certain to set in."

Pierre's eyes darted quickly from Julia to Simone. "I will do it," Simone said calmly. "I am sorry, Pierre." Reaching behind her she picked up a bottle of rum and handed it to him. Julia stood and wiped her forehead with the back of her hand.

Standing beside her, Simone said, "When he passes out from the rum I will remove the arm."

"Have you done that before?" Julia asked.

"Yes. Is he the last one?"

Julia nodded and leaned against the railing around the deck and took a deep breath. "Thank you, Julia," Simone said. "You are tired. Please get something to eat and rest for a little while."

"I'm fine, Captain."

"I insist and would appreciate it if you would not continue to argue with me."

When Julia looked up, prepared to say something, her words were stopped by the look in Simone's eyes. Instead she said, "Perhaps you are right. I will rest until you are ready to remove this man's arm, but expect to be awakened to assist you."

Taking Julia by the arm, Simone led her to her cabin under the wheel deck. "I have much to do. Please rest in my cabin until I am ready."

Once again Julia started to protest, but was overcome with exhaustion. Nodding, she entered Simone's cabin. Lying down on the soft bed, she was nearly asleep before her head hit the pillow. Simone drew a light duvet over her and couldn't resist observing the sleeping woman for a few moments before returning to her duties.

IT WAS STILL barely daylight when Julia was awakened by a light shaking of her shoulder. Momentarily disoriented, she rubbed her face and opened her eyes. Simone stood next to the bed. "We are ready," she said softly.

Julia swung her legs off the bed and glanced around. Spotting a water basin on a small table, Julia poured some water into the basin and splashed it on her face. When she turned around, Simone handed her a small towel. "Where will you do it?" Julia asked.

"On deck. It will be easier to clean up than the crew's quarters." Simone placed her hand on Julia's back as she escorted her back onto the deck. As she knelt down next to Pierre, Julia saw an empty bottle of rum lying nearby. Four crew members were positioned near the unconscious crewman, another held a torch for additional lighting.

"Where do I make the cut?" Simone asked.

"Here, just above the elbow," Julia said. She tied a tourniquet tightly around Pierre's upper arm, then took the injured man's hand and turned it slightly, holding it firmly on the deck at a right angle to his body.

Simone drew her cutlass and waited until the mangled arm was away from Pierre's body. Julia held her breath as Simone poured rum over the blade and nodded at the other crewmen. They grasped his remaining arm and legs and held them tightly. With a quick glance at Julia, Simone raised the cutlass over her head and brought it down in a single powerful stroke, severing the useless arm. She ran the blade through the flame of the torch, heating it, and then pressed the flat of the blade against the open wound to stem the flow of blood.

The scent of burning flesh made Julia lightheaded and she blinked back the white dots dancing in front of her eyes as she wrapped the fresh wound tightly. Infection would remain a concern and she hoped the injured man would survive until they reached Bayou LaFourche. She felt a cold sweat break out along her forehead and felt suddenly nauseous. She began breathing through her mouth to make the feeling go away. She raised her head to take a deep breath and saw one of the crewmen toss the severed limb overboard. It was the last thing she remembered before she was engulfed in darkness.

A COOL CLOTH covered her eyes and she raised her hand to move it. "No. Let it remain a little longer," Simone's voice said.

"What happened?" Julia mumbled.

"You fainted."

"I'm sorry."

"No need to be. We finished what needed to be done. Thank you." Julia felt fingertips brush along the side of her face and across her forehead.

"How is Pierre?"

"He is resting below. A friend is keeping watch over him tonight, along with a bottle of rum."

"I am fine now, Captain. I should return to my quarters. All I need is a good night's sleep."

"You may stay here, if you wish."

Julia reached up and pulled the cloth from her eyes. Simone sat beside her on the bed. It was dark in the Captain's quarters save for a single candle on the washstand near the bed. In the candlelight, Simone was breathtakingly beautiful as the dim light cast reddish-orange shadows across her face. Julia brought her hand up to touch Simone's face, but stopped herself. "You need to rest as well, Captain. It has been a very long day. Where is Joaquin?"

"He has been asleep for an hour or more already. When I was a child I could sleep through anything. It would be nice to have such a sleep again. Perhaps one day when I am away from the sea."

Julia propped herself on an elbow and turned sideways on the bed. Scooting to the far side of the bed, she said, "I sleep better when I am not alone. If you don't mind, I will accept your offer to stay here."

Simone rose and went to her desk. As she sat and opened her journal, she said, "I must write the day's events in my journal. Please rest."

WARMTH ENGULFED JULIA. She smiled in her sleep as she fell deeper into her dream. She felt safe, but could feel her body react to the images in the dream. She stirred slightly, her body seeking the source of her arousal. She sensed a presence behind her and edged her hips toward it until they fit into a solid curve. Movement against her back and warm breath along her neck sent a shiver through her. A strong arm encircling her waist pulled her closer and a voice sighed in contentment as a knee rose to rest along the back of her thighs. Her hips moved and her legs parted, seeking to increase the contact. She gasped as she felt a hand slip slowly up her side, stroking and teasing the curve of her breast. Soft lips of an unseen lover moved down the side of her neck and across her bare shoulders. Her body reacted to the teasing touches, setting her on fire inside. She tried to move to take in her lover's face, but was held in place by the strong arm around her. As fingertips trailed between her breasts and made their way down toward her hairline, she lifted her hips to greet them, to welcome them into the refuge of her body. She saw a flash of short dark hair as lips traveled around her neck. "Simone," she breathed.

SIMONE WROTE IN her journal, occasionally stopping to watch the sleeping woman in her bed. What would it feel like to drape an arm over Julia's waist, breathing in her scent? she wondered. There was something unusual about Julia Blanchard and Simone wished she could have the opportunity to discover her secrets one by one. Turning back to her journal she sketched Julia's face. It joined others she had drawn during their voyage, each attempting to catch the fire in her eyes, the up-turn of her lips just before they parted in a smile. Her attention to her drawing was interrupted by the sound of Julia breathing her name

"Julia," Simone said as she stood next to the bed. "Julia, are you ill?"

Julia blinked her eyes open to see Simone standing over her. "What is it?" she asked.

"I heard you call my name in your sleep while I wrote in my journal. Are you having a bad dream?" Simone asked as she ran her hand across Julia's forehead. "You are very warm."

"Yes. Yes, it must have been a dream," Julia said, sitting up. "I think perhaps I will take in some fresh air. Today has been quite stressful."

Simone offered Julia her hand and helped her off the bed. They stood close to one another awkwardly for a moment before Simone reluctantly stepped back. "Perhaps you should eat something light as well," she suggested.

"Yes, I will do that, Captain. Thank you," Julia said as she made her way to the door of the Captain's quarters.

Chapter
Thirteen

JULIA MANAGED TO keep her distance from Simone, as well as maintain her sanity, the remainder of the voyage. The flotilla of ships was favored by northerly winds that carried them toward their destination without encountering additional British ships. Over dinner Simone surmised the British fleet may have curtailed their patrols in the Gulf of Mexico in preparation for their invasion along the American coast.

It became a daily ritual for Julia to stand on the bow of *Le Faucon* each evening and watch the sun dip into the waters of the Gulf. She felt the sea breeze ruffle her hair and ran a hand through it. It hadn't been its current length in a very long time. She always kept it short, in part due to her work underwater, but primarily because she hated the natural waves that appeared to have an unruly mind of their own.

"We will arrive at Bayou LaFourche soon," Simone said.

Julia turned and smiled at the captain. "How can you tell?"

The captain stepped next to her and squinted into the evening sky. She ran a hand up Julia's back and brought it to rest near the base of her neck. Julia shivered slightly at the touch. Pointing up Simone said, "The birds. They are never far from land."

Julia gazed upward and watched gulls glide along the invisible air streams rising from the water. The autumn sea breeze cooled her skin and the warmth from Simone's touch spread quickly through her body. She took a deep breath to control her impulse to move closer against Simone, perhaps to be gathered protectively in her arms and... "Within a week we will be in New Orleans and you shall be free once more to resume your life," Simone said, breaking into Julia's private reverie.

"It has been quite an adventure. An unforgettable one."

"Will you return to your home in Georgia?"

"Yes. I miss it as you miss your home on Martinique. But I will return to it not the same person as when I left."

Simone looked down at her. "Perhaps this voyage has changed us both in some ways."

"When this is over, perhaps one day you will visit Savannah. Parts of it, especially the lush greenery, remind me of *Le Repos*."

"*Faucon,*" a crewman interrupted. "Your dinner is in your quarters."

"*Merci,* we shall be there shortly. Please inform Joaquin," Simone replied, not looking away from Julia's profile against the evening sky. She longed to feel the softness of the reddish-blonde hair under her fingertips and forced herself to turn away. She hadn't slept well since their encounter with the British ships. The lingering soft scent of Julia's body was imprinted on her pillow and bedding, yet she was unwilling to have it washed away. It crept into her senses as she slept, turning her rest into visions of desire. Offering her hand to Julia, she walked with her toward her cabin.

JOAQUIN STOOD IN front of Julia as the ships entered the deep water channel of Timbalier Bay. Laffite sent word there was ample anchorage for their ships out of sight of other vessels that might happen past the bay. Even in the rainiest season Bayou LaFourche would not accommodate anything as large as the British sloops of war. From Timbalier it was only a short overland trip to Bayou LaFourche. Secreted along the marshy shore of the bayou were several pirogues. Laffite and his immediate party made their way north through the swampy bayou toward the home of a business associate, Alexandre LaBranche.

Julia was awe-struck by the natural wild beauty of the area as crewmen poled through the waterway toward their destination. The tall grasses and marshes were home to a wide variety of birds and animals and she knew they were being observed as the boats moved quietly along. Everything was lush and beautiful while remaining wild and strangely eerie when seen through the gathering evening fog, not yet willing to surrender to the night. Snow-white egrets sailed over them and dipped close to the water before banking to settle in the shallow waters near solid land. Occasionally she heard the splashing sounds of fish jumping in and out of the water. Unseen currents moved without disturbing the surface. Julia felt incredibly relaxed and allowed her hand to trail in the water as the boat moved through it. A light touch on her shoulder drew her attention to Simone who was seated behind her. "There are alligators in these waters, *Mademoiselle.*"

Simone chuckled as Julia jerked her hand from the water as if it were scalded. Julia dried her hand on the hem of her skirt and pulled Joaquin closer to her. There was little conversation to disturb the remainder of the evening quiet.

Two hours later the small boats made their way into an open, wider expanse of water and Julia saw a huge mansion looming in the distance. She and Joaquin shared the pirogue with Laffite and Simone, while Kitty, Esperanza, and Anton were in the pirogue behind them. As they neared the eastern shore of the bayou plantation, Laffite stood and waited until they were close enough to step onto the small plantation dock. She heard voices not far away as she accepted Simone's hand and felt solid ground beneath her feet for the first time in nearly a month. The plantation home was a long two-story house in the French Creole style. Columns between the two stories supported a wide porch around the second floor. Considering its location near the river, Julia surmised the second floor served as protection from the river if it flooded. The silhouettes of numerous out building were scattered on one side and behind the main building.

The group followed Laffite up a small rise toward the mansion and were greeted by a distinguished looking man in his mid-forties. Laffite and the man hugged briefly and exchanged kisses on the cheeks. Turning to the rest of his party, Laffite said, "My friends, this is our host and my very good friend, Alexandre LaBranche. He was generous enough to offer us the use of his home." LaBranche was nearly as tall as Laffite, Julia estimated about six feet. Whiskers grew along the sides of his face to nearly his chin. Julia wondered if that was the style for gentlemen in the early eighteen-hundreds since Laffite had the same. When the introductions were completed, LaBranche ordered additional pirogues sent back to Timbalier Bay to bring the remaining crew to his home.

"Where are we?" Julia asked quietly as she walked beside Simone.

"This area is called the German Coast," Simone answered. "It provides a means for Laffite to smuggle merchandise into New Orleans without interference from customs officials or anyone intent on severing trade into the city."

"How far are we from New Orleans?"

"Not far. Perhaps twenty miles. No more than that. But this is not an area that can be easily searched unless you know the passages in and out as Laffite does."

Julia remembered seeing pictures of old Southern mansions and had visited a few which had been restored, but to actually see one in its own time period was amazing. She felt like a tourist as she gawked at the workmanship. Despite the darkness, she could clearly see the cypress boards near the entry held together by wooden pegs. Stepping into the front entryway, a disturbance behind her brought her attention back to the main portico.

"The servant's quarters are behind the main house. You and the boy will have to go there," an older black man with graying hair told Esperanza and Joaquin as he stopped them from entering the house.

"Take your hands off me," Esperanza spat at the man.

When the man motioned with his head for assistance, Simone walked back to the door. "Excuse me, sir, but this woman and her son are with me. They are free and the property of no man."

"My apologies, ma'am, but they cannot stay inside the main house," the man said calmly without raising his voice.

"Ah, I understand," Simone nodded. Turning to face their host, she twisted her lips into a smile that frightened Julia. "*Monsieur* LaBranche, my party and I will be returning to our vessels." Glancing at Laffite, she continued, "It is apparent my assistance and that of my men is not needed here." Bowing slightly, she spun around and escorted Esperanza and Joaquin down the wide front walkway of the mansion.

Julia admired Simone's refusal to turn her back on Esperanza and her son. Nodding to LaBranche and Laffite, Julia followed the trio ahead of her, as did Anton and Kitty.

As Simone helped Esperanza and Joaquin onto the pirogue once more, Laffite appeared on the wharf behind her. "Simone, may I have a word?" he asked calmly. Julia watched Simone join him. They walked a short distance along the bank before stopping to exchange words, some of which appeared to be quite heated. Although Simone regarded Laffite as a comrade-in-arms and couldn't have cared less about his smuggling operations, she never liked the fact that part of his wealth was derived from the auction of slaves. It would have been an equally lucrative venture for her to become involved with, but memories of her time with Rochat would never allow her to become part of an enterprise which subjected others to the same abuse and humiliation she endured.

Nearly an hour passed before the little group re-entered LaBranche's home. Simone personally escorted Esperanza and Joaquin through the front door of the house, her eyes defying anyone to stop them, and up the spiral staircase to their rooms on the second floor. Remembering what Simone told her about the probable fate of Joaquin's father, Julia thought having Esperanza share a room with Simone quite possibly saved LeBranche's life. A servant escorted Julia to her own room a few minutes later.

Dinner that evening was a quiet affair. Most of the discussion centered around getting into New Orleans as quickly as possible. Not wishing to subject Esperanza and her son to further inhospitable behavior, Simone lit a small black cigar at the end of the meal and said, "My party and I shall travel to New Orleans in the morning, Jean. I must deliver *Mademoiselles* Blanchard and Longmire to the Cabildo so they may be returned safely to their homes." Casting an apologetic glance at Esperanza, she continued, "My companion and her son wish to visit old friends in the city. We shall find accommodations there for the remainder of our stay and shall not be returning. I am certain you will be able to find me when necessary."

Throughout dinner, Julia saw LaBranche observing Simone's interaction with Esperanza and Joaquin. He was clearly uncomfortable sharing dinner with them.

She was startled when their host finally broke his silence. "Tell me, Miss Moreau, how long has this...lady been your companion?" he asked. Julia cringed at the contempt in his voice and shot a look toward Simone, awaiting her response.

Simone picked up her wine glass from the table and emptied it in one swallow. "My liaison with *Mademoiselle* Batista is in its fifth year," she said, setting the glass down. "A longer period than your own liaisons each year following the Octoroon Ball, I would hazard to guess."

Laffite threw his head back and laughed loudly as LaBranche's face reddened at Simone's implication. The remainder of the evening Julia watched Simone extend every courtesy to Esperanza. A touch here and there, designed to increase her host's discomfort. A whispered message followed by a smile, projecting the intimacy between them. Finally, to LaBranche's relief, Simone excused herself for the evening to escort Esperanza and Joaquin to their room. She nodded in Julia's direction and stopped for a moment.

"We shall leave before dawn tomorrow, *Mademoiselle* Blanchard."

Julia looked at her and smiled. "You were magnificent this evening, Captain."

Simone bowed her head slightly and returned to Esperanza's side.

Chapter
Fourteen

SIMONE'S PARTY LEFT LaBranche's plantation before dawn and made their way from the German Coast to New Orleans by pirogue, carrying little. They stepped onto the wharf near Canal Street, easily blending in with citizens busily going about their everyday business.

They were a group of nine including Julia, Kitty, Anton, Esperanza, Joaquin, Simone, the first mate, Henri Archambault and two additional crew members Simone trusted. As soon as Julia and Kitty were safely deposited at the seat of government in New Orleans, the Cabildo, Simone and the remainder of her party planned to spread out through the city and send any news of British movements back to Laffite. They walked slowly along Decatur seeing nothing that appeared out of place. If the citizens of the city were aware of the danger coming their way, they seemed oblivious to it.

The city was much smaller than Julia remembered, consisting primarily of only the elegant nine by twelve block area known as the *Vieux Carré*, filled with wrought-iron galleries, narrow streets and open cafes. Muted multi-colored buildings adorned with shutters and peaked dormers sat flush against the banquettes that ran in front of each building. Julia noticed, even two hundred years before her visit with Amy, the streets teemed with people. As she drank in the sights and sounds of the enchanting city's bygone era, she passed fashionably dressed women wearing plumed bonnets, accompanied by gentlemen in cutaway coats smelling distinctively of bay rum at nearly every intersection. Even early in the morning merchants rushed from place to place setting their wares out for the inspection of potential customers, while barely clothed prostitutes strolled brazenly along the venues. The calls of colorful wagon venders extolling the uniqueness of their goods could be heard down each narrow street, accompanied by the clickety-clack of the wagon's wheels over the cobblestones.

As the group made its way toward the former Spanish parade ground, Place d'Armes, in the center of the *Vieux Carré*, Julia's senses were inundated by the sights and smells along the few blocks from the wharf. From one block to the next she detected the scent of sugar cane, peanuts being boiled, the distinctive odors of various ales from taverns, imported spices from the Caribbean Islands and the sharp aromas greeting her from the French coffee houses. New Orleans in November 1814 was nothing like the city Julia visited with Amy. Although the streets of the French Quarter had changed considerably, Julia smiled as she recognized a few of the buildings. In modern New Orleans, the buildings were nothing more than establishments catering to tourists, selling souvenirs made in China or Taiwan rather than the businesses flourishing as she walked by them in the past.

As they approached the Place d'Armes, Esperanza stopped Simone. Smiling at her lover, Simone raised an eyebrow in an unspoken question.

"I would like to see what vegetables and fruit are at the markets," Esperanza said.

Withdrawing coins from a pouch under her tunic, Simone said "Let Joaquin find something special." Turning to Henri, she said, "Archambault, will you accompany Esperanza and Joaquin to the market and assist them?"

"Certainly, *Faucon*," Henri grinned. "When should we meet you again?"

"Here in two hours should be sufficient." Kissing Esperanza lightly on the cheek and ruffling Joaquin's dark hair, Simone watched the trio make their way along the crowded cypress boardwalk running the length of Decatur between the wharf and Place d'Armes. Turning her attention to the three large buildings across the open expanse of the parade ground, Simone said, "We should make our way to the Cabildo, *Mademoiselles*."

As they walked along the narrow streets skirting the Place d'Armes, Simone observed everything around them. "Laffite is correct," she said. "This city is worth fighting for."

"The British will attack in force before Christmas," Julia blurted out before she could catch herself.

Simone stopped and stared at Julia. "How can you know such a thing?" she asked suspiciously.

"Oh...well, that seemed to be what Mr. Laffite indicated last night at dinner," Julia said in an attempt to cover her statement.

Julia knew her time with Simone was quickly coming to an end, but as she looked at the beautiful open space in front of her, filled with oak trees and fading blossoms, she knew she wasn't ready to leave without experiencing the city as it once had been.

"I know you are anxious to deliver Miss Longmire and myself to the authorities, but might it be possible to enjoy a beignet and chicory first? I've heard they are quite delicious," Julia said, remembering the traditional deep-fried pastry and rich chicory coffee from her previous trip.

Gazing into Julia's hazel eyes, Simone smiled. "I could not possibly deny the pleasure of such a treat to anyone." Excusing herself, Simone spoke to Anton and Kitty for a moment. Julia looked around while she waited for Simone to return. St. Louis Cathedral without its familiar modern spires looked oddly unfinished.

"We will meet Anton and *Mademoiselle* Longmire in the alleyway between the Cabildo and St. Louis Cathedral in an hour or so," Simone said. Taking Julia by the elbow, she guided her across the open area and onto Rue de Chartres. Despite Julia's frequent stops to look over merchant's wares, they finally reached a charming café on Rue de Bourbon with outdoor seating. As they waited for their pastry and drinks, Simone took a deep breath of the cool morning air. The cobblestone streets still held traces of the heavy dew which covered them at sunrise and small patches of fog rose from the stones as they dried. She smiled at the activity around her. She found it to be an interesting city, one well worth defending.

"What are you thinking about?" Julia asked as a plate and cup were set in front of her.

"What a shame it would be if beignets and French coffee were replaced with crumpets and tea should the British seize this city," Simone replied as she lifted her cup to her lips and inhaled the inviting chicory aroma.

"Have you ever eaten a crumpet, Captain?"

"No, but the name alone is distasteful sounding. Beignet sounds much more alluring, don't you think, *Mademoiselle*?"

Julia laughed lightly. "I suppose that is true, but then even the worst possible things don't sound quite as bad in French. *Fumier* sounds much better than manure, for example."

Simone chuckled as she sipped her coffee. She wished there was enough time to learn more about the saucy woman with short reddish hair and sparking hazel eyes. She was certain she could easily lose herself in the eyes alone. As relaxed as she was beginning to feel, she knew she was only delaying the inevitable. Before the morning ended, Julia Blanchard would be gone from her life and she would never see her again.

She watched Julia savor the sweet flavor of the beignet, lightly dusted with powdered sugar and couldn't help but smile at the blonde's obvious delight.

JULIA'S ATTENTION TO her pastry was interrupted by the appearance of an ebony-skinned woman dressed in colorful skirt and blouse. Her skin stood out against the bright yellow blouse. Her ankle-length skirt of patchwork squares matched the patchwork turban wrapped around her braided hair. Huge tinkling earrings dangled from her earlobes, touching her shoulders as she made her way down the street, singing out in a distinctive Caribbean accent, "Sisters, get you chaaarms! De bery best in lucky chaaarms!" Julia giggled at the antics of the woman dancing along the street. The woman saw Julia and walked toward them, pausing just outside the low wrought iron fence surrounding the outdoor seating. Winking at Simone, the woman leaned toward Julia and held out a trinket.

"No, but thank you anyway," Julia smiled.

"Dis one, she has already too much luck, eh?" the woman said to Simone, who merely shrugged and said nothing.

Before they could say more, the woman joined Julia and Simone at their table, motioning to a waiter for a cup of coffee.

"How 'bout dis? For the price of one small coffee, Bernadette tell you what is in de future?" the woman propositioned with a toothy white smile.

Julia laughed out loud before she could stop herself, causing Bernadette to frown, creating a deep crease between her eyebrows. "De cards dey never lie."

Glancing at Simone, Julia saw a crooked smile as Simone lifted the cup to her lips again. Although she already knew more of the future than the woman could begin to imagine, Julia said, "All right. Tell me my future, Bernadette."

Bernadette withdrew a worn deck of cards from somewhere within the folds of her skirt and shuffled them as she watched Simone. Turning her attention back to Julia, Bernadette said, "Take five cards and make them face down." Fanning the cards in her hands, she waited as Julia selected her five cards. Setting the remaining cards to the side, she took Julia's hands and looked into her eyes for a moment before releasing them.

Flipping the first card over, Bernadette revealed an eight of hearts. "Dis card is de card of invitation, but of separation as well. You take a journey dat will make you leave de side of one who is special to you."

"That's a very general prediction, Bernadette. Everyone takes a journey at some time," Julia said, casting a quick glance at Simone.

"Dat true. Maybe other cards dey show de meaning." The second card was the queen of spades. Shifting her dark eyes quickly toward Simone, Bernadette said softly, "Dere be an alluring and tempting dark-haired woman, but you must be cautious."

"Why?" Julia asked.

"Her intentions dey may not be honorable."

Julia slid her eyes from Bernadette to Simone. "Really?" she said with a smile. While it was true Simone had a temper, Julia had never witnessed her do anything dishonorable. As she looked at Simone, Bernadette turned the third card, the three of hearts. "Dis card warns you to be careful. You heart, it may be in danger."

"So far, these are fairly depressing cards," Julia chuckled.

Frowning, Bernadette turned the fourth card. "'Nother heart."

"Is that good?" Julia asked.

"Dey are de cards of love. De nine says your desires, dey come to pass."

"Before or after my journey?" Julia asked, watching Simone.

"Cannot tell you dat," Bernadette shrugged. With a quick turn of her wrist she flipped over the final card. Her eyes widened when she saw it. Standing abruptly she gathered her cards and stuffed them back into the folds of her skirt.

"Wait," Julia said. "What does the last card say?"

"You buy charm for to protect youself," Bernadette said.

"The card told you that?"

Bernadette backed slowly away from the table. "You don' belong here. Card is de death card."

"The death card?" Julia said. "My death?"

"You already dead," Bernadette said, lowering her voice and making the sign of the cross. She turned and virtually ran from the café.

"Well, what did all that mean?" Julia asked, attempting to keep her voice light.

"She's nothing more than a street vender. No one takes them seriously. We must be going," Simone said as she drained her cup and placed coins on the small round café table.

As they wandered slowly along Rue de Bourbon toward the Cabildo Julia took in everything around her. She read the notices announcing the next event at the Theatre d'Orleans on Rue de Bourbon, wishing she could think of something to say. She didn't believe in fortune-telling, but hoped she would one day see Simone Moreau again.

Chapter
Fifteen

GIVING THE *NORTHUMBERLAND* to Anton had been the final straw. Archambault had worked as hard as any man to prove his loyalty to *Faucon*. She promised him his own ship, the next one captured. Now she had lied and broken the unspoken pact between them. For what? To move her brother ahead of him, grooming him to take over when she made the decision to step down.

Now he was reduced to playing nursemaid to Simone's bitch and her bastard son. He was beginning to think Simone no longer had what it took to command her crew. They had captured a few ships and were now on this fool's errand against the British, a fight the Americans could not possibly win. And what would be their prize? A piece of paper allowing them to do what they were already doing, accompanied by nothing more than gratitude? His belly and his pockets could not be filled by gratitude.

The more rum he drank the darker his thoughts became. He wasn't getting any younger. He needed to capture enough to live comfortably. If I get rid of *Faucon*, her bitch and the bastard child, he thought, I can take *Le Faucon de Mer* and claim Simone's home on Martinique. It would be easy enough for him to seize. No one there other than her horses and cousin to oversee her property. The more he thought about the possibilities, the more he realized how much better off he would be if there were no *Faucon*.

He overheard Simone arguing with Esperanza more often recently, especially since the English woman was brought on board. Even he could see how Simone acted toward the blonde woman. He would never understand why a woman would seek Simone's company or attentions, but she did draw attractive women to her. Simone was a difficult woman to figure out. Not simply because she enjoyed the company of other women, but because she could be more vicious than any of the men on her crew. He had seen her run an unhappy member of the crew through with her cutlass and slit an enemy's throat without a second thought on more than one occasion. While still a young woman she had murdered Captain Rochat in his own bed.

"May I buy you another?" a man asked as he sidled up next to Archambault.

"You can buy me an entire keg if you wish," Henri chuckled as he gulped down the remainder of his drink. "Join me and stay until your money is gone."

When the man was settled and another round of drinks ordered, he held his hand out to Henri, "You are Henri Archambault, first mate to Simone Moreau, are you not?"

Henri took the offered hand and looked at the man. He was younger than Henri with a ruddy smooth-shaven face set off by a slender nose and thin lips. But it was his eyes Archambault noticed first. They were as black as midnight in color. He could see his own reflection in the blackness as he answered. "I am. And who might you be, *Monsiour?*"

"I am LaRue," the man said as he took a drink. The man leaned closer to Henri and looked around the tavern. "Join me at a table, my friend."

After paying for a refill, Henri made his way to a far table and sat down heavily. "What is so secret you cannot speak of it?" he asked.

LaRue eyed Archambault cautiously before speaking. "*Faucon* is causing more problems for the British than she is worth. She takes chances that will eventually lead not only to her destruction, but that of her crew as well."

"Go on," Archambault said as his mouth went dry and he stared at the man.

"The British are preparing to attack the Americans at New Orleans."

"I care nothing about the Americans."

"The British are concerned, and rightly so, that interference from *Faucon*, Laffite and other privateers will unnecessarily distract them from their goal. The Americans have already stupidly attacked and destroyed Laffite's headquarters on Barataria, but failed to destroy his ships. Despite that betrayal, Laffite is likely to ally himself with the Americans."

"Is there a point to this history lesson, LaRue?"

"If Laffite has convinced *Faucon* to join him against the British, together they could cause a problem."

Henri chuckled. "I have had quite a bit to drink so you will have to pardon me if I am unsure what you are referring to."

Leaning closer, LaRue said, "The British are offering a goodly reward to anyone who turns *Faucon* in to them."

"And what would that be? A fast death over a slow one?"

"I was told you could deliver *Faucon* to the British...for a price," LaRue said, his eyes meeting Archambault's.

Startled, Henri said, "You are suggesting I betray Simone!"

LaRue smiled. "Not directly. Perhaps if she were placed in a position which would result in her capture, no one would be the wiser and you would profit handsomely."

Henri stared at LaRue and swirled rum in his mouth before swallowing. "What do they offer?"

"I can guarantee your own ship and crew and one hundred pounds," LaRue stated.

"Two hundred pounds," Henri said.

"Agreed. When can you bring her here?"

"She is already here. She came into the city this morning, but she would never be stupid enough to simply walk into a trap."

"How many ships?"

"Four in addition to Laffite's five. They are planning to join forces with the Americans on land. Her crews added to Laffite's would total nearly a thousand men."

"But if *Faucon* were to be lost and you were to replace her, that force could be cut by half."

"If you are planning to capture *Faucon*, you will have to act quickly before the remainder of her men arrive in the city."

"Do you have a suggestion?"

"*Faucon*'s woman and child are with me now. She would die to free them if they were to be captured." Henri shrugged and motioned to a tavern girl for another drink. "The woman and boy are nearby at the market. I was sent by *Faucon* to protect them." He gulped his drink and shrugged with a grin. "But I am only one man."

LaRue chuckled. "Excellent, Archambault."

"Where will you take them?"

"The British have a small encampment ten miles south of the city where they await the arrival of reinforcements soon. They have their headquarters nearby on a commandeered plantation. The woman and boy will be there."

Archambault rose from the table. "I will rejoin the woman and boy. Tell your men I must be injured during the struggle to take them. *Faucon* will not believe my story otherwise." Laughing, he added, "But tell them not to get carried away."

STROLLING DOWN RUE de St. Louis, Simone guided Julia onto Rue de Royale. Three or four blocks ahead Julia saw St. Louis Cathedral rising slightly above the buildings to either side. When they reached the entrance to the alleyway behind the cathedral, Julia saw a familiar full head of red hair halfway down the short block. Venders and merchants were selling goods from small stalls that lined the alleyway, but Julia suddenly lost her desire to inspect their wares. As they came closer, Kitty and Anton appeared to be in the midst of a discussion that left Kitty in tears. Simone approached the couple and spoke to Anton briefly before rejoining Julia.

"Is there a problem?" Julia asked.

"*Mademoiselle* Longmire is reluctant to leave," Simone answered as she looked around.

"Unless I am mistaken, Kitty is very much attracted to Anton," Julia said.

"So it would seem. It is time," Simone said as she looked in Anton's direction and caught his eye. Nodding in reply, he brought Kitty into an embrace and spoke to her. Julia watched the tender scene and sighed.

"If that is your wish, Captain," she said.

Her eyes blazing, Simone said, "It is not my wish, but I can make no other decision." Taking Julia's arm, she strode purposefully toward Anton, pushing away her own feelings. As they passed Anton and Kitty, the couple fell in behind them through the crowded stalls filled with contraband goods toward the Cabildo. Simone would be able to think more clearly once she was certain Julia was in safe hands. Placing her hand gently against Julia's lower back, Simone made her way up the two low steps of the old Spanish building housing the new American government.

"*Faucon!*" a voice called. Simone paused and looked over her shoulder for its source. Finally she spotted Archambault quickly weaving his way through the people strolling on the Place d'Armes. He stopped beneath a large live oak not far from the building and leaned against it to catch his breath. Simone and Anton ran to join him. As soon as Simone saw his bleeding face, she knew something was wrong.

"Archambault, what has happened?" she asked as she examined the deep cut above his right eye.

"I am sorry, *Faucon*. I only turned away for a moment," Henri gasped.

Sensing the worst, Simone grabbed him by the arms. "Where are Esperanza and Joaquin?" she asked, dreading the answer.

"The British, they have them," Henri answered, lowering his eyes and shaking his head.

"That is not possible," Anton said. "We have seen no evidence the British have entered the city."

"British agents," Henri said. "They are seeking information."

"Esperanza and Joaquin know nothing," Simone said.

"The British know you are here, *Faucon*. I heard them speaking when they believed I was unconscious."

Anger surged through Simone's body and she grabbed her first mate by the front of his shirt, shoving him forcefully into the tree behind him. "Why did you not stop them?"

Pushing Simone away, Henri retorted, "How do you think I was injured?"

Julia watched the discussion with Archambault from a distance as long as she could stand it. She and Kitty reached the three barely in time to stop Simone from drawing her pistol. "What has happened?"

she demanded.

"The British have taken Esperanza and Joaquin," Anton answered.

Looking at the first mate, Julia ásked, "Where have they taken them? Do you know?"

Staring angrily at Simone, Henri brought his sleeve up and wiped at the blood that seeped from his wound. "I do not answer to you, English woman," he spat.

The force of Simone's backhand snapped Henri's head back and he staggered from the blow. Pulling him back within inches of her face, Simone seethed, "Where, Archambault?"

"I heard the English say there is an encampment below the city where they await reinforcements."

Releasing Archambault, Simone turned to Anton. "You will take *Mademoiselles* Blanchard and Longmire to the Cabildo as we planned and then rejoin Laffite. Archambault and I will return with Esperanza and Joaquin as quickly as possible," Simone said. Turning back to Archambault, she continued, "You will come with me, Henri. We will find horses at the blacksmith shop."

Henri nodded. As Simone turned to leave, Julia stopped her. "I...be careful, Simone." Bowing slightly, Simone took Julia's hand, turned it over, and kissed her palm. A moment later, she and Archambault disappeared down the alleyway toward Rue de Royale. Anton took Kitty's arm and started toward the Cabildo once again. He hadn't taken more than two steps when Kitty stopped abruptly and refused to budge.

"I have chosen not to leave," Kitty stated.

"But *Faucon* has ordered it," Anton said.

"I am not some common seaman who can be ordered about. I am perfectly capable of making my own decisions. And I have decided to wait here until the Captain returns."

Smiling, Julia stepped next to Kitty and added, "I concur."

Faced with two recalcitrant women he said, "There will be hell to pay for this disobedience."

"Is there a place we can stay while we wait?" Julia asked.

"I will see if perhaps the nuns at the Ursuline Convent will provide you a safe place to sleep," Anton said.

"Go to a nunnery?" Kitty snorted. "I think bloody not!"

SIMONE THREW A saddle onto the back of a horse at the blacksmith shop that served as a legitimate front for Laffite's smuggling business. She tried to think of a way to extricate Esperanza and Joaquin that would allow them all to leave freely, but knew what she had to do. Their safety was more important than her own. "Archambault," she said as she tightened the girth beneath the animal's belly. "Find Raul and Francois, then follow me. You must make certain Esperanza and Joaquin return to the city safely."

"But what about you, *Faucon*?"

"I will be fine," she said as she mounted the horse.

"But *Faucon*..."

"Do as you are told, Archambault!" She kicked the horse in the sides and quickly left the livery behind the blacksmith shop. A few minutes later Henri Archambault swung onto the back of a second horse and left just as quickly. *Faucon* had issued her last order to him.

Chapter
Sixteen

SIMONE'S HORSE COVERED the miles along the river road
south away from the city swiftly. Dozens of rambling thoughts ran
through her mind as she made the journey. She was concerned for the
safety of Joaquin. The boy was surely frightened. She was convinced
the British would release them if she surrendered herself. She would
have to be alert for an opportunity to make her own escape.

It was almost an overcast mid-afternoon when the appearance of a
soldier dressed in white pants and red coat forced Simone to rein her
horse to an abrupt stop. The soldier aimed his musket at her as she
announced boldly, "I am *Faucon*. I believe I am expected." Her horse
breathed heavily beneath her and danced in place as the soldier
motioned her forward with his musket. Simone saw soldiers moving
around when she entered the gate of the plantation grounds and tried
to estimate how many there might be. It couldn't have been more than
an advanced party. She reined her horse to a halt in front of the steps
leading onto the broad porch of the plantation house where three
British officers stood with their hands behind their backs.

"It is a pleasure to meet you at last, Miss Moreau," one of the men
said.

"Captain Moreau," Simone corrected with a smile. "I believe you
are holding my companion and her son. Surely you have made a
mistake."

"You are here, so obviously I have not. Please, join us inside."

Simone swung her leg over the horse's back to dismount and
strode up the steps. When she reached the porch, one of the men made
a movement with his head and armed soldiers appeared on either side
of Simone. "You will excuse our rudeness, madam, but we must
relieve you of your weapons," he said tightly.

"A prudent precaution," she said as she pulled her pistol from her
waist and handed it butt-first to a nearby soldier. She slowly withdrew
her cutlass from its scabbard and let her eyes linger on it a moment
before smiling benignly and handing it to a second soldier. "Do you
wish to search me further, *Monsiour*?" she asked.

"Bring her!" one of the men ordered sharply, turning to re-enter
the house.

Simone shrugged off hands that attempted to grab her and walked resolutely inside. She followed the men down a short hallway, observing everything around her before finally turning into a large first floor study which now served as an office. The first persons she saw were Esperanza and Joaquin. She smiled at them confidently. A soldier stood next to them.

"*Faucon!*" Joaquin called out, leaving Esperanza's side and running to Simone. She hugged him to her as his arms flew around her waist. The soldier guarding the boy rushed to separate them. Simone looked at him coldly. "If you touch the boy, you will die," she warned. Looking down at Joaquin, she smoothed his hair. "Are you well, *mon petit?*"

"*Oui.* We are not hurt. I knew you would come."

"You will be leaving here soon. Go to your mother now." Looking at the officer seated behind a large desk, Simone asked, "What is it you wish from me that could not be accomplished without kidnapping my companion and her child?"

"What do you know about the defenses the Americans are preparing in New Orleans, Miss Moreau?"

"I only arrived this morning. But I would advise you to leave. You cannot defeat the Americans. Their army grows larger daily."

"She is lying," Archambault announced as he stepped into the room. "The Americans do not have a leader at the moment. It is true they have many weapons, but no flint or powder to fire them."

Simone spun around to face her first mate. "Henri? What are you doing?"

"Not taking orders from you any longer," he sneered. "I am taking command of *Le Faucon* and leaving." Glancing at the man behind the desk, he asked, "You have my money?"

"Traitor!" Simone spat, leaping toward him. As soldiers restrained her, Archambault stepped closer, raised his arm and snapped her head back as he viciously backhanded her.

"That is for striking me a few hours ago," he said. He raised his hand to strike her again, but was stopped by the dapper-looking older man behind the desk.

"That is enough, sir," the officer said calmly. "We need to question her while she is still able to speak."

Simone wiped blood from her mouth and was escorted to a chair. She sat and crossed her legs, casting a smile at Esperanza and Joaquin. "You may let the woman and her son leave," she said as she appeared to relax. "They know nothing and have served their purpose by luring me here."

"No, Simone!" Esperanza said.

Simone raised her hand to stop further protestations.

"Perhaps later," the officer replied. "When you tell me what I want to know."

"There is little of value I can tell you." Glaring at Archambault she said, "As I am sure this pig has told you, I have only arrived in the city today."

"If you cooperate, I will let your friends leave. You, however, shall remain as our guest until your trial for piracy against British ships on the high seas," the officer said with a bored look. "I am sure you are aware of the punishment for such an act."

"*Oui.* Either way, I shall die, so what would be the point of telling you anything?"

"So this woman and child you are so fond of may live."

"They have done nothing to you, sir. There is nothing to be gained by holding them. Surely an honorable man such as yourself would not needlessly injure a child or deprive him of the succor and comfort of his mother."

"Very clever, Miss Moreau, but you will tell me what you know. One way or another." At a slight nod of his head the soldier guarding Joaquin seized the boy by the hair and drew a knife from his waistcoat. He pulled Joaquin's head back and laid the knife against the boy's throat.

"You will tell me what I want to know or the boy dies," the man behind the desk said calmly. "We are at war. Unfortunately, civilians will be injured, some needlessly through stubbornness." He watched Simone's reaction while he struck a match and lit his pipe.

Simone controlled her desire to protect Joaquin and allowed her eyes to move around the room. Everyone appeared calm except Archambault who would have liked to be holding the knife himself.

"You are a coward, Henri. You have not the strength to face me yourself and leave your dirty work to these British dogs."

"You were captured and killed by the British during a valiant attempt to rescue your bitch and her whelp." Archambault shrugged. "Unfortunately, there was nothing I could do to save you or them."

Without looking at the officer in charge, Simone said, "The woman is a cook on my ship and her son is my cabin boy. They know nothing of the plans to defend New Orleans. Release them with a safe escort back to New Orleans and I will tell you what I know."

"You will tell me now. Otherwise I will have the boy killed and turn the woman over to Mr. Archambault to dispose of as he sees fit."

"She would fetch an excellent price on the auction block," Archambault said with a sneer. Running his tongue around his lips he grinned at Esperanza, his eyes appraising her body. "No one will care if she has been a little used first."

"She is a free woman and servant to no man," Simone snapped.

"She will only remain a free woman if we take this city and cut off the port for slave trading, Miss Moreau. You can save her by telling us what we want to know."

"I have your promise, sir, they will not be harmed?" Simone asked.

"You do, but we shall hold them here until we secure the city," the commander nodded.

Simone cast a glance at Esperanza. The soldier released his grip on Joaquin. Their eyes gleamed with defiance. Simone smiled when Esperanza rearranged her skirt and cast a glance toward the floor, giving her a barely perceptible nod.

"Take the woman and the boy and lock them securely in a room," the commander ordered.

Once Esperanza and Joaquin were escorted from the room, Simone grudgingly told the British commander what she knew concerning the American defenses in New Orleans. Not even Archambault could deny what she said. She hoped her delays and evasiveness would give Esperanza sufficient time to escape and reach the city. From the questions she was asked, she believed the main British force would land nearby within the following week or two. When General Jackson arrived in the city, he would have limited time to make the necessary preparations to stave off the invasion.

ESPERANZA JERKED HER arm from the grip of the soldier escorting her and Joaquin to another room. She would have to act as quietly as possible, hoping Simone would use her diversion to make her own escape. The soldier shoved her to make her move faster. She turned and smiled at him, knowing he would not see the dawn of another day. They reached the top of the main staircase. She glanced around looking for possible escape routes as she waited for the soldier to open the door. Pushing the door open he shoved her into the room and grabbed Joaquin by the arm. The boy looked at his mother and understood what he needed to do. He struggled briefly against the soldier and bit his hand. The soldier released him and turned to face the boy who was backing out the door away from him. Quickly he grabbed Joaquin by the neck and pulled him inside the room. "You filthy whelp," he hissed. His hand fell away from Joaquin and his eyes widened. He whirled around and stared at Esperanza, opening his mouth to call for help, but no sound came. He stumbled toward her, his arms reaching for her.

Joaquin saw the knife protruding from the soldier's back and jerked it free. He kicked the door closed and advanced on the still-standing man. The soldier had Esperanza by the throat. "Kill him," she said, her voice calm. Joaquin stared at the bloody knife in his hand. Standing behind the soldier he drove the knife into the back of the soldier's thigh. The man released Esperanza and his hand flew to his leg. Joaquin withdrew the knife quickly and tossed it to his mother. Without hesitation she brought her arm in an arc in front of her and slit the soldier's throat. Blood from his throat sprayed a red mist onto Esperanza's face and blouse. Breathing heavily she said,

"Now we leave."

"We cannot leave *Faucon*," Joaquin said.

"She will make her escape when she knows we are safe." Taking her son by the arm she cracked the door open. "No matter what happens don't stop. Do you understand, Joaquin?"

The boy nodded and followed Esperanza out of the room and down the upstairs hallway. Esperanza entered another room and went to the window overlooking the British encampment. "We will wait here until they are asleep. Then we will let Simone know we are safe. Our escape will provide the diversion she needs." Esperanza turned and dropped to her knees, grasping Joaquin's upper arms. "Simone is depending on us. We must not disappoint her."

SIMONE DEFLECTED QUESTIONS from her interrogators until well after dark. When her interrogation began, guards in the room watched her intently. Now with the passage of several hours and deprived of sleep, they seemed less alert and almost bored. The office in which she was being held had two large windows overlooking the side lawn of the two-story mansion. When she arrived she noticed the open area surrounding the main house eventually fell away into a marshy area along the side of the house.

Simone wasn't sure how much time had passed when she saw two silhouetted figures crossing the open field. She rubbed her eyes and suppressed a yawn. A map of the area lay on the desk. She had pointed out the locations of barricades established outside the city. Now the three officers were conferring with one another at the desk and the guards were engaged in a conversation. Moments later she saw several horses running, followed by a horse racing through the encampment, shouts alerting the sleeping soldiers. The officers and guards looked out the windows in disbelief.

Simone seized her opportunity and shoved past the officers. She rushed by the startled guards, pushing them over furniture before they could react, and flung her body through a window. Regaining her feet, she crouched as she ran toward the marsh, a shower of musket balls falling around her. She was within reach of the safety offered by the dense undergrowth when searing pain ripped through her side. She stumbled forward and dove into the tall marsh grasses with the shouts of the officers and guards coming from behind her. She knew she would have an advantage once she reached the swamp adjoining the marsh a few yards away. The soldiers pursuing her spread out in an attempt to surround her. Holding her side, she sprang over the boggy ground, ignoring the burning pain, and into the swamp until her feet sank deeper and deeper before becoming mired in the thick bottom mud. As she struggled to extricate herself from the quagmire she heard the soldiers following her panting as they began to close on her position. Looking quickly around, she saw her only chance for escape. Painfully pulling her body onto the low hanging branch of a nearby cypress, she concealed herself among the Spanish moss draped over the branches overhead. Halfway up, she heard a familiar accented voice. As much as she wanted to escape, her desire for revenge was greater.

With the cloak of darkness blocking out moonlight from the thickness of the swamp and mud caking her clothing and skin, Simone found and withdrew the small dagger concealed in the top of her boot. She grimaced as she pressed a hand against her wound. The musket ball had created a large hole in her side, but hatred fueled her and she waited. Crouched in the tree, she finally saw him. As he passed beneath her hiding place, she dropped to the soft ground behind him and covered his mouth. She pulled his head back and drew the blade of her dagger deeply across his throat, hissing into his ear. "You die a man without honor." As his body dropped heavily in front of her, she looked at the lifeless body of the man she once trusted with her life. Hearing the sound of cursing from soldiers nearby as they struggled to push through the heavy mud, Simone quickly gathered moss and covered Archambault's body, leaving it to rot.

As quickly as her injury allowed, she climbed once again onto the cypress and drew its hanging moss around her, resting her head against its cool trunk to bring her laboring breath under control as the British floundered past her. She pulled a chunk of moss loose and clenched her teeth together tightly as she packed her wound to staunch the bleeding. Occasionally, musket fire followed by a scream and the sound of thrashing water penetrated the darkness, sending a chill down her spine.

By the time the sky began to lighten she hoped the soldiers had either abandoned their search or become lost in the swamp only to become a meal for an alligator. She slid carefully from her hiding place and quickly searched Archambault's body, relieving him of his pistol, ammunition, and cutlass. The hair along the back of her neck prickled unexpectedly and she looked around. The water a few yards from her rippled toward the patch of ground where she stood and she backed slowly away from Archambault's body. She barely made it behind the thick trunk of the cypress when the water erupted in front of her. The animal moved at an amazing speed, launching its body from the water. Its bright white maw sank into the body and began dragging it away. "*Bon appétit*," she muttered as she began pushing northward through the cold water of the swamp and marshes toward New Orleans.

ANTON MADE ARRANGEMENTS with Laffite's attorney and friend, Edward Livingston, to allow Julia and Kitty to stay at his home during the remainder of their stay in New Orleans. Julia slept fitfully, her worry about Simone making its way into her dreams. What if she never saw Simone again? What if she never had the opportunity to tell her of her feelings?

She was awakened by loud voices from the courtyard and went onto the balcony to see what was causing the disturbance. She was shocked when she saw Anton engaged in a frantic conversation with Esperanza. Rushing along the balcony until she reached the stairs, Julia hurried across the courtyard and grabbed Anton by the arm. "What is wrong? Where is Simone?"

"The British have her," he answered tersely. "Esperanza and Joaquin managed to escape."

Julia looked at Esperanza, who was obviously distraught. Blood finely covered her blouse and was smeared on her caramel skin. Shifting her eyes to Joaquin, Julia reached out for him and hugged him to her. "They are exhausted, Anton. We have to get them cleaned up and fed. They need to rest."

"We must gather the crew and rescue Simone," Esperanza said, tears leaving a reddish trail along her cheeks. "Anton, you must go for Laffite."

"I will leave at first light. Julia is right. There is little we can do now."

Joaquin looked up at Julia. "*Faucon* will escape. She will arrive soon," he said confidently even though his voice tremored.

"I know she will, Joaquin," Julia said without conviction as she stroked his hair. "Let's get you fed and ready for bed now." Looking over her shoulder, she said, "You cannot help Simone if you are too tired to move, Esperanza. Until Anton returns with help there is nothing to do but wait and hope she returns safely."

TWO OF THE longest days she could remember living dragged by as Julia waited for Simone to return. Alone at night she feared the worst, but refused to give up hope. To keep herself occupied, she continued tutoring Joaquin to take both their minds away from thoughts of Simone. They were in the middle of a mathematics lesson when Mr. Livingston rushed into the dining room.

"Jackson has arrived!" he announced.

Julia and Joaquin accompanied Livingston to the street and joined a gathering crowd of citizens trying to get their first glimpse of the man they hoped would be their savior. Julia had seen many pictures of Andrew Jackson astride his white horse leading a charge against British soldiers with barely a mark on him. The sight that greeted her didn't look remotely like the heroic figure in the history books.

Jackson sat in an open carriage as it made its way slowly down Rue de Royale toward the building he would use as his headquarters.

He looked incredibly gaunt and pale, his face covered with wrinkles making him look much older than a man in his late forties. A thick head of white hair was combed back from his thin face. He waved unresolutely to the crowds that greeted him without smiling. *This is the man who saves New Orleans?*

Livingston glanced at Julia, seeing the worry on her face. "General Jackson has been quite ill with dysentery for several weeks, but he will be up to the task, my dear," he said.

Nodding, Julia said, "I am sure he will be successful in defending the city, Mr. Livingston."

"I am meeting with him shortly as he addresses the citizens and must go. He has assured me he will defeat the British or give up his life in the endeavor. I have known him for many years and his word has always been good. Is there any word concerning Captain Moreau?"

"Not yet," Julia answered. "When will Laffite arrive?"

"Soon. I must convince the General to meet with Jean as soon as possible."

Chapter
Seventeen

THE STREETS OF the city were dark as Simone staggered through them toward Laffite's blacksmith shop on Rue de Bourbon. Damp clothing clung to her skin. She couldn't remember the last time she had been so cold. Scattered flickering streetlights did little to penetrate the darkness hanging over the city. Laffite's men would know where to take her. Her side throbbed ceaselessly and it was difficult for her to breathe without pain. While she stopped the bleeding from her wound by packing it with mud and moss, it was a temporary measure at best. More than two days had passed since her escape and frequent stops to gather her strength or seek temporary warmth made the journey even longer. She was feverish, but continued moving. If she stopped again she might not be able to get up. She was barely recognizable as she stumbled into the side entrance of the blacksmith shop. The two men inside were startled and stared at her for a moment before she collapsed.

The next time she opened her eyes, she could barely make out the glow of a low oil lantern. Her side burned and she groaned as she brought her hand across her abdomen to touch the wound.

"No, don't," a soft voice said as a warm hand swept down her arm.

Simone jerked away from the touch, crying out from the pain coursing down her side. A flash of blonde imprinted itself on her feverish eyes before she succumbed to the darkness once again.

"SHE'S BURNING UP with fever," Julia said. Wringing out a cloth in cool water, she pressed it against Simone's forehead. "Are you certain the doctor cleaned the wound well enough?"

"There are many things in the swamp," Esperanza said, watching the concern on Julia's face. "If something made its way into her blood, there is no way for the doctor to remove it. *Faucon* will have to fight it. The mud she placed on the wound kept her from bleeding to death, but could kill her."

"She will not die!" Julia said, her eyes flashing as she looked up at Esperanza. "She is a strong woman."

"Only time will tell." Esperanza said.

"One of us should be with her at all times, talking to her. If she hears our voices, they will guide her back to us," Julia said as she gazed at Simone. She had never seen the strong, arrogant woman look so vulnerable.

Esperanze placed a hand on Julia's shoulder. "I will send Joaquin up to speak to her in a while. You must eat something less you fall ill as well."

"I am fine," Julia said as she wrung out the cloth again and placed it along Simone's neck. The truth was she had been terrified when Laffite's men brought Simone by carriage to Livingston's home. In the four days since Simone was brought to the house, Julia spent virtually all of her time watching over the captain's unconscious body. The wound from the musket ball tore a festering hole in her side. Aside from the germ-laden swamp, there was the possibility the musket ball lodged in her body had begun to poison her as well. Julia was heartened by the fact Simone seemed to be breathing easily while her body worked to heal itself.

As Esperanza withdrew from the room, Julia looked at Simone. The peacefulness of her face was occasionally broken by a light groan or frown and Julia couldn't imagine what might have been in her dreams.

"You'll be fine, Simone," Julia said softly. "Do you understand me? I couldn't bear not having you with me. We will win this battle and all return safely to Martinique. There's nothing for me to go home to so you're stuck with me for a while longer."

Julia rested her head on the edge of the bed and soon was overcome by exhaustion. Mental pictures of Simone standing tall and strong on the deck of her ship flipped through her mind. Other than the single kiss the day they first met, nothing more had happened between them other than in Julia's dreams. But she had seen more in Simone's eyes and didn't know what word to put to what she saw. Want. Need. Desire. She was certain Simone must have seen the same in her eyes and couldn't deny she had fallen in love with Simone based on little more than a look. Not even after a night of desperate passion had she felt the same way about any other woman. Smiling in her sleep, she was startled by a hand stroking her hair and sat up quickly. Pale eyes looked at her. "Oh, my God, Simone," she breathed.

"Why are you here?" Simone rasped.

"To care for you."

"I ordered you to leave. The British are south of the city awaiting their main force."

"I couldn't leave while you were injured. I know you are used to everyone jumping when you issue an order, but I am not a member of your crew."

"You are my...captive," Simone said.

"And you are mine," Julia whispered as she looked into the depths of Simone's eyes again, eyes that spoke more than words could ever hope to.

Over the next few days Julia, Esperanza, and Kitty, usually accompanied by Joaquin, assisted Simone in getting up from her bed in order to increase her strength. At first she was too weak to take more than two or three steps, but with each day, her strength slowly returned. Her appetite gradually improved and she regained some of the weight she lost during her ordeal. Julia enjoyed the times she spent with Simone, supporting her as she took halting steps around the enclosed garden courtyard of the Livingston home. She came to look forward to the times Simone gripped her shoulders to steady her body. Despite the cold weather, the sunlight seemed to rejuvenate the injured woman and occasionally she would rest halfway through her walk to soak in the sunshine, the color slowly returning to her face.

JULIA SLIPPED QUIETLY through the partially opened door, the only light from a small oil lamp on the dresser of the room, its wick set low, casting the room in a soft reddish glow. She hadn't intended to nap so long, but the exhaustion of the past two weeks finally caught up with her and she slept for several hours. The weather outside was humid and a cold, skin-penetrating rain began to fall, reminding everyone that even New Orleans was capable of experiencing winter. The household staff in the Livingston's home was already beginning to make preparations for the Christmas holiday that would be upon them in two weeks. It was Julia's favorite season of the year. She loved the smell of Christmas, the scent of freshly cut pine boughs and spices from foods simmering in the kitchen. She remembered holidays as a child when she and her brother frolicked in the snow surrounding their Virginia home, pelting one another with snowballs until their clothing became wet and heavy before warming themselves with their mother's homemade hot apple cider. Taking a deep breath, she could almost smell the cinnamon melting into the warm liquid.

Shifting her eyes to the far side of the room, a smile crossed her lips. Simone was still resting and Julia carefully approached the bed to set a mug of warm cider on the small table beside it. She couldn't stop herself from being amazed at how beautiful Simone was in repose, nor could she prevent her fingertips from lightly tracing the contours of Simone's cheeks and gently squared jaw. She didn't detect further sign of the fever that had ravaged Simone's body a week earlier and the doctor was amazed at how well the wound in her side was healing. Brushing aside a short lock of hair, Julia smiled down at Simone as she slept and turned to leave the room.

"*Bonsoir*," Simone said softly, causing Julia to look back at her, meeting the light golden eyes she had come to expect.

"I didn't mean to wake you," Julia replied.

"I was awake when you entered the room, but waited for the touch of your hand against my brow. I missed seeing you when I awoke earlier."

"I took a little nap while you were resting. Are you hungry?" Julia asked in almost a whisper. Looking down at her hands she knew there was so much she wanted to say to Simone. How scared she had been when she saw the ugly, festering wound in her side. How she couldn't go on living without her. But she couldn't bring herself to say any of the things she had said only to herself.

"I ate a light supper with Joaquin earlier. Please, come sit with me," Simone said as she pushed her body farther up on the bed. Quickly Julia went to her side and placed pillows behind her back. Simone grunted lightly at the effort. As she leaned back against the pillows, her face softened and she took a deep breath. "What is that delicious aroma?" she asked.

"Oh, I brought you a cup of apple cider. The weather is quite chilly today." Julia picked the cup up and held it to Simone's lips. As she drank, Simone brought her hands up to cover Julia's. When she swallowed and felt the warmth of the liquid flow down her throat, she smiled.

"It tastes even more delicious than it smells. Thank you. Did you make it?"

"Yes. Although not quite as good, it is almost like the apple cider my mother makes this time of year."

"One day I shall have to thank your mother for teaching you to make it."

Julia continued holding the cup as Simone's hands covered hers. The warmth of her touch spread through Julia as if it were warm cider. Catching herself, she moved to set the cup back onto the table. She reached behind her to pull the wooden chair that had been her place since Simone's return closer to the bed.

Still holding Julia's right hand, Simone shifted slightly and said, "No. Please sit here beside me. I am much better now. Tell me what has happened while I was recovering."

Sitting on the edge of the bed, Julia turned her body to face Simone. "Joaquin and Esperanza have been worried about you, especially Joaquin," she said.

"What happened was not his fault, nor Esperanza's," Simone said as she looked at Julia's hand in hers and stroked the back of it lightly with her thumb. "We were betrayed by someone we trusted."

"General Jackson has arrived in the city with his men and everyone seems to be in better spirits because of it. Mr. Livingston has sent word to Laffite and they expect him to arrive within the week," Julia continued. Simone nodded at the news as she turned Julia's hand in hers and let her fingers travel to Julia's wrist, brushing the sensitive skin softly.

"Anton...Anton has gone with a small party of men to the German Coast to meet with Laffite and bring your men back as well. Kitty is beside herself, naturally. They have become quite an item," Julia chuckled.

Bringing her eyes up to meet Julia's, Simone smiled. "An item? This is a good thing?"

"Sorry," Julia answered. "I meant I think they care for one another." She couldn't pull her eyes away from Simone's.

"She loves him?" Simone asked as her fingers stroked farther up Julia's arm.

"I believe she does," Julia said. She put her hand over Simone's to stop it from continuing its slow tortuous journey. "Please, Simone. You don't know what you are doing to me."

"If it is half of what looking at you stirs within me, then I cannot imagine anything more painfully sweet," Simone said, her voice deep and husky. Raising her hand to Julia's face, she let it linger along her cheek.

Leaning into the touch, Julia whispered, "It is a most exquisite pain."

Sitting up farther and leaning forward, Simone brought her lips within centimeters of Julia's, pausing a fraction of a second before pulling Julia gently to her, kissing the edges of her lips and feeling the pulse in her neck increase. She teased her with the tip of her tongue until Julia's lips parted. A moan came from Julia's throat as she savored the first intimacy between them and encouraged Simone to explore her mouth fully and deeply, her tongue as anxious as Simone's to discover the pleasures within. It was the slowest, most gentle, sensuous kiss Julia could remember experiencing. She wasn't ready for it to end when Simone finally broke their connection and held her cheek to Julia's.

"Lie with me," Simone whispered, her breath hot against Julia's ear, sending a tremor through her body.

"Your injuries...," Julia breathed back.

"I shall surely die if I cannot touch you, *mon amour*. I will deny my feelings no longer."

Julia stood and began unlacing the bodice of her blouse. Simone took in the tempting cleavage. Gazing down at Simone, Julia said, "I must forewarn you I am incapable of being a passive lover."

"Then give of yourself freely and with as much passion as you feel," Simone said with a smile as the blouse rose over Julia's head and dropped to the floor. Placing a hand on Julia's waist, Simone drew her closer, kissing along her side as her skirt began to fall away. Julia saw the smoldering desire in Simone's eyes and brought their lips together once again, restraining herself from devouring her. She knew it must have hurt as Simone pulled the shirt she was sleeping in over her head and drew Julia close against her, breathing in her scent, their breasts brushing against one another. Julia moved onto the bed, kissing Simone and straddling her lower body as she wrapped her arms around her lover's neck and cradled her head to hold her in their kiss. With Simone's hands exploring her naked body, Julia's mind went blank and she drank in the exquisite lightness of her touch and the feel of soft lips against hers, a feeling she had been unable to erase from her mind since the day they met on board the *Viper*. Now those lips were used not to demonstrate control, but in complete surrender to passion.

Julia arched her neck back, exposing it to Simone's searching mouth. Relishing the maddening slowness of Simone's tender caresses, Julia gasped as she felt Simone enter her quickly and then withdraw. She opened her eyes, breathing heavily as Simone brought her fingers to her mouth and licked them. She felt as if she was drowning in the pupils that expanded with ever-growing desire. "Like your cider, you, too, are more delicious than your scent," Simone said as their lips met again.

Tasting herself on Simone's lips was more than Julia could bear. "Simone, please," she choked out. "I..." But her plea was answered before she could speak it as Simone sought her mouth again, her tongue thrusting into it in rhythm with the thrust of her fingers entering Julia's body. As she rode Simone's hand, her thumb finding the swollen clitoris with each stroke, Julia was lost on an ocean of indescribable pleasure, its waves crashing onto the shore of her body just as relentlessly. She clung to the only thing that kept her from drowning. The safety of her lover's arms.

THIN SHAFTS OF light crossing the floor though a crack in the closed shutters of the bedroom window greeted Julia as she blinked her eyes open. Disoriented for a moment, she moved. A hand sliding up her hip and across her waist, pulling her into the warmth of the body lying behind her brought her back to reality and she smiled contentedly. This time it was not a dream.

"It is too soon to get up, *mon amour*. I have only now fallen asleep," Simone mumbled against Julia's hair.

Moving the covers enough to turn, Julia rolled over to gaze into Simone's eyes. Stroking back disheveled black hair she leaned closer and gently kissed her lover, bringing a crooked smile to Simone's lips. "I have to move to look at you. You are very beautiful when you sleep and I love looking at you." Trailing her fingers down Simone's arm, she said, "Go back to sleep so I can stare at you a little longer."

"How can you expect me to sleep when you touch me in such a way?" Simone said with a chuckle.

"You will have to get used to it."

"I shall never tire of it. Even when we have grown old and gray, many, many years from now." A grimace crossed Simone's face as she drew her arm up and propped her head on her hand.

"Are you all right, Simone?" Julia lifted the cover and looked at the bandage covering the wound. "I should change that."

"No, no. I am fine. There is a miraculous healing quality in your kisses and touches. I shall have to keep you in case I am injured again." Leaning down, she kissed Julia's forehead and began making her way down her cheek toward her mouth, her hand drifting up Julia's abdomen and stroking the warm silken softness of her breast.

"Oh, no, you don't!" Julia laughed, holding her at bay. "You are going to rest now and I am going to find some breakfast for us."

Simone groaned as she fell back onto her pillow. "Is this what I have to look forward to as we grow old and gray? Being rejected by the woman I desire? And in my own bed?"

Julia stood and looked around for something to cover her naked body. "First of all, my dear Captain, this is not your bed," she said as she bent to look at the foot of the bed. "And second...aha," she continued as she found a nightgown and pulled it over her head, "second, we will have many more nights to look forward to together in the years to come." She moved to the side of the bed and lowered her mouth to Simone's. "And third, I hope you will always desire me as you did last night. Only a fool would reject you," she whispered as she kissed Simone. "I am no fool."

AFTER ASSISTING SIMONE into the shirt she slept in and finding a robe to wear over her nightgown, Julia opened the shutters a few inches and let fresh air into the bedroom. Closing the door behind her, she walked along the second story balcony and took wrought iron steps into the open courtyard she was sure was filled with flowering plants in the spring and summer months. Crossing the paved walkway which was hidden from the street by a high gated fence, she hummed quietly to herself as she opened the door leading into the kitchen and dining area of the French-style home. Perhaps when, or if, she returned to her home on Tybee Island, she would repaint it in bright colors to remind her of her stay in the real New Orleans. She frowned as she shook her head. She would never return to Tybee Island. To go home would mean losing Simone and that was unthinkable. This was where she belonged. Simone was the woman with whom she would spend the remainder of her life.

Glancing into the dining room, she spotted Joaquin sitting at the main table. Entering the large room, she smiled down at him and rested a hand on his shoulder. "Good morning, Joaquin. Did you sleep well last night?"

He looked up at her and nodded. "Is *Faucon* well this morning?"

"She is growing stronger each day. Perhaps after she has a little something to eat she will feel even better."

"May I take breakfast to her?"

"Of course you may. I know she would very much like to see you. Help me?"

Joaquin helped Julia prepare coffee, juice, and cut up fruit and set it on a tray. "*Monsieur* Livingston brought beignets this morning," Joaquin said.

"Then beignets it shall be. Tell Simone I will be up in a little bit to help her out of bed." Julia smiled as she watched Joaquin carefully carrying the tray across the courtyard while she prepared a cup of chicory for herself. She watched the boy enter Simone's room. Suddenly the hair along the back of her neck prickled and she rubbed at it absently. Feeling as if someone was watching her she turned to find Esperanza standing in the shadow of the doorway between the kitchen and dining room. "Good morning, Esperanza," she said quietly.

"Good morning, *Mademoiselle*. Is Simone rested this morning?"

"Yes. I think we might be able to let her join us downstairs later. I'm sure she would enjoy being with other people for a change. She is still a little weak, but improving with each day." Although from her performance the night before, Julia thought any lack of stamina on her lover's part now was more likely from exhaustion than her injury.

Esperanza slowly walked across the kitchen and folded her arms over her chest as she gazed out the window into the courtyard. Without looking at Julia, she spoke. "Simone saved my life five years ago. Since that time she has cared of me and my son. I have been her lover for four of those years." She glanced quickly at Julia then shifted her eyes away before taking a deep breath. "I have had her body many times," she said in a low voice. Facing Julia she continued, "But I have never had her heart. She has saved it for someone else and now, unless I am mistaken, she has given it away."

Julia could think of no response to what Esperanza was saying and could only stare into the cooling cup in her hands. "I cannot say I do not envy you," Esperanza went on. "Simone is a woman of deep passion, but has never looked at me the way she looks at you. She cannot deny her desires even though she has tried. What lives in the heart cannot be denied. Now you must care for her. She deserves nothing less."

"I—I don't know what to say, Esperanza. It was never my intention..."

"No one can predict these things. I wish you no ill-will. But it would be a lie to say I will not miss her."

"What about Joaquin?"

"He is my son by birth alone. I care for him, but not as Simone does. I would never attempt to keep them apart."

"I hope one day you and I will become friends. You have a place in Simone's life as well," Julia said.

"I have done terrible things to you."

"Nothing more than any woman in love and seeing it slip away wouldn't have done. No one has been harmed."

Esperanza pushed herself away from the counter and extended her hand to Julia, who took it gratefully.

Chapter
Eighteen

WHEN JEAN LAFFITE entered a home his presence commanded everyone's attention. His appearance at the home of Edward Livingston late on the afternoon of December sixteenth was no less an event than if he had suddenly made an appearance before the city's constable. A flurry of activity began as soon as he swept into the house and would, no doubt, continue until his departure. Tossing his hat and coat to Livingston's housekeeper, Laffite strode into the living room. Simone was reclining on the divan chatting with Julia. Laffite stopped in front of Simone and, placing his hands on his hips, smiled down at her.

"On your feet, woman!" he demanded. "We have business to discuss."

"Captain Moreau is still recovering from her injuries, Mr. Laffite," Julia protested.

Laffite's smile widened, flashing amazingly white teeth beneath his black moustache as he shifted his gaze to Julia.

"If I should become injured I pray I would have as beautiful a nurse," he said. Shrugging, he took a nearby side chair and pulled it closer to the sofa. "But, alas, I would most likely be saddled with Pierre once again."

Julia looked quizzically at Simone who smiled and said, "His brother, my dear."

"I am pleased to see you survived your encounter with the British, Simone. How much longer will you be recuperating?"

"I am fine now, Jean."

"The British fleet arrived at Lake Borgne four days ago."

"How many ships?"

"My observers say the line of ships stretched beyond the horizon. The Americans had little with which to combat them. Pesky resistance at best."

"I will not risk my ships or men to fight an armada, Jean. There is no cause worth a fight that cannot be won."

"You must come with me tomorrow. Livingston has arranged a meeting with General Jackson at his headquarters. We must convince him to accept our assistance in repelling the British. Together we command a thousand experienced fighters and cannoneers."

"You will be arrested as soon as you show your face, Jean. These ideals you have become so enamored of surely are not worth the risk of your life."

Laffite waved a small hand in dismissal. "Livingston will be arriving soon with the necessary paperwork to assure my continued freedom. They forget that I am Jean Laffite, a French-born citizen in a French city. There are few Americans here, my friend. I have asked that you be included in the paperwork to protect you as well."

"Thank you, Jean. I plan to leave the city soon to begin a new life," Simone said, looking at Julia.

"Go with me tomorrow to speak to Jackson. Then if you still wish to retreat I will not prevent it."

Taking a deep breath, Simone nodded. "Very well. But I can promise nothing."

ACCOMPANIED BY LAFFITE'S friend, Major Latour, Simone and Laffite, along with Edward Livingston, traveled to Jackson's headquarters on Rue de Royale by carriage the following afternoon. Simone was not optimistic they would be received favorably by the American commander as they waited to be seen. Jackson had turned down all previous offers of assistance from Laffite, openly declaring him and his men nothing more than bandits and common criminals. Julia told Simone General Jackson was ill, but continued to assure her the Americans would defeat the British. Her confidence seemed unshakable although Simone didn't know the basis for her lover's beliefs. Nothing Simone had observed convinced her the city could be successfully defended.

An aide to General Jackson escorted the small party into Jackson's office. As they entered the room, Simone saw an old man slowly push his body up from where he was lying on an overstuffed divan. Livingston stepped forward and waited until the emaciated-looking man stood erectly in front of them. Jackson's blue eyes slowly scanned the small group in front of him. "General, may I present *Monsiour* Jean Laffite and Captain Simone Moreau. They have come to offer their services in defending the city of New Orleans from the British."

In a stronger voice than Simone would have thought possible, Jackson replied. "I have already rejected the assistance of these individuals, Mr. Livingston. I do not believe there is anything to be gained by further discussion."

Laffite stepped forward and touched Livingston on the arm before he could reply. "Excuse me, *mon Général*, it is not my intention to grovel before you and beg for the opportunity to be wounded or killed," Laffite began as he stepped closer to the tall American leader. "However, if you will allow me to present my offer once again I am confident we can reach an agreement. Edward, perhaps you would be so kind as to pour us each a glass of brandy to ward off the chill in the air."

Laffite looked around the office at maps and diagrams which hung on the walls. When Livingston handed him a glass of brandy, he drank it down in a single swallow. "Please, have a seat, *Général*," he said. "I have heard you are ill. Please."

Simone accepted a glass from Livingston and watched Jackson closely. When they entered the room he appeared somewhat hostile to their appearance. The look on his face was now one of interest as Laffite spoke. She always found Laffite to be a charming and persuasive man. Perhaps Jean was not turning out to be what Jackson was expecting. Surely he expected a pirate, complete with eye patch and a scarf tied around his head. Now he was no doubt surprised at the well-mannered gentleman standing before him.

"Let us evaluate what is available to defend our city," Laffite said, walking about the room, still gazing at the maps. "The city itself affords some natural protection by virtue of the swamps surrounding it and the river. It would be difficult for an army to simply march into the city other than from the south, here," he said as he pointed to an area which had been cleared for plantations. "As I am sure you are aware, *Général*, the British fleet has already made anchorage near Lake Borgne to the north of the Chandeleur Islands. If I commanded the British troops that are landing, even as we speak, it would merely be a matter of transporting them across Lake Borgne and moving them through the marshes to this point south of the city. What does your naval commander have to stop them?"

"Commodore Patterson had five gunboats defending Lake Borgne, but they were no match for the British gunboats bringing troops across. I have ordered all passages through the swamps along the southern shore of the lake blockaded," Jackson said wearily.

"It is likely the major batteries of British troops will form here, near the Villere plantation. Captain Moreau was detained near that location briefly by an advanced party. Before they can be fully reinforced, we must attack them."

"My men have enough rifles, pistols and cannons, but there is scarcely a flint to be found for the rifles and little gunpowder or ammunition for the cannons."

Chuckling, Laffite said, "If I am not mistaken, sir, many of your cannons were, until recently, my personal property. However, despite that, I am prepared to provide you with an unlimited supply of flints and more gunpowder and ammunition than you will need from my personal stores. Your navy has two ships with excellent firepower."

"Commodore Patterson tells me the most heavily armed corvette, the *Louisiana*, cannot leave the wharf because she does not have enough crewmen to man her sufficiently. Only the sloop-of-war

Carolina has a crew sufficient for the task."

Looking at Simone, Laffite said, "The members of our crews are all experienced sailors and trained cannoneers. Your troops will need guides to lead them through the swamps. I offer you not only the services of my men and those of Captain Moreau, but the ammunition and gunpowder you need."

"What do you demand as repayment for this generous offer?"

"Captain Moreau and I ask for nothing more than amnesty for ourselves and our men. We also request Letters of Marque allowing us to serve the American government once the safety of New Orleans has been secured."

Jackson rubbed his face with a long thin hand and looked from Laffite to Simone. "Is this arrangement satisfactory to you as well, Madam?"

With a simple nod Simone committed her crews to the service of General Jackson in defending the city. By the time they left Jackson's headquarters Simone was assigned as a gun captain aboard the sloop *Carolina*. Anton would be aboard the newly completed and much larger *Louisiana*. Laffite was named Jackson's aide-de-camp, charged with supervising the defenses into the city from his former headquarters on Barataria Bay to the southwest.

DESPITE THE DANGER gathering outside the city, the citizens of New Orleans tried valiantly to maintain as normal a life as possible. Julia couldn't remember the last time she'd felt so contented. She'd found the love she always wanted. She loved and gave of herself passionately and she knew, without a doubt, she was loved in return. Nothing could dampen her spirits as preparations for the annual Winter Ball continued unabated in the Livingston household. The people of New Orleans, a celebratory holiday notwithstanding, appeared reassured since the arrival of General Jackson. Periodic skirmishes had not reached the city and remained confined to a line ten miles south of the city. She knew the city itself would never be involved in the direct fighting, that Jackson and his makeshift army would be successful in protecting the city and repelling the British, thereby securing the valuable southern port. She knew General Jackson would go on to even greater things, his political future resting on his legend as the hero of the Battle of New Orleans. Her knowledge of what was to come helped her remain calm.

The Livingston household staff spent days preparing the elegant home for the Livingston's annual party. Boughs of evergreens lined the staircases and mantles and the entire house glowed with the spirit of the season. Julia bartered to purchase a small gift for Simone. She hadn't seen Simone in three days due to the preparations on board the *Carolina*. Laffite kept his part of the agreement with Jackson and a steady flow of ammunition and gunpowder to the two warships had begun. When Simone appeared unexpectedly at Julia's bedside late the night before, she had been appropriately welcomed. Julia smiled at the memory. She had never felt so wanton in expressing her feelings before. A smile crossed her lips as she thought about her lover sleeping soundly in their upstairs room.

Julia was preparing a cup of chicory, a substance she was quickly becoming addicted to, when Mrs. Livingston joined her in the kitchen.

"Ah, good morning, Miss Blanchard," Mrs. Livingston greeted her. "Are you looking forward to the party this evening?"

"It sounds delightful. I wish I had something more suitable to wear, but Kitty and I have been mending and cleaning our things."

Mrs. Livingston tilted her head and looked at Julia. "You know," she said as she blew on her coffee to cool it slightly, "I think I might have something that would fit you perfectly. Unfortunately, I have indulged in too many rich foods over the past two or three years and don't have time to have it altered. Once I was a slender little thing such as you. If it fits, you are more than welcome to wear it this evening. It would look wonderful with your hair color and complexion."

"I appreciate the offer, Mrs. Livingston, but I—"

"I would feel slighted, my dear, if you refused my offer. I insist."

BY SEVEN ON the evening of December twenty-second, guests began arriving through the courtyard of the Livingston home. Candles cast pinpoints of light through the gardens and across the wrought iron galleries. Julia was nervous as she looked at her reflection in a standing beveled mirror, turning from side to side. She would never have thought she could wear such a garment and feel comfortable. The material was soft flowing maroon velvet. The center of the dress, which had an alluringly revealing neckline, was a cream, satin-backed material, criss-crossed with gold and black embroidered filigree outlining inset maroon pieces. Black and gold filigree ran around the gown at mid-calf. From there to the floor the gown glittered with black and gold metallic threads in a delicate embroidered pattern.

She adjusted the long sleeves of the gown, pulling a small loop over each middle finger assuring the sleeves remained in place. A crème inset ran the outside length of each sleeve. Satisfied with her appearance, she pulled a crème cashmere shawl embroidered with black, maroon and gold edging around her shoulders, letting it drape over her arms and down her back. She knew Simone would be surprised, but hoped it proved a pleasant one. Although not something Julia would have ordinarily worn in her other life, it made her feel amazingly feminine.

She made her way along the gallery and onto a second floor

landing leading to the carved staircase to the main floor. As she paused at the top of the staircase, she saw dozens of guests milling around below her. It was like everything she had read about in history books as a girl. No one would ever believe her.

Laffite sipped from a flute of champagne and brushed the wetness from his mustache with the back of his forefinger with a smile. "Now that Jackson has seen the error in his earlier judgment, I am positive New Orleans will never fall into the hands of the British, Edward. We shall continue with our business as always."

"I hope you are correct in your assessment, Jean," Livingston said. "I can think of nothing more upsetting than having the city overrun with those pompous, overbearing gentlemen."

Laffite was an imposing figure, his height accentuated by his solid black clothing. He prided himself in his appearance and never appeared ruffled, even in a fight. His confidence cast an aura around him that often gave others pause when considering whether to confront the man. His wealth only added to his legend. He was considered quite a catch and frequented the Octoroon Balls and other gatherings, bringing him into contact with numerous attractive young ladies. He had spotted a young woman earlier whom he intended to favor with his attentions. He glanced over the heads of the group around him in an attempt to locate her. As his eyes scanned the guests, he stopped when he saw a woman making her way slowly down the staircase.

"A rare beauty," he said. "I envy your good fortune, Simone."

Simone smiled as she joined Laffite in observing Julia. She stepped away from the group and weaved her way through the other guests, stopping at the foot of the staircase. Julia paused for a moment, taking in the wondrous look of her lover awaiting her. Simone wore tan pants that ended in a split just above her black boots. A solid white shirt inside a white buttoned vest was tied in a large bow at her neck. The dark chocolate waistcoat, which fell to mid-thigh in the back, set off the color of Simone's eyes. The open collar of the waistcoat stood up in the back, ending at the hairline of her short black hair.

As Julia reached the last step, Simone took her hand, turning it over to kiss the palm. Moving a step back, she walked around Julia, taking in the vision before her. "You look magnificent, *ma chère*."

"*Merci, mon amour*," Julia smiled. "I was concerned you might be displeased."

"You are very beautiful, Julia. That you would wear this to please me only makes me desire you more."

Julia ran her eyes down Simone's body, biting her bottom lip in a teasingly coy manner. "And, if I may say so, Captain, you look unbelievably handsome this evening."

Simone slipped her arm around Julia's waist and drew her closer. "Laffite is jealous, you know," she whispered. Glancing at the other guests, she said, "They are all jealous that you are with me."

"I will always be with you, my love," Julia whispered in return, leaning into Simone's embrace.

"And I with you. Would you care for something to drink?"

"Not just yet. But I would love to feel your arms around me in a dance."

Simone laughed as Julia took her arm. "Perhaps later you will dance for me as you did on La Margarita."

"Not unless Esperanza is preparing the drinks. But I do not need anything to encourage me to perform a dance of seduction for you."

As Simone took Julia's hand for the dance, she said, "I may be leaving the festivities early this evening if you continue to tease me."

"I was rather hoping you would." Julia smiled up at the handsome woman. As much as she liked the gown Mrs. Livingston had given her for the evening, it would never compare to what she was certain Simone would give her once it was removed.

Chapter
Nineteen

SIMONE LAZILY RAN her hand across Julia's back, smiling as she took a deep breath and inhaled the lingering scent of passion surrounding her. It had been a perfect night. She thrilled at the sound of her name on Julia's lips. She was consumed by her need to feel the soft smoothness of Julia's skin beneath her fingertips as she watched her eyes melt into soft green pools under her touch. Simone had never known such a helpless, insatiable desire for anything or anyone in her life. It was powerful and she was certain she would die if she lost it. She closed her eyes and buried her face in the tangled short hair beside her. In the quiet she heard a familiar sound in the distance and sat up abruptly. She grabbed a shirt and slipped it over her head as she left the bed, crossing the room to open a window. The deep bells of St. Louis Cathedral were ringing continuously and the sound of gunfire echoed throughout the city. She went to the door leading onto the gallery and leaned over the railing.

"What is happening?" she called as she saw Livingston pulling a coat on while rushing across the courtyard.

"The British! They have arrived!" he answered.

She turned to get dressed and saw Julia standing in the doorway. "You have to leave, don't you?" Julia asked.

"The British are outside the city. I must return to the *Carolina*," Simone said as she went to Julia and wrapped an arm around her.

Julia watched quietly as Simone dressed. "I will wait here for your return."

Looking over her shoulder, Simone said, "Please go to the Ursuline Convent. You will be safe there until I return. Promise you will go, Julia, so I do not worry."

"I promise. Kitty told me they are establishing an infirmary inside the convent and I can help."

Tucking in her familiar white shirt, Simone said softly, "Julia, always know that I love you." Crossing to the bed, she leaned down and kissed her tenderly. "I will carry you in my heart always."

Julia picked up a small wrapped package and handed it to Simone. "In case you can't return in time for Christmas."

"I am sorry, *mon amour*, but I have nothing to give you in return,"

Simone said as she ran her fingers over the package.

"You have already given me everything I've ever hoped for. Now go before I start crying."

Kissing Julia one last time, Simone turned away and hurried down the gallery to Livingston's carriage where she joined the attorney and Anton.

SIMONE COULD SEE the masts of the ships long before she and Anton reached the wharf where they were moored. Although they were not assigned to the same ship, Simone was impressed by the firepower aboard the *Carolina*. Two decks of twenty-four pounders, as well as smaller ten pounders had been brought aboard. They were capable of laying down a swath of destruction against the British line she was certain the enemy would not be able to answer. Moored next to the *Carolina* was the newer, larger ship, the *Louisiana*. Completion on the second ship was delayed after she made the trip from the shipyards in North Carolina, arriving in New Orleans barely ahead of the British blockade.

The members of the *Carolina* crew watched as Simone strode up the gangplank onto the big ship, her hand resting on the butt of her pistol. Stepping onto the deck, she nodded to a few of her men before knocking on the captain's door. She was unaccustomed to not being in command, but would obey the captain's orders to assure the safety of the ship as it performed its mission. It only took the captain, Lieutenant Henley, a few minutes to explain Commodore Patterson's plan. Simone agreed the plan was brilliant as she left to make the final preparations for the upcoming battle.

She checked and rechecked everything around her assigned cannon and those near her. There was nothing left to do except wait for the order to come from the captain. She sat with her men on the deck, leaning against the hull and closed her eyes. They would have to wait for night to fall if their plan was to be successful.

"*Faucon*," a woman's voice said quietly.

Simone opened her eyes in the waning twilight. "Esperanza! What are you doing here?" Dressed in baggy breeches and a loose fitting shirt, Esperanza's hair was pulled back and pinned at her neckline.

"My place is beside you," Esperanza answered.

Pushing herself up, Simone took Esperanza by the arm. "You must leave immediately and return to the Livingston's home. Joaquin needs you."

Esperanza stopped and jerked her arm away. "Julia will watch him until we return."

"You do not belong here."

"I do as much as you, Simone. I will not leave you."

"The captain of this ship will not allow you to remain. It was hard enough to convince him I should be here."

"Then I shall hide until the ship sails. Once underway he would never stop to return me to the wharf."

The word came unexpectedly and Simone saw the gangplank being withdrawn as the crew began hoisting the *Carolina*'s sails. "Stay close to me," Simone said as she quickly returned to her assigned cannon. "You must remain completely silent until the word is given to fire."

The *Carolina* was ordered to move downstream and anchor off shore as close to the British positions on the eastern bank of the river as possible. As the sails began sliding up the masts, Simone double-checked the lines attached to each cannon caisson and ordered each crew to preset their elevations to cover as wide and deep an area as possible. All cannons on the port side were loaded and ready to fire.

By seven o'clock, the eighty-five-foot long sloop was slipping slowly downriver, her lamps unlit. The night fog rose from the river as the sloop moved, like a ghost, through the thick mist toward the British encampment. An eerie sense of anticipation settled over the crew as they waited silently. Nearly an hour passed before Simone heard the sound of the anchor falling into the water. She turned, crouched low, and saw the British campfires less than a hundred yards from the ship. Soldiers on the bank were calling out to the ship and firing weapons into the air to draw the crew's attention.

She wasn't sure how long they waited before she felt and heard the gun ports on the deck below her snap open. Quickly she lit her spark rod and glanced at Esperanza. A loud voice broke through the night. "Fire!" Simone touched the rod to the powder of her cannon. Simultaneously, all the cannons on the port side of the ships erupted in a burst of orange flame and blue-gray smoke as grapeshot tore through the British position. The concussion rolled the ship toward its starboard side. Jumping up, Simone directed her crew to reload and continue firing at will. She saw men on the bank running to escape the withering cannon fire. Tents caught fire and men and earth were thrown through the air. The ship continued firing for more than an hour. By the time the order to cease firing came, Simone and her crew were exhausted, their ears ringing from the level of noise. As the crew gathered itself, red, white, and blue rockets lit the area followed by an attack of Jackson's cavalry which had been gathering and waiting nearby as the *Carolina* carried out its deadly attack.

As the ground fighting continued, the *Carolina* withdrew to the western shore of the river and set anchor once again out of the range of musket fire from the British on the opposite shore. As the sun began to rise the following morning, the *Carolina* launched its second barrage of the British position. By mid-morning the larger sixteen-gun *Louisiana*, now manned by Laffite's cannoneers, dropped anchor a mile upstream and joined in the devastating attack on the British.

Both ships continued firing, buying time for Jackson to fortify his makeshift line of defense along the Rodriguez Canal. In the pre-dawn hours of December twenty-seventh, Simone was finally satisfied there were no other preparations to be made before the day's barrages began. She sat on the deck and rested against the railing. She closed her eyes and breathed in deeply. The scent wafting off the water from the river and surrounding swamp was heavy and fetid. While the decks below often held a musky, moldy odor, the water of the river gave off a distinctive aroma even on deck. In the distance she heard sporadic rifle and pistol fire along the banks of the river, followed occasionally by the sound of voices yelling. Reaching into her pocket she withdrew the small gift Julia had given her. She untied the bow and opened the box. She smiled as she lifted out a small pewter sculpture of a horse rearing onto its hind legs. It reminded her of one more reason to survive.

She felt someone slide down next to her and turned her head. A smile crossed her lips as she looked at the woman who shared her life and her bed the last four years. She chuckled when she noticed the clothing Esperanza wore. "Where did you get those?" she asked, slipping the sculpture inside her shirt.

"I stole them. Do you not think I am fashionable?"

"You would look beautiful no matter your clothing," Simone said, pulling Esperanza to her and kissing her on the cheeks.

"I shall miss you, Simone," Esperanza whispered as she rested her head against Simone's shoulder.

"Man your stations!" the captain called out from the bridge of the *Carolina* before Simone could respond.

Casting a reassuring smile at Esperanza, Simone helped her stand and looked over the railing. A nearby crewman poured a small amount of black powder in the firing point of the cannon and inserted the firing tip. Simone lit the end of her spark rod and waited.

"Fire!" the captain bellowed. Simone crouched down and touched the spark rod to the wick and stepped quickly to one side as a cannonball exploded from the barrel, forcing the body of the cannon backward. Crewmen grabbed the ropes on either side of the weapon and began hauling it back to the rail to prepare for another round.

The air on deck was thick with the smell of burned gunpowder and smoke from the cannon barrels. Esperanza swept hair away from her face and prepared to fill the magazine once again. Unexpectedly the deck of the *Carolina* was struck by return fire from British cannon batteries which had somehow been moved to a position at nearly point-blank range.

As the wick was slipped into the firing mechanism of their cannon once more, Simone yelled, "Stand back!" A second round of cannon fire struck the *Carolina*. She looked around as fires began to ignite around the deck and she pulled Esperanza toward the starboard side of the ship.

"Leave the ship, Esperanza," she ordered. "They have our range and are firing hot shot."

"Not without you, Simone," Esperanza said stubbornly.

"I will be right behind you. I have no desire to die this day. Move quickly before the fires spread."

Esperanza nodded and climbed onto the ship's railing, looking down for a foothold. Simone held her by the waist and prepared to lower her from the deck. She wasn't sure what happened as Esperanza cried out and fell away from the ship, into the water below. Simone leaped onto the railing and clung to the cargo netting until she located Esperanza. She jumped from the burning ship, quickly submerging in the muddy water. When she surfaced she turned in a circle until she found Esperanza once again. Grabbing her under her arms, Simone began pulling her toward the western shoreline, joining other crew members swimming away from the doomed ship.

Midway to the western shore, Simone was startled by the sound of wood splintering as an explosion ripped the *Carolina* apart, raining burning debris onto those in the water. Simone shielded Esperanza from as much as possible as shards of wood rained over them.

BY THE TIME Simone reached water shallow enough to stand in, she was exhausted from fighting the river's current. Two equally battered crewmen came to help her pull Esperanza onto the bank. They all lay on the muddy slope catching their breath as they watched the final moments of the *Carolina*. Simone looked upstream and saw the *Louisiana* retreating toward the city. She hoped Anton had not been injured in the fighting. A moan drew her attention back to Esperanza. She rose onto her knees, brushing long black hair away from her former lover's face before assessing her injury. To her dismay, blood spread across the woman's abdomen and she was impossibly pale.

"Where are you injured?" Simone asked softly.

Esperanza's eyes darted over Simone's face and she gripped her arm with a bloodied hand. "Take care of Joaquin, *mon amour*," Esperanza said. "Tell him...tell him I did care for him."

"You can tell him yourself," Simone said as she unbuttoned Esperanza's shirt. She drew in a short quick breath at the sight of the gaping wound. Shrapnel cut a swath through the caramel skin leaving a torn wound almost as large as Simone's fist.

Knowing there was nothing she could do, Simone sat on the bank and rested Esperanza's head on her lap, holding her. "I am sorry, Esperanza," she choked out.

Looking up at Simone, a peaceful looked passed over Esperanza's face and she managed to raise her hand to touch Simone's lips. "I have loved you well, *mon Faucon*," she said in a fading voice.

"More than I deserved, *ma chère*," Simone replied as she took Esperanza's hand and kissed the fingertips. "You deserved better."

AS SOON AS the damage to the *Louisiana* was assessed and repairs begun, the captain allowed the crew to return to their bunks for a much needed rest. Now with the loss of the *Carolina*, their ship would not be able to withstand the British batteries from a closer distance. The captain advised them the defenders of the city would be taking a stand at the Rodriguez Canal, which was still being fortified. The role of the *Louisiana* would be to provide additional cannonfire in that fight. He believed the city would be lost if the British overran the makeshift American position south of the city.

As the rest of the crew fell into their bunks, exhausted from the fighting, Anton slipped onto the deck and left the ship. Moving as quickly as possible, he found a horse which was left unattended and took it. It was twilight before he made his way to the Ursuline Convent, two miles south of the city, where injured soldiers and militiamen were being cared for. He entered the two-story white structure and wandered from room to room on the first floor searching for Kitty and Julia. He stopped an older nun to ask about the two women.

He looked into a large room that had been turned into a temporary infirmary. He saw Kitty's red hair and longed to go to her, but there was more serious, more urgent news to deliver first. He nodded to Kitty briefly when she stood and saw him. Then he saw the head covered with short blonde hair leaning over a patient on the far side of the room. Resolutely, he made his way toward her. As he stopped next to the cot Julia glanced up.

"I shall be right back," she said to the patient. "You are doing just fine."

She kept her eyes on Anton as she came around the cot. "Are you injured, Anton?" she asked.

"No. I am well. Julia...I...are Joaquin and Esperanza with you?"

"Joaquin is taking supper. I am not sure where Esperanza is. She left and asked me to watch Joaquin until she returned. What has happened?"

"The *Carolina* has been destroyed," he said.

Julia's hand flew to her mouth and tears threatened in her eyes. "How?"

"We were told cannon fire struck the ship's magazine causing an explosion."

Fearful of the answer, Julia forced herself to ask, "And Simone?"

"She was lost," he said solemnly. "I am sorry."

Julia looked down and shook her head. "It cannot be. The British will not take the city. The Americans will win."

"Perhaps, but Simone and the *Carolina* are gone."

"Did you find her afterward?" Julia asked hesitantly. "Where is her...she?"

"The *Louisiana* retreated back to the city after the explosion. British troops now control the area. There was no opportunity to look."

"Then you can't possibly know for certain she was killed." Julia's voice rose as she challenged the news of her lover's death.

"No one could have survived that explosion, Julia. You and Kitty must leave the city at once. We all want to believe the British will not win, but the odds are not in our favor. I must insist that you and Kitty take the boy and leave at first light. I will arrange for one of Laffite's men to guide you before I return to the *Louisiana*." He reached out to rest his hand on Julia's shoulder. "Is there anything more I can do for you?"

"I will make arrangements for Joaquin to leave the city if you wish, but I will remain here. If you wish to do anything for me, bring Simone's body for me to see. I won't leave this city until I see her again." Until she saw Simone's body she would never believe her lover was dead. She could not have traveled so far in time and place to finally find the love she had been looking for only to lose her so cruelly.

Julia glanced across the room and saw Kitty pacing and wringing her hands as she watched them talk. "Now go to Kitty before she worries herself sick." She patted his hand and said quietly, "Thank you for coming."

Julia turned away before Anton could see the tears rolling down her cheeks and made her way through the maze of cots and into the nun's chapel at the far end of the first floor. There she leaned against the cool wall and slid down its rough surface until she was on the floor, crying uncontrollably.

Chapter
Twenty

SIMONE RELUCTANTLY LEFT Esperanza's body hidden in the tall marsh grasses near the western bank of the river and moved farther inland from the bank. She walked north toward the city and away from what remained of the *Carolina* as quickly as she could. She hadn't gone far when she heard voices and slid into the marsh grasses, her body shivering against the dampness. She gripped her dagger tightly in her hand as the voices approached. Recognizing a familiar French-accented voice, she stood and looked at the men who had just tramped by her. "*Bonjour*, Pierre," she said to Laffite's brother.

"Simone!" the stout man exclaimed as he swung around. "You are alive!"

"That much is obvious, my friend. Why are you here?"

"We heard the explosion and came to see what happened."

Looking over her shoulder, she said, "The *Carolina* has been destroyed. The British must have gotten a battery closer during the night. Hot shot hit the magazine."

"Are you hurt?"

"No, but I am anxious to return to the city." She gratefully accepted a cape from one of Pierre's men and pulled it over her shoulders.

"The Americans are preparing for their final stand. It may be wiser to see if they are successful. Jean believes the British may attempt to land soldiers on this side of the river to attack from the rear."

"Then I shall stay with you until the fighting is finished."

Despite her desire to return to New Orleans, Simone spent the remainder of the week with Pierre Laffite and his men. Periodic skirmishes on the east bank told them the fighting was far from over. Pierre sent men through the swampy area of the west bank to warn them of an attack from their rear. Simone was beginning to regard their vigilance as unnecessary and chafed to return to the eastern shore.

The morning of January eighth the sound of cannon and musket fire pierced the air from the eastern bank of the river. One of Laffite's scouts returned to the group to report a large contingent of British soldiers making its way around the American position by way of the western bank. Pierre sent a messenger to his brother before turning his group to meet the new threat.

They were unsure of the number of British troops landing along the western bank of the river, but it didn't take long for them to realize they were badly outmanned and outgunned. Pierre and his group retreated to an area where a small battery of American artillery was set up and waited. They were spread painfully thin along a narrow line. Simone didn't like the looks of their situation. There were no more than nine cannons aligned to meet the British forces who had easily overrun the first line of defenders a mile south of the American artillery. The American commander on the west bank waited until he saw the British advancing within range of his cannons and opened fire. Volleys of musket fire followed, but for every British soldier that fell another quickly took his place and continued to march relentlessly toward the Americans.

"Disable the cannons!" Simone called out. She ran to the gunpowder barrels and tipped them over, rolling them toward the river to render the gunpowder useless. Others joined her in the attempt to make the cannons, which were sure to be used against them as they retreated, useless. As her final barrel teetered on the edge of a slope running to the water, she stood and was grabbed from behind. She spun around, pulling her cutlass from its scabbard barely in time to deflect the bayonet of a British soldier. She jumped back slightly and held her weapon in preparation to fight. The soldier was young and the sight of a woman on the battlefield startled him momentarily. Using his hesitation to her advantage, she shoved the barrel down the slope as she slashed the man's arm. She could have easily killed him. Turning away from the wounded soldier she bolted into the marsh to join her comrades.

The Americans managed to regroup less than a mile away, but without the aid of their artillery they could offer little more than token resistance. They hid within the marsh grasses and caught their breath before the next attack. But it never came. A man ran toward them and was quickly surrounded by a motley group of wet, dirty, and bloody volunteers, pirates, and American soldiers. He threw is hands into the air quickly. "The British are leaving!" he announced.

"But they are winning," Pierre said. "What has happened?"

"Jackson is winning on the eastern bank. They are returning to reinforce the British line. The British commander has been killed."

Simone shoved her cutlass into its scabbard and sat down heavily, putting her head in her hands. "The city is safe?" she asked, looking up at the messenger. Jubilation broke out among the survivors of the fighting on the western bank.

Early that afternoon, Simone smiled when she saw Jean Laffite striding through his beloved swamps and marshes, leading several hundred Americans. Julia had been right. The Americans did manage against all odds to reject the British attempt to take New Orleans. She borrowed a spyglass from Laffite and gazed across the wide river. The fields and banks were littered with the bodies of the dead and wounded. Both sides fought valiantly. New Orleans was saved and Simone was ready to leave it and begin her new life with Julia.

SIMONE RETURNED TO the city with Laffite and his men, relieved to see little damage. Jackson and his men did not allow the British closer than ten miles from New Orleans. News of the American victory spread quickly among the citizens and the streets were jammed with celebrations. They pushed their way through the crowds of revelers. There was only one destination on Simone's mind.

"A great victory, eh, Simone?" Laffite asked.

"*Oui*," she answered with a smile. "The time for fighting is over."

"Come with us. This city is growing much too civilized. Barataria is gone. There will be good hunting farther to the west," Laffite said.

"I cannot believe you would leave here."

"With my Letter of Marque from the Americans the gold from Spanish ships will make us all wealthy. Join us and I guarantee it will be worth your while."

"I have no interest in fighting the Spanish. Peaceful days lie ahead for me on Martinique, my friend." Simone said. "If the captains of my other ships wish to accompany you I will do nothing to stop them, but I shall return home."

Simone and Laffite hugged briefly. "I wish you the best of luck. If you should grow tired of peace and quiet, sail west and you shall find me."

"*Au revoir, mon ami*," Simone said, patting Laffite on the back.

Making her way across the Place d'Armes, she saw a familiar face and quickened her steps. "Anton!" she called out. Her brother heard his name being called, but was unable to locate its source until Simone pushed past a group near the center of the open area.

"Simone!" he exclaimed when he finally saw her. They made their way quickly to one another and hugged fiercely when they met.

"I...I thought you were lost when the *Carolina* exploded," he said.

"I made it over the side before the explosion. Esperanza was killed," she said, fighting back the sorrow she felt from the loss. "Where is Julia?"

"She has returned to Livingston's home. I tried to convince her to leave the city, but she refused to believe you were lost. Kitty and Joaquin are with her."

"I must go to her, Anton," Simone said as she began to move away. "I will see you later, yes?"

SIMONE WALKED AS quickly as the crowds permitted toward Edward Livingston's home on Rue de Dauphine. When she reached the courtyard gate half an hour later she paused to catch her breath. Stepping into the courtyard she looked around and made her way to the stairs leading to the second floor. Halfway up, she could wait no longer. "Julia!" she called out. "Julia!"

A door farther down the gallery opened and Kitty stepped outside, her hands flying to her mouth. "Praise God!" she said as she rushed toward Simone and hugged her.

Taking Kitty by the arms Simone asked, "Where is Julia?"

"In the chapel on the other side of the courtyard. Her prayers have indeed been answered," Kitty beamed.

Simone rushed back down the wrought iron stairs and across the courtyard. She opened the wooden chapel door and stepped inside, stopping to quickly dip her fingers into the font of holy water. She genuflected and made the sign of the cross. It had been many years since she had entered a church, but she had never had more reason to be grateful. She saw Julia kneeling at the railing near the altar, a bank of flickering candles illuminating her face.

With the fighting near the city many people spent extra time in chapels or St. Louis Cathedral praying for the safety of their city. When the door to the chapel opened Julia ignored it as a common occurrence, continuing with her prayers. Until she saw Simone's body she would never believe her lover was dead. She wasn't sure she would be able to look at a mangled body and recognize Simone without being destroyed herself.

"Julia," Simone said softly.

Now I am hearing things, Julia thought with a frown. Simone is gone.

Simone stepped closer to the railing. "Julia, *mon amour.*"

Julia spun around and nearly fell from the shock of seeing Simone. Her clothes were torn and filthy with mud and blood. Julia stared at Simone for a moment longer as if she were an apparition before standing and running to her. She was swept up by welcoming strong arms and held closely in a warm embrace. Simone set her down and Julia pulled her into a deep frantic kiss, unwilling to release her for fear she was nothing more than a dream. The kiss returned to her was all the assurance Julia needed. Simone was alive!

"Anton told me you were dead," Julia croaked. "Oh God, my love, are you injured?"

"No. I am well," Simone answered. Wrapping an arm around Julia's waist she said, "I want to feel you with me, but not in this place."

Julia turned back toward the altar and made the sign of the cross. "Thank you," she mouthed as she rejoined Simone.

They walked out of the chapel. A cold wind whipped across the courtyard and they clung to one another. Simone stopped when she saw Joaquin standing near the dormant fountain in the center of the courtyard. "I must speak to him," Simone said solemnly. "Esperanza was lost."

Julia saw the tears forming in Simone's eyes. She nodded. "I will prepare a bath for you."

Simone kissed Julia lightly and watched her climb the stairs to the second floor. She walked to Joaquin and knelt in front of him, drawing him into a tender hug, kissing his cheeks and wiping away his tears. "Sit with me, Joaquin. We must talk." Simone sat on the edge of the fountain. Joaquin joined her and she wrapped an arm around his shoulders. Tipping his chin toward her she said, "I am sorry, Joaquin. Esperanza was killed during the fight against the British."

"Was she...brave?"

"Very brave. You should be proud of her. She sacrificed her life to help save the city, but I was unable to save her."

"May we bury her on Martinique?"

"Of course. We will return her to the home she loved best."

"I...I will miss her, *Faucon*," Joaquin said. Tears streaked his cheeks.

Pulling the boy into her arms, Simone whispered, "We shall all miss her spirit."

"What will become of me now?"

"I will care for you, *mon chou*, as always. You will live with us on Martinique. I shall be proud to call you my son. Your mother's last words were of you. She loved you in her own way. Now go into the chapel and light a candle in memory of her spirit."

Simone watched Joaquin enter the small chapel and wiped away her own tears. She loved the boy as if he were her own and made a silent vow to give him the best life she could. Straightening her shirt she stood and climbed the stairs toward her future.

Chapter
Twenty-one

THE FIGHTING AT New Orleans was costly. Simone lost twenty-five of her crewmen as well as Esperanza. Following a week of rest and preparations, Simone helped Julia and Joaquin aboard *Le Faucon de Mer* for the final journey home to Martinique. The feel of Julia beside her filled her soul with happiness despite the losses they had suffered.

The day after her return to New Orleans Simone and four of her crew members crossed the Mississippi River to the western bank. She personally cleaned her former lover's body before sealing it in a simple wooden casket. Across the river the British were also going about the grim task of preparing their dead for burial. They had all fought valiantly, but the toll was more than Simone could comprehend.

As the ship weighed anchor and slowly made its way out of Timbalier Bay toward the open sea, Simone stood on the wheel deck. "Take us home, Gaston," she said to her new first mate. "The most direct course you can navigate."

"*Oui*, Captain," the man nodded as the ship cleared the channel entrance to the Gulf of Mexico.

A brisk winter breeze filled the sails. Simone wrapped a cape around her shoulders and walked to the stern. Her black hair fluttered around her head as she sat and watched the *Northumberland* fall in behind her. This would be her last voyage. *Le Faucon* had been her home for too many years.

A smile crossed her lips as she gazed back at her brother's ship. He and Kitty married the day before they left New Orleans. St. Louis Cathedral was filled with rugged looking crewmen as they exchanged their vows. Most of their men practiced no religion and seemed uncomfortable and uncertain as to the proper behavior. They were much more comfortable at the celebration afterward.

The captains of Simone's other two ships made the decision to remain with Laffite. They knew no other life and she wished them well. They were loyal to her and deserved their rewards for such loyalty. Her thoughts were interrupted by the feeling she was being watched. She turned her head toward Gaston and saw Julia staring at her. Motioning her closer, she pulled Julia against her for warmth and covered them both with her cape.

Julia had been unusually quiet as they made their final preparations to leave New Orleans, but offered no explanation. Simone had been reluctant to question her then. "What is troubling you, *mon amour?*" she whispered. "You seem unhappy."

"No. I am indescribably happy, but...there is something you need to know about me."

"Is it something serious? No matter what it is, it could never diminish my love for you," Simone said, brushing her lips against Julia's neck. "We have survived much worse, I am certain."

"It's chilly up here," Julia said. "Can we speak about it in your cabin?"

"It is *our* cabin now and I would enjoy being there with you." Simone stood and offered her hand to Julia. She left an order with Gaston not to be disturbed and escorted Julia down the steps to the main deck. Had Julia changed her mind and now had no wish to accompany her to Martinique? Simone refused to think of such a possibility. As they entered their cabin Simone pulled Julia to her. She was shocked when Julia pushed away from her and walked to the windows overlooking the sea behind them.

Simone followed her and placed her hands on Julia's shoulders. "Have I done something to upset you?" Simone asked. "If so, you have my deepest apologies."

"No. You are everything I have ever desired. The problem is with me," Julia answered.

Simone took a deep breath and wrapped her arms around her lover. "Tell me what you believe is wrong and I will do what I can to change it."

Julia laughed. "You can do many things, my love, but this isn't something you can fix. No one can."

Simone turned Julia to look at her. "I love you, Julia, but I cannot play these guessing games. I have given you my heart and now you are ripping it apart."

Julia looked down for a moment. When she looked up again she saw the worry in Simone's eyes, and stroked the side of her face. "I don't belong here," she finally said softly.

"Of course you do! You will always belong here with me," Simon said with authority.

"Do you remember Bernadette?"

"That foolish old tarot reader in New Orleans? What of her?"

"She said I didn't belong here. Being near me frightened her."

"She was an old fool. Nothing more than a street vender stealing money from the gullible," Simone said dismissively.

"But she was right, Simone. I don't belong here."

Simone dropped her hands and took a step back. "Do you wish to leave?"

Closing the distance between them, Julia shook her head. "No, no. I never wish to leave you. You are everything I have wanted my whole life."

"Then what is wrong?"

Julia took Simone's hand and pulled her toward the bed. When they both were seated Julia took a deep breath and turned to face Simone. "I am from a different time, Simone. I don't know how I came to be here, but I am."

Simone stared at her lover and opened her mouth to speak, but could think of no response. Julia smiled. "I am from a time in the future. I live on Tybee Island on the Georgia coast. I am a marine archaeologist. I was diving alone when my boat was stolen by...by pirates." The more she said, the faster the words tumbled from her mouth. "Pirates in my time are mostly drug smugglers. They took my cabin cruiser and left me in the open sea to die. When I was rescued by the *Viper* I was certain I was dreaming, seeing things that weren't really there. But now the dream has gone on for over six months. I...I can't explain how I came to be here in this time, with you." She stopped and looked at Simone. "Now you know. The woman who loves you is insane. You are a figment of my imagination. None of this can be happening, but it is." Suddenly tears sprang to Julia's eyes and she buried her face in her hands. "I don't want to lose you, but I'm afraid if I ever awaken from this dream you will be gone. I couldn't bear that, Simone. I love you too much to go on living without you."

Simone took Julia's wrists and pulled them away from her face. She wiped the tears from Julia's cheeks and leaned closer until their lips met. At first, even after the passionate nights they had already spent together, Julia was tentative. As Simone's kiss became more insistent, Julia's lips parted and she wrapped her arms tightly around Simone, pouring every ounce of emotion within her into the kiss. Breathless when the kiss came to an end, Simone whispered, "A kiss such as that cannot be only in a dream, my love." Her hand brushed over Julia's breast and she felt the nipple harden. "Your body would not react to my touch in a dream. As long as you breathe I shall be with you."

"I hope you are right."

Simone lowered Julia onto the bed, kissing along her neck. "Let me show you other things that cannot occur within a dream."

As she felt Simone's body move over hers, a feeling of dread and profound loss swept through Julia. She had dreamed these very things and felt them as much in her dreams as she was now. Please don't let me ever awaken, she silently prayed.

JULIA FELT BETTER after telling Simone the truth, or at least what she thought was the truth. They spent the next two weeks strolling the deck of *Le Faucon de Mer*, discussing their future together. Neither of them brought up the future as Julia knew it although they did discuss Julia's family and occasionally the work she was doing. Simone seemed fascinated by the excavation Julia described even though Julia was certain Simone was merely humoring her insane lover. Nevertheless, she had told the truth, knowing they might never discuss it again once they reached the island sanctuary.

A week from Martinique Julia leaned against the railing and gazed out over the orange and yellow sunlight streaming across the water's surface from the horizon. Nothing was more beautiful than a sunset on the waters of the Caribbean. A kiss against the back of her neck brought a smile to her face. "If you are not Captain Simone Moreau then you are in serious trouble, crewman," she laughed.

"In a week I will only be Simone Moreau," her lover said as she joined her to look out over the calm waters.

"The water is very still this evening," Julia commented.

"Yes, it is. Almost too calm. Without a wind we will make little progress."

"In a hurry to get home?"

"The journeys we are most eager to complete always take the longest. Or so it seems," Simone said with a smile. "Our dinner is ready."

Julia took Simone's arm as they made their way to their cabin. "You know, Simone," Julia started. "The things I miss most about the future are my cargo pants and t-shirts. Oh, and my sneakers. They were so comfortable!"

"When we reach Martinique I will see that you have pants at least," Simone smiled.

"Would you really?"

"Of course. I want you to be happy. But I do not know the things you call 'sneakers'. Are they for stealth?"

"I suppose so. I'm unsure how they acquired their name."

SIMONE WAS AWAKENED from a deep sleep by a thumping sound and sat up in bed. Looking at the windows on the far side of the cabin she saw water streaming over them.

"Is something wrong?" Julia asked, her voice heavy with sleep.

"No. Go back to sleep. I will see what has happened."

Simone slipped on her pants and boots, throwing her cape over her shoulders before she stepped onto the main deck. Cold rain pelted her face. The ship was listing slightly into the wind as she made her way onto the wheel deck. "What is happening, Gaston?" she said loud enough to be heard over the wind.

"The wind began increasing almost an hour ago, Captain. We have only just been struck by the rain. It is becoming more difficult to pilot the ship now that the wind has begun to swirl." The first mate clung to the wheel to maintain control of the vessel.

Simone went to the railing overlooking the main deck. "Lower the sails!" she ordered. "Gaston! Turn into the wind to let the wind from the sails!"

The wind velocity seemed to grow stronger by the minute as Simone and Gaston both attempted to hold the wheel away from the wind. She wiped rain from her face and watched her crew slowly making their way up the lines to take in the sails. If the wind filled them and continued to grow one or more of the masts could be broken or severely damaged at the very least. She glanced over her shoulder, but the rain made it impossible to see the *Northumberland*. It was a slightly smaller ship and she hoped Anton's sails were already lowered.

"Simone! What is happening?" Julia's voice called out.

Simone maintained her hold on the wheel. She couldn't believe Julia was standing halfway up the steps to the wheel deck. "Go back inside the cabin! You will be safe there! I will join you when this storm passes!"

Julia nodded and turned to descend the steps. It seemed as if a hole suddenly opened on the surface of the water and the ship plunged downward. To her horror Simone saw Julia fall the last two or three feet to the main deck. "Go to her, *Faucon*! I can hold the wheel alone for a few moments, but hurry!" Gaston said over the wind and rain.

Bracing her body, Simone carefully made her way to the main deck. As she reached Julia a wave of water poured over the deck, knocking both women off their feet. Simone held Julia's hand tightly, attempting to regain a foothold on the slickened deck. "Don't let go!"

It took every ounce of strength Simone could summon to maintain her grasp on Julia as they began to slide closer to the main deck railing. "Raul! Francois!" Simone called out. "Hurry!" She looked around and she saw the men making their way toward her, hanging onto ropes to pull themselves along. They were no more than a few feet away when a second wave washed across the deck, dragging Julia over the side, still clinging to Simone's hand. Simone's shoulder slammed into the railing support, sending jolts of pain through her arm. Fighting against the pain she managed to grab Julia with her other hand as well. "I've got you!"

Simone felt someone grab her legs and hold her in place. They would be all right. She only had to pull Julia back a few feet onto the deck. She felt her grip beginning to slip, her muscles screaming from the strain. "Pull me back!" she called over her shoulder. "Quickly!"

"Simone!" The sound of her name caused her to look over the railing at her lover. "I love you, Simone! Never forget that!" Julia shouted up to her.

"Don't leave me!" Simone called back. "Hang on a moment longer!"

"I can't. I don't belong here," Julia said, her strength finally giving way as she lost her grip on Simone's hands and fell toward the churning water below her.

"No!" Simone screamed, pulling herself up to the railing. "Julia!!" Only the grasp of Raul and Francois prevented her from throwing herself into the water after her lover. Unable to break their hold, her knees buckled and she fell to the deck sobbing. Finally the men picked her up and carried her back into her cabin. She was soaked to the bone and shivering, but not from the cold. She curled into a tight ball as the men drew the coverlet over her and left her to grieve.

When she opened her eyes again the sun was shining brightly. Her clothes were still wet, but she ignored them. She stumbled onto the main deck and glanced around, hoping the night before had only been a nightmare. From the averted looks of her crew she knew the truth. The ship seemed to have sustained only minor damage and they suffered only one casualty from the storm, the one who mattered most to Simone.

Chapter
Twenty-two

"RICKY! WAIT FOR me! I'm gonna tell Mommy!" The little girl scampered as quickly as her six-year-old legs would carry her along the shoreline. She saw her brother stop and examine something in the sand and tried to speed up. He had been teasing her all afternoon. He was bored with watching his little sister and decided the best way to get rid of her was to wear her out. It always worked with their new puppy. Just run his little legs off until he fell over exhausted.

"Hurry up, Pammie!" He was getting tired of the cat-and-mouse game himself. He squatted down and used a stick to loosen the damp sand around a sea shell. He picked it up and carried it to the waterline to wash the sand from it. It had seemed almost white, but the water brought out a pinkish hue. It wasn't as pretty as some others he had found, but was a good size to add to the shell collection in their aquarium back home. By the time he stuck it in his pocket, Pammie made it to him.

She grabbed his hand and squeezed his fingers hard. "Ow!"

"You're 'sposed to stay with me," the pint-size towhead said with a pout.

"I know. I was just playin'. Ready to head back? Dad will have our burgers off the grill by the time we get to the tent and I'm starving."

The sun was dropping quickly toward the horizon, sending orange and red streams of light across the top of the water. Pammie shielded her eyes and smiled. "Good night, Mr. Sun." Looking up at her twelve-year-old brother, she asked, "Does the sun sleep under the water all night long?"

"It never sleeps under the water, Pam. It's always in the sky. When we don't see it here anymore it's because it's shining somewhere else. That's how we know it's time to rest."

"Oh," she said as she thought about that idea for a moment. Her eyes suddenly brightened. "I'll race you to that log down the beach, but you gotta give me a head start."

Ricky squinted down the beach and tried to figure the distance. "Okay, but only to five this time. Ready? Go!"

He smiled as his sister dug her little feet into the sand and sprinted away. He knew he could catch her, even if he counted to ten. Counting silently to five, he let out a war whoop and set out after her. She looked back over her shoulder and squealed with laughter which only slowed her down. A few seconds later, he flew past her, closing on the log. Laughing, he turned back toward the log. A few yards from it, he stopped quickly, breathing hard. He spun around just in time to catch his sister and swing her up into his arms.

Squatting down on one knee, he said, "Get on, Pammie. I'll give you a piggyback ride back to camp."

She glanced past him at the log. "What's —"

"Just get on! We have to get back right away!"

THE SUN WAS well below the horizon as the Jeep Wrangler began its trip down the beach, guided by Ricky Lawrence and his father. The sheriff's deputy shined a high power beam along the shoreline while a second deputy drove.

"How far from our camp were you?" Ricky's father asked.

"I don't know," the boy answered with a shrug. "I didn't think it was this far though."

"Are you sure it was a body?" the driver asked. "Not just some seaweed caught up on a log or something?"

"It was a body!" Ricky insisted, trying to see any familiar landmark in the dark. "With blonde hair."

"Could have just been a bleached out log," the driver muttered.

"There!" Ricky hollered suddenly. "Over there!"

The deputy swung the beam down the shoreline and backed it up to see the object lying at the edge of the water. "Wait here," he ordered as the two deputies jumped out of the Jeep and hurried to the waterline, flashlight beams bouncing on the figure. The closer they got, the more they knew the boy was right.

Kneeling on either side of the lifeless body, they looked at one another briefly before one of them reached down to feel for a pulse on the woman's neck. Quickly, he drew his hand back. "Fuck! It ain't much, but I think I felt a pulse. Call for an ambulance!"

As the second deputy sprinted back to the Jeep, the other placed his hand on the body's waist and carefully turned her over. The sight of the woman's face startled him and he barely stopped himself from falling over. "She should already be dead," he said to himself. "Jesus! What a mess."

By the time the county paramedics arrived, the woman stopped breathing and the deputy lost the weak pulse he found earlier. He and his companion began CPR, but they weren't confidant their efforts would be successful. As red and blue lights swept across the lonely strip of sand along the North Carolina Outer Banks, paramedics relieved the deputies. They quickly dragged her away from the water and stripped the rash suit from her motionless body, charged their defibrillator and carried on a non-stop conversation with the local hospital emergency room doctor. With each jolt, her body jumped involuntarily on the sand.

"Call in and see if we've had any missing person reports around here," the sheriff ordered as he watched the struggle to reclaim the woman's life. "We'll probably be havin' to notify a next of kin."

After the third jolt, a paramedic felt once again for a pulse as everyone held their breath. A grin spread across his face. "We got her back, but it's weak," he said. "Let's get an IV going and get the hell outta here!"

Ten minutes later the ambulance made its way up a sandy hillock toward the only road on the island. The woman was unconscious, but had a faint heartbeat. Her breathing was labored and the mask feeding her oxygen didn't seem to be helping very much. It was twenty miles to the nearest hospital and the conversation between the paramedic and the hospital continued. Aside from the fact the woman definitely had sun bleached strawberry-blonde hair they couldn't give any further description. Her face, arms, and legs were heavily blistered and badly swollen. Her lips were cracked open and there was a fear that if the swelling continued from the burns, the skin on her feet and hands might split open as well. Her eyes were swollen shut and they struggled to insert a breathing tube. Despite the cool of the evening, her body felt hot to the touch. Her arms were heavily blistered and it took the paramedic several minutes to find a vein to start an IV.

The paramedic leaned over her to check the IV drip providing fluids for her ravaged and dehydrated body. "Think she's gonna make it?" the driver called back.

"I dunno," he answered. Looking down at her, he frowned. She might wish she hadn't made it, he thought. He wished he could stroke her head to let her know someone was with her, but there was no unburned spot on her head. "How much longer?"

"Five minutes!"

"Make it two and I'll buy you a six-pack!" the EMT laughed.

Suddenly the woman's body went limp. The medic searched for a pulse. "Contact the hospital," he instructed the EMT. "Tell them the victim is in cardiac arrest and we're starting CPR."

THE REAR DOORS of the ambulance flew open and the paramedic jumped out, pulling the gurney with him. A doctor and two nurses were next to him before the legs of the gurney were set. "We've got her. Vitals."

The paramedic began rattling off the patient's meager vital signs. "She went into cardiac arrest en route. We shocked her once and got a pulse back."

"Might be swelling in the brain from the heat her head has endured. You did good, Johnnie," the doctor said as they rolled the gurney into an empty bay and lifted the woman quickly onto a treatment table. The doctor glanced briefly at the paramedic. They had done everything they could, but it didn't look good.

Chapter
Twenty-three

JULIA SMILED AS she felt the coolness against her lips. She didn't need to open her eyes to recognize the touch of Simone's lips brushing against hers in the cool evening sea breezes wafting over them as they strolled over the deck of *Le Faucon*. Longing filled her soul, followed by desperate loneliness as she remembered. Simone was not there. Julia would never feel her warm embrace again. Tears formed beneath her eyelids and stung as she squeezed her eyes tightly, pushing them away and down the sides of her face.

The nurse softly applied cooling aloe gel mixed with an antibiotic cream to the burned areas of her patient's face hoping to successfully avoid any widespread scarring. She saw the tears as they made their way toward the pillow beneath her patient's head.

"I am so sorry, sweetie," she said. "I'll be through in just a few more seconds and let you rest."

Julia took a deep shaky breath. The fingers lightly touching her face were soothing. "H...hur...ts," she mumbled as she exhaled. The soothing touch stopped immediately. Julia felt the loss of it and tried to frown. Unexpectedly, a voice spoke softly in her ear. *Simone?*

"Can you hear me?" the voice asked. "If you do, can you wiggle your fingers?"

Julia's brain sent messages to her hands. She could feel them try to move, but wasn't sure they had. Her fingers felt heavy and stiff and she didn't know what was wrong. Frustration ran through her. She needed to do something. Where was she? This couldn't be what happened when you died, she thought. It hurts and it's not beautiful. Their family priest promised it would be beautiful! Her head began to throb as she concentrated on convincing any part of her body to do what she wanted. Suddenly, as if the flood of orders had all been released simultaneously, her arms and legs began to jerk and twitch, causing them to brush against the tent covering her body. As the pain seared through her, she tried to rescind her brain's orders, but they were just as slow to respond as the first orders had been.

Seemingly out of nowhere hands pressed gingerly against her arms and legs, pinning her down. A steady flow of tears burned their way along her cheeks and temples as she opened her mouth and took in jerky breaths. Finally her movements slowed and then stopped. Voices around her spoke excitedly to one another and then fell silent.

"My name is Dr. Gorman," a quiet voice close to her ear said. "You're in a hospital in Wilmington, North Carolina. Can you tell me your name?"

TALBOT AND GINA were packing for their trip to Georgia to ready Julia's home for sale when the call came. Julia was alive! Tal couldn't remember a moment of their trip from Richmond to North Carolina. Now as he searched for a parking space close to the hospital entrance, Gina could barely contain herself. He was as anxious as his wife to see and touch his daughter again.

Gina opened the car door and stepped out, not waiting for her husband to open it for her as she usually did. By the time he caught up to her she was in the hospital lobby. He took her arm and stopped her. "Gina, wait. Please!"

"What is it, Talbot?"

"When I spoke to Dr. Gorman, he described Julia's injuries. I just want you to be prepared to see her. It may not be a pretty sight," he said as gently as he could.

"She's alive and that's all that matters. I don't care what she looks like! She will heal," Gina said as she smiled up at her husband.

They held hands and cast reassuring glances at one another as they waited for the elevator to reach the fourth floor. Approaching the counter at the nurses' station, Talbot cleared his throat. "We're Julia Blanchard's parents," he said. "Which room is she in?"

"Just a moment," the nurse said. Walking across the station, she paused for a moment and spoke to an older man with thinning gray hair. He nodded, closing the chart he was writing in and followed the nurse to greet the Blanchards.

"You made very good time," he said as he extended his hand. "I'm Dr. Gorman. I spoke with you on the phone."

"Where is she?" Gina asked impatiently.

"I'll take you to her, but she still has a long way to go. We will be running more tests over the next few days. The burns on her body are quite severe and may require plastic surgery in the future. Will she be staying with you when she is discharged?"

"I don't know, Doctor," Talbot answered. "If not, then we will be staying with her."

Gorman chuckled. "Well, she is apparently a very determined young woman. Otherwise, she would have died. Follow me."

Talbot nodded and put his arm around Gina's waist, giving her a light hug. "We told her you were coming," Gorman said with a smile. "We made her as presentable as possible."

"Thank you, Doctor," Gina said. Taking a deep breath, not sure what to expect, she slowly pushed the door open. They walked quietly toward the bed and saw Julia's red, swollen face resting on the stark white pillow.

"Please don't stare at me," Julia said softly, her eyes still closed. A tear traced its way along her cheek as she spoke, burning the raw flesh.

"Oh, Julia," Gina said as she burst into tears. "You're beautiful!"

Julia forced her eyes open in a reddened slit and managed to raise the corners of her mouth into a semblance of a smile. "I bet you say that to all the lobsters," she quipped, eliciting a relieved laugh from her parents.

"We've been worried sick about you, young lady," Talbot said with a frown. "You scared your mother half to death."

Regina stared at her husband in disbelief. "Don't make it sound like you weren't worried yourself, Talbot Blanchard," she admonished. "That detective in Savannah is probably still recovering from the tongue lashing you gave him."

A laugh escaped from Julia even though she tried to suppress it. "Ow, ow, ow," she groaned. "Damn, it hurts to laugh."

"Then don't do it, dear," Regina commented calmly, leading to another burst of painful laughter from Julia.

"Oh God! It hurts and feels good at the same time," Julia sputtered.

A tear escaped Julia's eye and drifted along the side of her face. Unexpectedly, her father stepped closer to her and reached his hand out tentatively, brushing the tear away. He gently took her hand in his and leaned down. "I'm so proud of you, my precious jewel," he whispered, using his childhood nickname for her.

Julia squeezed his hand, ignoring the pain from her burns, and whispered back. "I love you, Daddy."

When Tal raised his body again tears filled his eyes, but Julia could see the love and concern in them. Regina watched them and smiled. It wasn't like her husband to be so emotional. Clearing her throat she said, "Dr. Gorman says you're going to be here for a while, Jules."

Julia shifted her eyes toward her mother. "How long is a while?" she asked.

"Perhaps a month. It depends on how quickly your body mends."

Julia noticed her mother appeared nervous. "What's wrong, Mom?"

"Nothing. You're alive and that's all that matters," Regina said.

"You know I can tell when you're lying," Julia said. "Now what's wrong?"

The emotions Regina had been hiding away since Julia's disappearance bubbled to the surface. "What the hell were you thinking, Julia Diane Blanchard? Going out on that damnable boat alone? How could you have been so... well, stupid?" Regina ranted.

"Mom —" Julia tried.

"I just don't understand it. It isn't like you to be so careless."

"Regina," Talbot said softly.

"What?" she retorted. "You asked the same questions. You were furious at Julia."

Talbot looked at his daughter. "Yes, I was. But I was afraid."

"Mom!" Julia said, interrupting her parents' discussion.

Regina closed her eyes and took a deep breath. "Yes, dear."

Julia held her other hand out to her mother. When Regina took it, Julia said, "I wasn't thinking and it got me in trouble. What I did was incredibly stupid and I am so grateful I survived. The whole ordeal taught me more than I can ever tell you. I learned what love truly is and how deep it can be."

"You learned that from floating around on the ocean?" Talbot asked.

"The sea has many secrets, Dad. It revealed the meaning of love to me, but I don't expect anyone to believe me or understand anything that happened to me while I was out there. I just know that timeless love does exist. I never thought I would know that kind of love." Julia closed her eyes. "I'm the luckiest woman on Earth because I've known timeless, endless love."

Julia's voice began to drift as she spoke. Tal and Regina looked at one another and realized she had fallen asleep, a relaxed smile on her lips. They withdrew their hands from hers before stepping quietly away from the bed.

"How's my patient doing?" Dr. Gorman said when he saw them step into the corridor.

"She's hallucinating," Talbot said. "Is that normal?"

JULIA LEANED HER head back on the head rest of her parents' SUV and watched familiar countryside finally began to appear. It seemed as if she had been gone forever. The lush green of summer was beginning to change into vibrant fall colors. As a surprise going away present from the hospital staff and Dr. Gorman, she was given a brand new pair of Ray-Ban wrap-around sunglasses to protect her eyes which were still sensitive to bright sunlight. Although they assured her they hadn't been permanently damaged by her ordeal, they would still need protection from bright sunlight for a week or two longer.

She glanced across the front seat at her father. She knew he was glad she had finally been released from the Wilmington hospital. Her month long recovery had dragged by slowly and allowed her too much to think. Both parents would have preferred she return with them to their home, but understood her need to get back to a normal life and put the ordeal behind her. She rubbed absently at the bandage still remaining on her left arm. Until her skin healed completely, Julia didn't want to be seen by anyone from the Institute. She couldn't tolerate being stared at and needed time alone with her memories. But were they really memories? Or nothing more than the delusions of a woman facing the certainty of her own death? It couldn't have been real.

"You'll have to call Frankie when you get home," Gina said. "She's so anxious to see you and tell you about the project."

"She'll have to wait until I look a little more human and less like a medium rare steak."

"You look fine, dear," Gina chuckled.

"I can work from the house if Frankie sends the information they've gathered to me. I'll call her in the morning. I'm too tired this evening."

"It'll be almost dark before we get there," Talbot said. "I hope your friend has been keeping the house up."

"What friend?" Julia asked.

"I don't remember her name."

"You can't mean Amy. I threw her out. She's the reason I went to the *Peach* site that weekend."

"I told her to move out at your memorial service, but she hired an attorney to claim the house as her residence," Talbot grumbled.

Julia rode silently the rest of the trip, but could feel the tension and anger building inside as the car crossed the bridge onto Tybee Island. Talbot swung into the gravel drive leading to her home. "I'd appreciate it if you and Mom would stay in the car for a few minutes," she said.

"Of course we will, dear," Gina said.

Julia stepped out of the vehicle and slammed the car door shut. She leaned down and tapped on the passenger-side window. When her father lowered it she said, "This shouldn't take long. Wait five minutes, then call the local sheriff and ask him to swing by." Taking a deep breath, Julia straightened her shirt and slacks and walked up the front steps to her house. She could see lights on in the front room and tried the door knob. When she found it locked, she took a key from her pocket and slipped it in the lock, but it didn't work. "Bitch," she muttered as she pressed the doorbell and waited.

The door swung open a minute later and Julia winced as Amy hugged her. "Thank God!" Amy said. "I was so worried about you, sweetheart." Amy scrunched her nose in distaste when she saw Julia's damaged face, a reaction not missed by Julia.

As much as Julia loved having someone in her arms, Amy wasn't the one she wanted. Grasping her by the upper arms, she moved her away. "Is that why you had the damn locks changed?" she asked.

"No! I was afraid someone else might have taken your keys."

Stepping around her lover, Julia moved into the front entry and removed her sunglasses, squinting as her sensitive eyes adjusted to the lighting inside the house. Amy closed the door as she followed her inside. "I told you to be gone by the time I returned, Amy. I was gone a little longer than I anticipated, so you've had plenty of time to get out. Why are you still here?"

"We both said a lot of things in the heat of the moment, Julia. I made a mistake and I'm sorry I hurt you. It will never happen again, darling."

"You're damn right it won't because you won't be here. Pack a bag and leave. Come back tomorrow if you want to get the rest of your shit, but you're not staying here tonight. This is my home and I'm not leaving again."

"My attorney said—"

"I don't give a damn what your attorney says. This is my house! You might have made a claim on it when you thought I was dead because no one would have known the difference, but I'm alive. So get out!"

"Please, Julia. I need a few days to pack my things. I'll stay in the guestroom."

"My parents will be using the guestroom," Julia said. She took a deep breath and looked at her former partner. "I forgive you, Amy, for cheating on me. I was spending a lot of time on the project and I know it took away from the time I could have spent with you."

A smile crossed Amy's lips. "I still shouldn't have done what I did. I know how important your work is to you."

"I admit I felt something for you, but I know now it was never love. I know what real love is and we never had that." Julia blinked hard as her memory of Simone and their time together resurfaced. "Real love hurts more than you can imagine when you lose it. I was mad when I left, but the strange thing is, I just now realized I didn't miss you. I'm sorry."

A knock at the front door interrupted their conversation and Julia stepped around Amy to open it. She smiled when she saw her friend and island sheriff, Alphonse Delarosa. "Welcome home, Doc," he said. "I was told you might need some assistance."

"Thanks, Al." Looking across the room at Amy, she said, "Do I need assistance, Amy?"

"No. I'll be gone in less than an hour."

Chapter
Twenty-four

SIMONE SPENT THE remainder of the journey to Martinique in her cabin, refusing company and eating and drinking little, lost in grief. She heard the ship's anchor chain rumble until it struck bottom. She stared out the windows at the back of her cabin absorbed in her thoughts. Her cabin door opened and she heard footsteps behind her.

"No one enters my cabin without my permission," she snapped without turning around, angry anyone had dared to intrude on her solitude and private grief.

"Forgive me, *Faucon*," Joaquin's small voice said. "We have arrived."

Simone turned and looked down at the boy, feeling his sorrow. She knelt and opened her arms to him. "I lost her as well," he mumbled into Simone's shoulders. She felt the wetness of his tears soaking through her shirt and cried with him even though she thought she had no more tears to shed. Holding him tightly, they sank to the floor and cried together until there were no more tears.

AT *LE REPOS* Simone continued her silence, speaking only to Joaquin, for another week. Anton watched her come and go from the house and wished there was something he could do to alleviate her grief. Two weeks passed, broken only by a simple service as Esperanza was laid to rest in a garden near the main house. The only times Simone joined Anton and Kitty was over silent evening meals. Even the usually talkative and gregarious Kitty seemed afraid to speak. In the middle of their meal, Simone placed her knife and fork on her plate and smiled at Joaquin, who returned a smile and nodded at her.

"I have an announcement," she said, her voice calm and even. "I am leaving Martinique."

"Where are we going, *Faucon*," Anton asked with a glance at Kitty.

"You misunderstand, my brother," Simone answered. "*I*, and only I, am leaving Martinique."

"But where will you go?" Kitty asked.

Looking warmly at her brother she said, "It is my wish for you and Kitty to remain at *Le Repos* and care for Joaquin. I have discussed this with him and he understands my decision. He cannot go where I am going as long as the Americans continue to allow slavery. When he reaches his majority, *Le Repos* will become his property to do with as he sees fit. I will leave you ample funds to build a house of your own for you and your family on the property."

"Of course we will care for Joaquin, but where are you going?" Anton asked again.

"I shall take *Le Faucon de Mer* and sail to the coast of Georgia."

Anton cleared his throat. "I know you have suffered a terrible loss, Simone, but you cannot bring Julia back to you."

"You do not know what I do about Julia, but you are correct. I know I will never see or hold her again in this lifetime, but I can be closer to her by living where she lived."

Looking at Joaquin she said, "I will take all but four of the Arabians with me. It will be up to you to increase the number of horses in your care here. Can you do that, *mon fils*?"

"I can," Joaquin answered confidently.

"You should remain here and at least attempt to rebuild your life, Simone," Anton said.

"I have no life here," she snapped. "My life is with Julia, no matter where she may be. She refused to believe I died in New Orleans. As long as she lives here," she said, slamming her fist forcefully against her chest, "I have not lost her."

"Even you cannot sail *Le Faucon* alone," Kitty said.

"Twelve of my crew, along with their families, have agreed to sail with me to begin a new life. Once we reach Georgia I will no longer have a need for the ship."

Anton opened his mouth to speak again, but Simone held her hand up. "My decision is made. There will be no more discussion. I leave in one week's time. Let us enjoy one another's company in the time we have left to us."

THREE AND A half months had passed since Simone boarded *Le Faucon* with Julia and set sail from New Orleans for her home in Martinique. Now she watched the coastline of the island grow smaller as the ship left its safe harbor on its final voyage. Anton and Kitty would remain on Martinique to care for Joaquin. Following the battle to defend New Orleans there were days Simone wasn't able to comprehend how the greatest army in the world suffered such a devastating loss. Perhaps Laffite had been right. The Americans fought for an ideal, a way of life, while the British fought merely to control property. Now as she watched the lush green of Martinique fade away behind her, she knew she would miss it. But her future awaited her on the far side of the horizon and all she wanted was to be closer to Julia, even in some small way.

A dozen members of *Le Faucon's* crew, together with their families, sailed with her toward a new life. *Le Repos* would be in good hands with Anton. It was a fitting reward where he and Kitty could rear their children in safety and peace. As she rested against the deck railing and heard the gentle whinnies of the Arabians below deck, she tried to comprehend what the future would hold for her. She would have preferred having her days filled with her beloved horses, her nights filled with passion in the arms of the woman she loved. Perhaps her memories would be enough.

THE VOYAGE WAS the most uneventful one Simone could remember. Without the constant threat of the British intercepting her, she felt well-rested. The journey proved difficult for the horses, however. Even though they were well-fed and watered, the lack of exercise left them weaker than she would have liked. She walked them each day in the small confines below deck. She would take *Le Faucon* as close to shore as possible, but they would have to swim the final distance to shore when the ship reached its destination. She was currying and feeding the big animals as she did every day since their departure from Martinique.

"*Faucon!*" an excited crewman called as he slid down the stairs from the main deck.

"What is it, Raul?" she asked as she continued humming softly to keep the horses calm.

"Land, *Faucon*. We have arrived!"

"How can you be sure?" she asked, dropping the brush and walking quickly to meet him.

"It is the lighthouse. Gaston has checked the chart four times," Raul answered, a wide smile cutting across his weathered face.

Simone ran up the steps leading to the main deck, taking them two at a time. Once topside she moved quickly to the wheel deck, smiling at Gaston who was manning the wheel as she picked up her spyglass. Scanning the horizon, she could see the coastline in the distance and the flashing light that marked its location.

"There are many light beacons along this coast, *Faucon*," Gaston said.

"You have checked the charts. Is this the place?"

"I believe it is."

Smiling at the young man, she said, "You have become my best navigator, Gaston. If this is not the exact location for which we search, it will be close enough. We must prepare."

Le Faucon became a flurry of activity in the fading light. Turning the ship toward shore and lowering the largest sails to slow their approach, Simone piloted the vessel as crew members called out the water's depth. Satisfied they could get no closer, they set anchor. The horses were led through a cargo door in the side of the ship and into the water. Simone was grateful for calm water as the long boats guided the animals to shore. Two trips later, the crewmen's families and goods were ferried safely ashore.

Simone and a single crewman returned to *Le Faucon* for the final time. As they reached the ship, Simone grabbed the cargo netting and looked down at Raul. "As soon as I drop my personal belongings to you, row away from the ship. Light your lantern and I will swim to you."

"I can wait for you here, *Faucon*," Raul protested.

"No. If I don't join you in an hour, return to shore and make sure the animals are cared for." The resolute look in her eyes warned Raul to obey without further protest.

Simone climbed onto the main deck and walked to her cabin. She removed her journal from the desk, wrapping it in paper she waxed during their voyage and stuffed the pewter sculpture Julia had given her into a small bag along with her clothing. Glancing quickly around, she saw nothing else she wanted. It would all become a part of her past, just as *Le Faucon* would.

As soon as she dropped her bag down to Raul and watched him row away, she struck a match and lit the wick on the lantern hanging outside her cabin door, using it to guide her into the decks below. *Le Faucon* was a well-built ship and she wasn't sure how much damage it would take to send her to the bottom of the sea. She and her crew had worked three days moving four cannons into the belly of the ship and setting them up. She stopped on the cannon deck and grabbed a bag of powder to fire the cannons one last time.

As she made her way toward the keel, well below the water line, she smelled the ever-present mold and mildew permeating the wooden hull. Two cannon were already set to fire at a downward angle through the left side of the hull, two for the right. She would have to work quickly before water pouring in through the damaged hull became deep enough to make the powder too damp to ignite. She filled quills with gunpowder, setting one as a fuse in each cannon. She lit a patch of wadding on a spark rod and took a deep breath, glancing in the direction of the stairway out of the keel. Standing away from the recoil of the first cannon, she lit the fuse. Immediately, the cannon roared, the cannonball shattering the wooden hull. She reached out to brace her body as the ship shuddered its protests and water began rising swiftly around her feet. Stepping back again, she touched the fuse of the second cannon with the spark. The cannon recoiled and turned slightly as the wooden wheels slipped in the ankle-deep sea water. It slammed back against Simone's leg, knocking her off her feet. As she struggled to stand in the rapidly rising water, she estimated she wouldn't have time to fire the final two cannons before the water overtook them and waded through thigh deep water toward the steps, pulling herself up and out of the filling compartment.

As the weight of the water began to pull the bottom of the ship down, she ran up the three upper decks and finally emerged onto the main deck. The ship creaked and groaned pitifully, but the sea around her remained calm. The sails had been dropped while they unloaded the Arabians and it occurred to her she would never hear the sound of sail cloth snapping in a good breeze again. She swung a leg over the deck railing and onto the netting as the vessel shifted and began to list. Halfway down the netting, she turned and dove away from the ship, hoping the masts wouldn't snap and fall in her direction. Stroking under water as quickly as she could, she popped out of the water and stopped. Watching as *Le Faucon* began to sink, bemoaning its fate, tears began trickling down her cheeks. Treading water as she watched, she finally turned away and began swimming toward Raul's lantern. Even without Julia, this would be her new home.

Chapter
Twenty-five

JULIA HAD ONLY been back in her own home two weeks. She finally convinced her parents she would be fine alone, in fact, she preferred it that way. Now as she rambled around in the empty home, the time dragged by. She wanted to talk to someone about what happened to her, about the places she saw, about the rogue who stole her heart, but knew no one would believe it had been anything more than an elaborate fantasy concocted in the mind of a woman desperately clinging to life. As the evenings began to come earlier, Julia walked along the light sandy beach on Tybee Island. In each small inlet she wondered if Simone had returned safely to Martinique. If she had been real, was she suffering her loss as much as Julia was. Occasionally a light breeze tousled her hair as she lowered her head to walk along the beach, hearing the swell and break of the water as it rolled up to shore over the gentle slope of the Continental Shelf.

She strolled up a small grassy hillock and shoved her hands in her jacket pocket as she looked out over the water. Marsh grasses swayed gently and everything seemed peaceful. Sitting on the edge of the hillock, Julia stretched her legs out in front of her and inhaled the salty fragrance of the sea air escorting the waves inland. Since her return to Tybee Island she hadn't been able to get Simone out of her mind. Her logical mind told her nothing could have happened. It defied all the laws of nature she believed in as a scientist. But her heart refused to accept the logic her mind was demanding. She refused to believe the love she always searched for might have been nothing more than a figment of her imagination. If she closed her eyes and listened to her inner voice, she could hear Simone's softly accented voice carried by the breeze around her and feel her touch when the same breezes shifted the fabric of her clothing against her skin. Her stomach clenched thinking of the reality only she had known.

JULIA WALKED INTO the Atlantic Marine Institute again nearly a month after her return to Tybee Island. She pulled her chair closer to her desk, but hesitated before powering up the new computer in front of her. Frankie promised every word concerning the *Peach* was loaded on the laptop, replacing what she lost when the *Discovery* was hijacked.

Data skimmed up the monitor, and Julia smiled. Frankie had uploaded descriptions and pictures of everything salvaged from the wreck in her absence. She clicked on each itemized entry, her eyes scanning quickly through the pictures. As she glanced at and passed by one picture, she suddenly stopped and backed the page up, staring at a slide that made her heart stop. Side-by-side before and after pictures revealed an item tagged RGP # 78. The description listed it as a pewter tankard, origin unknown. It was hard to identify in the condition in which it was recovered, but the cleaned version clearly showed an ornately engraved "M' on one side. Although age and salt water had changed its appearance, Julia buried her face in her hands after seeing the familiar tankard.

"Julia? Are you all right?" Frankie's concerned voice asked from the office doorway. "Maybe you came back too soon."

Wiping her eyes, Julia looked up at the frowning face. "No, I'm fine, Frankie. You have all done a wonderful job with the recovery."

"There's a lot more there. The bow of the ship is still partially buried, but you can see the shots of the masthead near the end of the slides," Frankie said, the excitement building in her voice as she talked about the *Peach*.

"What does it look like?" Julia asked, closing her eyes.

"It appears to be an eagle with its wings swept back and seeming to look up to the sky. Pretty cool looking, but a lot of ships from that time period had something similar."

"You and Damian have done a lot of work. Really good work."

"Did you check out the pictures we took of the hull?"

"Which ones?" Julia asked.

Frankie squatted next to Julia's desk and moved the computer cursor to a file labeled *Questions*. "Not a very scientific label, but we couldn't think of anything else at the time," she chuckled. She clicked the file open and a series of pictures began to open.

"What do you think?" Frankie asked.

Julia squinted at a close-up picture taken of the ship's hull. "Is this below the water line?"

"Abso-freakin'-lutely. And the hole was made from *inside* the ship." Frankie's voice was brimming with excitement, the kind that came from discovering something no one had before. "We think the ship was either sabotaged or deliberately sunk by the crew, maybe to avoid being captured. Check this one out," she said clicking on another slide. "I thought Damian was going to kill himself getting this shot."

"What the hell..." Julia started.

"It's probably against the rules of excavation, but Damian cleared away a depression in the sediment and somehow managed to squeeze into it. Isn't it a great shot! You can clearly see the directionality of the wood surrounding the hole. It's definitely out."

Julia stared at the picture. *Was it possible? Had Simone really existed? Did she sail to Georgia and scuttle her own ship?*

"You might want to come down to the lab and take a peak at the cannon we just finished partially cleaning. It's the last one you recovered before you were...before you disappeared," Frankie said.

Julia clicked out of the folder and returned to the first set of artifact slides. Her stomach was in knots and she gripped the mouse to prevent her shaking hand from showing. "Where did you find this tankard?" she asked as she looked back at the computer monitor.

Frankie smiled when she saw it. "I found it by accident a few yards from the main vessel. Something caught my eye during an ascent and I had to go back to investigate. It's a beauty, isn't it?"

"Yes. Very beautiful," Julia murmured. "I'd like to see it as well."

"Then let's get to the lab, woman."

JULIA ENTERED THE lab and pulled on a work smock and gloves before she joined Frankie at a work table. Obviously a lot of time-consuming work had been performed on the cannon since the last time she saw it. It was still beautiful, a powerful reminder of a time long past.

"There's an engraved plate near the breach," Frankie said.

Reaching out, Julie placed both hands lightly on the barrel and swung a lighted magnifying glass over the breach. She blinked away the burning sensation of tears forming as she ran her gloved fingers over the pitted plate. It was Louis Rochat's cannon! The one that never performed correctly. The one Simone kept to remind her of what happened to her at Rochat's hands. As she stared at the cannon lying in its cushioned cradle, Julia suddenly hated it. It represented a terrible time in her lover's life and, even as a historian and scientist, she knew she would never be able to look at it the same way again. The cannon and tankard were not part of an elaborate hallucination. Simone's ship was resting on the bottom of the Atlantic Ocean no more than twenty miles from Julia's home.

"We think the name of the ship is engraved on the plate," Frankie said, breaking into Julia's thoughts. "*Le Faucon de Mer.* The Sea Hawk, if my French isn't too rusty."

"Yes. Yes it is," Julia managed to murmur as she ran her hand over the plate. Glancing at Frankie she said, "I mean it probably is."

"Damian's researching for some mention of the ship, but hasn't come up with anything definitive yet." Frankie shrugged. "We might never know for sure."

But Julia did know. "I want to make a dive at the site," she said suddenly. "Today."

"ARE YOU SURE you're up for this?" Frankie asked as Julia tightened the straps holding her tanks across her chest. "It's been what, three months since your last dive."

"I haven't forgotten how. My experience doesn't mean I've lost my love for the sea or my work, Frankie," Julia said. "My article about the excavation is almost complete, but a couple of new shots of the ship now that more of it has been uncovered can't hurt. Time for me to get back on my horse and ride."

Julia took a deep breath as she and Frankie began their dive to the *Peach*. A detailed grid marked the location of everything remaining on the ocean floor. If her article resulted in more money being allotted to the project, the Institute might resume salvaging the remaining cannons, but there wasn't much else of interest left. When the hulk of the *Peach* came into view, Julia paused in her descent to gaze at it. She hadn't been to the site in nearly three months, but nothing seemed to have changed other than the exposed figurehead gracing the bow of the wreckage. She swam slowly along the starboard side of the hull, knowing in her heart the shipwreck was *Le Faucon de Mer*. In her mind's eye she pictured what it once looked like. Frankie separated from her to move down the port side. When Julia reached the newly exposed bow of the *Peach* she unhooked an underwater camera from her utility belt. She took pictures from both sides before moving away from the bow to take a picture from the front. As she looked through the viewfinder she nearly dropped the camera. Lowering it from her mask, she stared at the ship. Standing on the bow, Simone brought her hand up and held it out toward Julia. The gentle current moved her hair as if it were the wind. Julia squeezed her eyes shut tightly, afraid to open them. She felt overwhelming loss and sadness run through her and began to cry. She couldn't control the deep wracking sobs suddenly interfering with her breathing. She was in trouble, but couldn't stop. From out of nowhere Frankie was at her side. She shook Julia and pointed upward. Julia nodded and hung onto Frankie as they began their ascent. Looking at the *Peach* slipping away below her, she saw amber eyes following her. She vowed never to return to the ship again.

AS SHE HAD on so many nights since returning to Tybee Island, Julia found herself drawn to its sandy beaches. The cool October wind floating off the ocean ruffled her short hair and she shivered slightly. But it wasn't only the fall sea breeze making her shiver. She was certain the *Georgia Peach* was *Le Faucon de Mer*. She had been on the ship, walked its decks, seen it in its glory, with its stunning captain standing on the wheel deck smiling into the sun and wind. Was it possible Simone had journeyed to the coast of Georgia searching for Julia? In the distance, the beacon of the Tybee Island lighthouse swept relentlessly out to sea, guiding lost sailors home once again. Longing to regain what she lost, while not sure it ever existed, Julia felt warm tears trickle onto her cheeks. *If you made it this far, come back to me now and let me touch you just one more time.*

Chapter
Twenty-six

IT WAS A brisk mid-November Sunday. Julia spent the morning writing reports on the progress of the cleaning and preservation of artifacts brought up from the *Peach* site by Damian and Frankie. She had refused to accompany them on their dives, but couldn't give them a believable explanation for her refusal.

For over a month she spent her nights, alone in the quiet of her home office, combing the Internet looking for any mention of Simone Moreau or *Le Faucon de Mer*. But not even her deepest searches revealed anything about the woman or her ship. Julia wracked her memory for possible avenues for her search. Montserrat. Moreau. The Battle of New Orleans. Martinique. There were nothing more than vague generalities concerning the pirates and privateers operating in the Caribbean in the late-eighteenth and early-nineteenth centuries. Her hopes were raised when she stumbled over a brief notation in a footnote mentioning Captain Louis Rochat. Other than the observation he hadn't been a very nice man, something she already knew, his footnote in history revealed nothing of value. She read biographies of Jean Laffite and Edward Livingston. Finally, following nearly a month of frustration, she was forced to abandon her search and attempt to return to reality.

By noon Monday she sat at her desk at the Institute putting the finishing touches on her article describing the excavation of the *Peach* and the efforts of Institute scientists to preserve another small piece of history. The Board of Directors of the Institute had already announced a public display of the artifacts scheduled to open the following January. She would have to supervise the construction of displays and the printing of materials to distribute to the press and brochures for visitors to the display. She wished she could tell them what she actually knew, but there was still the chance it had all been a hallucination based on people she may have seen at some point in time and brought into the fantasy her mind created. Thinking about the possibility that any portion of her adventure may have been true gave her a thumping headache. She closed her eyes and massaged her temples with her fingertips.

"I brought your mail up from the lobby," Frankie said, strolling into Julia's office.

"Anything interesting?"

"Maybe this one," Frankie said, turning a cream-colored envelope over in her hands. "Looks like an invitation to a wedding or something."

"I don't know anyone getting married. Probably junk mail. Just toss it in the circular file in the corner."

"It's not addressed to Occupant or Current Resident. Nice handwriting though. Hey! There's one of those cool wax seals on the back. I haven't seen one of those since I was in high school."

Julia's headache wasn't getting any better and she wasn't in the mood for inane conversation about handwriting or junk mail. "Then open the damn thing and then toss it."

"Oooh. Someone's a little touchy this morning," Frankie said.

"I've got a horrendous headache brewing. Sorry."

"It's nearly time for a lunch break. Maybe you're just hungry," Frankie offered as she laid the envelope on the corner of Julia's desk.

"Maybe. Well, aren't you going to open it?"

"It's not addressed to me."

Snatching the rich-looking envelope, Julia glanced at it briefly before running her index finger under the back flap and popping open the wax seal. "Someone wasted a lot of money just to try and sell me swampland in Arizona. So where do you want to go for lunch?" she asked, sliding what looked like an invitation from the envelope.

"How about Billy Bob's?"

"Burgers again? Don't you ever get tired of eating that crap? Your arteries have got to be clogged with fat by now."

"I'm still a starving grad student until January, remember?"

Julia read the engraved invitation and picked up the envelope, studying the front and back, carefully examining the wax seal. There was something unsettling about it she couldn't put into words. "Ever heard of a place called Montserrat Farms?" she asked.

"Nope. I'm not into cows and pigs."

"It's an invitation to a horse show featuring quote 'the finest in Arabian horses this side of the Mississippi River' unquote."

"Someone wants to sell you a horse! Boy, do they have the wrong gal, unless it's a seahorse," Frankie said, moving to read over Julia's shoulder.

Julia ran a fingertip over the raised monogram embossed on the top center of the invitation. "Does this look familiar to you? The initial, I mean," she asked.

"It's fancy, that's for sure. You gonna go?"

"I don't know. How about you and Danny go with me? It's the weekend after Thanksgiving. Unless you've got other plans."

"We can't afford plans and neither of our parents can afford to fly down until Christmas. So why not? Might be an interesting way to kill an afternoon."

JULIA HAD ACCEPTED the invitation, but now as she waited for Frankie and her husband Danny to pick her up, she was having second thoughts. The Savannah area had been her home for the last six years and she had never heard of Montserrat Farms. Of course, there was no reason she would have. The breeding horse and fox hunt crowd were not a part of her world.

The weather hovered in the mid-fifties, comfortably pleasant for late-November. Julia rubbed her forehead absently, once again absorbed in thoughts concerning events that couldn't have happened. She was grateful when the chiming of her doorbell brought her back to the present. Grabbing a lightweight down vest from the hall tree, Julia opened her front door to greet Frankie.

"You're early," Julia said.

Glancing at her watch, Frankie shrugged. "Maybe we'll get a chance to see the horses up close and personal if we get there a little early."

"Do you ride?" Julia asked as she pulled the front door closed behind her.

"I have, but certainly nothing as disciplined as dressage," Frankie said while they walked to Danny's car. "I've seen it on TV, of course, but can't imagine the amount of patience it must take to train a horse that well."

"It takes a special rapport between the trainer and the horse," Julia said, opening the back door of Danny's Jeep Cherokee.

Montserrat Farms was located in the gentle countryside ten miles west of the Savannah city limits. Julia exchanged idle chit-chat with Frankie and Danny for the relatively short drive. She loved the area the map indicated as the farm's location. Two miles from the main entrance to the farm, a stark white fence enclosed pastures, occasionally interrupted with copses of trees covered with Spanish moss. A half mile from the entrance, Julia smiled at the sight of foals frolicking in the pastures. She frowned to push away thoughts of Simone with her horses when Danny signaled to turn onto the main road of the farm.

A long straight road led them to the main buildings which were canopied by large old trees that had lost their foliage for the winter. In a few months the trees would begin to fill with new leaves again, creating a shadowy tunnel for visitors.

"It must take a small army to keep the grounds looking this good," Danny observed. "Must be a well-paying business."

Finally, the Jeep rounded a gentle curve and they saw several buildings ahead. Looking around, Julia identified three long brick, red-roofed buildings that looked as if they might be stables. The three buildings formed spokes around a matching octagonal building she assumed was a training arena. Smaller buildings, all with similar architecture, dotted the grounds. As Danny pulled into a marked parking area and turned off the ignition, she opened the back door and climbed out, stretching her legs.

"I don't think I'm going to need this vest," she said, pulling it off and tossing it back inside the Jeep.

Frankie shaded her eyes with her hand to look around and said, "That must be the main house. Cool architecture. Looks a little like the old homes we saw in the Caribbean on our honeymoon, doesn't it, Danny?"

"Well, it's not your typical architecture for around here, that's for sure," Danny agreed.

Julia turned to follow Frankie's gaze. Surrounded by brick-outlined gardens and standing in a small grove of trees, a paved walkway led to a two-story building with a red roof. Crème-colored shutters stood open on the second-story windows. A screened-in front porch covered the entire front of the house. Turning away quickly, Julia lowered her head to catch her bearings as she leaned an arm against the side of the Wrangler.

"You okay, Julia?" Frankie's concerned voice asked.

Taking a deep breath, Julia pasted a smile on her face and nodded. "Yes, I'm fine. It's just that that house seems familiar in some way. As if I've seen it before somewhere."

Taking Frankie's hand, Danny said, "Let's wander down by the stables before we find a seat in the arena."

Julia followed the couple and wasn't surprised that the horses they saw were magnificent animals. *The fastest and most beautiful in the world*, Joaquin had announced proudly. There was something noble and haute about the way they stood quietly and regarded the strangers staring at them. By the time the trio made their way into the arena and climbed into a seating area running three quarters of the way around the earthen floored arena, Julia began to relax and chatted amiably with Frankie and Danny about their work at the Institute and Frankie's doctoral dissertation. There was still work to be done on the *Peach*, but nothing urgent enough to prevent Frankie from completing her studies. She was a careful and meticulous scientist and had feelers out to several agencies and museums for possible positions.

At exactly two o'clock a stately-looking older man strode into the arena and brought a wireless microphone to his mouth. For a moment Julia half-expected to hear a booming voice such as the ones used by ringmasters in the circus. But there was no music and the man, dressed in a black top hat, black riding jacket over a stark white shirt, camel riding pants and dark brown riding boots, spoke with a melodic, soft voice.

"Welcome to this exhibition of the dressage quadrille. The art of dressage has been practiced in Europe since before the time of Charlemagne. Developed as a military tactic for battle, the earliest practitioners of dressage strenuously trained young military officers in the maneuvers you will see today. Armies, traveling in columns of two to four horses, were trained to act in absolute unison when facing an enemy.

"The most famous schools for training in the dressage were the Saumur in France and the Spanish Riding School in Austria. The Spanish Riding School was primarily what its name implies, a riding school, while the Saumur incorporated military tactics as well as riding skills. Today in modern competition riding for the dressage, judges look for a number of points on which to evaluate riders and their horses. Judges look for proper spacing between the animals, how well they move together as a unit as well as the alignment of the animals both laterally and longitudinally. Other things taken into consideration are the impulsion or energy of the horse, the degree of submission of the horse to the rider, and, for groups, how well they perform as a unit. For the single dressage, important points to watch for are the even gait of the horse, the alignment of the rider over the horse, and most importantly, the seemingly undetectable commands the horse receives from its rider, as if the horse knows exactly what it is doing without assistance.

"Today you will see a demonstration of both group and single dressage. The groups will perform two, three and four column maneuvers, crossing one another's path closely, fanning into a position as if to meet an enemy in battle, and the cloverleaf pattern. In the single dressage, the horse and rider will make their way around the arena in straight and oblique lines, change gaits at various points to show the virtually motionless control the rider exhibits. Hesitation to obey a command from a rider would receive negative scores from judges in any competition. There is a degree of trust and rapport that must exist between the horse and rider in order to give a flawless performance.

"While many of you may be familiar with the famous Lippizaner Stallions of the Spanish Riding School, the horses you will see performing today are all Arabians which were sired, raised and trained here at Montserrat Farms. They are the descendants of horses brought to this country nearly two hundred years ago. Although many are now owned by others, most are stabled at Montserrat Farms when not competing and they have been rewarded many times for their skills. Ladies and gentlemen, the dressage quadrille!"

For the next hour and a half horses entered the arena single file, in pairs, threes, and fours and performed a series of complex maneuvers in which they passed through a column of horses and reformed. Their turns, movement, and pace were so well synchronized they seemed to

Julia like waves moving across the arena. Although she was certain the riders were making minute commands with their hands, they were undetectable, and the riders seemed to be no more than mannequins placed on the backs of the powerful animals. Each round of maneuvers was explained as they occurred and received appreciative applause at the end. After a short intermission for drinks, the single dressage began. The riders and their mounts were introduced as they entered the ring and went through their paces. Some of the riders were obviously young students, but their performances were virtually flawless. It was apparent to the observers that their instructor had been successful in training them to a high degree of competency. After the last rider acknowledged the audience and the applause faded away, the announcer stepped back into the center of the arena.

"Ladies and gentlemen, the final exhibition this afternoon will be performed by the dressage instructor and owner of Montserrat Farms. She is the winner of numerous national and international competitions and a three-time member of the United States Olympic Dressage Team. Please welcome into the arena, *Mademoiselle* Dhuperior riding Jackson."

The moment she was introduced, the rider walked her sleek, dark brown Arabian, its mane braided along its neck and wrapped in white, into the arena and sat motionless until the applause died away. The rider wore a solid tan riding outfit with a dark brown top hat and riding boots. The horse and rider stood as motionless as a statue while the announcer explained that the snow-white wrappings on the lower portion of the horse's legs helped judges see imperfections in the animal's gait as it moved around the dark earthen floor of the arena. At the end of the explanation, the horse began moving, as if by its own volition, changing its gait into something Julia thought resembled a skip. Turning at the center of the arena, the rider sat ramrod straight and motionless as Jackson moved effortlessly in an oblique line, his front hooves crossing one another to perform the sideways movement, first to the left and then to the right. Julia paid particular attention to the impassive-appearing rider. Her body never moved and no matter how closely she looked, Julia could detect no wrist movements commanding the animal into the next maneuver. Following a fifteen-minute exhibition, the rider stopped her horse facing the audience. In the first discernable movement Julia was able to detect, the rider patted her mount and coaxed him into a bow, bringing appreciative applause from the audience. Grasping her top hat by its rim, the rider removed it and bowed her thanks to the crowd and smiled as she accepted their appreciation.

Julia stopped clapping, gasping when she saw the rider's face fully. A gleaming shock of short black hair combed forward from the crown framed the woman's face. Without an explanation to her companions, Julia stood abruptly, unable to look at the woman a moment longer and left the seating area as quickly as possible. The rider replaced her hat and turned her horse to leave the arena as the remainder of the audience rose to leave their seats.

WHEN FRANKIE AND Danny caught up to Julia, she was bent over the hood of the Jeep, her head resting on her forearms. She felt like she was going to hyperventilate and struggled to control her breath. Frankie's hand on her back startled her.

"Are you all right?" Frankie asked, concern evident in her voice.

"Yeah," Julia answered, fighting to take oxygen deeply into her lungs. "I...I don't know what happened, but I suddenly felt almost claustrophobic in there and had to get out. I'm sorry."

Rubbing a hand gently over Julia's back, Frankie smiled. "The show was over anyway. So at least you didn't miss anything."

"That's good," Julia said. *I'd already seen more than I wanted to.*

"I guess you're not planning to come back this evening for the reception then," Danny said.

"What reception?" Julia asked, looking up at Frankie.

"The invitation said there would be an open house and reception later this evening," Frankie said. "You should stay home and get some rest. Skip the free food and booze."

"I'm fine now, but I'm not planning to return for a reception. You two can come back, though. Don't let me spoil your evening."

"Well, actually," Frankie started as she glanced at Danny, "we sort of have other plans for tonight."

Swept by relief, Julia chuckled and patted Frankie on the back. "That's almost too much information, Frankie."

As soon as Danny dropped Julia at her home, she walked to her bedroom and flopped onto her bed, staring at the ceiling. She couldn't get the woman's face out of her mind and was afraid to go to sleep, fearing she would see it again in her dreams. Glancing at the clock on her nightstand, she sat up and went into her kitchen to prepare something to eat. She needed to do something to stop the thoughts that wouldn't quit running through her brain. She was convinced she might easily go insane. Her thoughts were giving her a headache and whatever was left of her heart would not stop grieving for something that had never been...couldn't have been. Looking down at the snack on her plate, she knew she couldn't live like this anymore. Dark bread, wedges of cheese and fruit were left abandoned as she walked resolutely into her bedroom and changed her clothes.

TURNING HER CAR into the long drive leading to the main house of Montserrat Farms, Julia tried to steel herself to face what awaited her. It would either be nothing or...the impossible. The main house was awash in lights outlining the enclosed porch and eaves. Torches on either side of the walkway and gardens lit her way. Subtle, but elegant Christmas decorations adorned the porch. The front door was open and Julia sucked in a deep breath of fresh cool air before she entered the house. She was greeted immediately by a young woman who offered to take her coat.

She proceeded into the main room which was open and furnished with comfortable looking settees and wing-back chairs. The corner to her right was filled by a beautifully understated Christmas tree that nearly touched the top of the vaulted ceiling. An elegant chandelier brightly lit the entire room. Against the far wall a buffet table was manned by two young men in uncomfortable looking starched white jackets. She scanned the room as she accepted a glass of wine from a passing waiter. She closed her eyes as she savored the first taste of an excellent full-bodied burgundy.

Choosing a place near the back of the tree, Julia looked carefully around the small groups of men and women chatting amongst themselves while enjoying their hostess's food and wine. Eventually a man stepped away from a group near the far corner of the room to retrieve wine refills. Then Julia saw her and shrank farther behind the tree. She couldn't take her eyes off the woman. She was dressed in a well-pressed white evening shirt tucked into form fitting black pants which, in turn, were tucked into the tops of the dark brown riding boots she wore during her exhibition. She was breathtakingly handsome. Her arm hung loosely around the shoulders of a young man who appeared to be in his early teens. Curly black hair coiled around his young caramel-colored face. Oh, my God! Can this get any more bizarre than it already is? Julia thought, closing her eyes. She worked to control her rapid breathing and the urge to flee grew overpowering. When she opened her eyes, looking for a quick escape route, they were met by a pair of piercing golden eyes traveling down her body and back to her face again, a slow, crooked smile moving across the woman's lips.

The woman bent slightly and said something to the boy and then bowed to the people surrounding her. Stepping away from the group, she began making her way, panther-like, across the room toward Julia. She needed to flee before the woman reached her and looked quickly to her left and right for an exit. Julia set her wine glass on a small table and darted into a hallway leading from the main room. Glancing over her shoulder she hoped the hallway would lead to the front entryway so she could make her escape. Discovering no exit she stopped in front of a closed door, turned the knob, and stepped quickly inside, closing the door as quietly as possible. She pressed her body against the wall next to the door and held her breath.

The room was dark except for a single small light. It took her eyes a moment to adjust to the dim lighting. She blinked several times before glancing around the room for a better place to hide. The room was filled with floor-to-ceiling bookcases on three walls. Portraits in ornate frames filled the majority of the remaining wall space. Across the room she saw a large desk and ran to it, kneeling to hide beneath it. She glanced up to check the door and stopped. The light which partially illuminated the room came from a small spotlight suspended from the ceiling a foot from a large, almost life-sized portrait.

Julia stood and stared at the picture. A moment later she walked slowly around the desk and drew closer to the portrait hanging in front of her. She knew her mouth must have been hanging open in disbelief, but she couldn't drag her eyes away from the stunning picture. Her hand went to her mouth, her eyes burning as they fought back unwanted tears. She stared at the uncanny likeness of herself hanging before her. Her hair was short and reddish-blonde. She wore a floor-length maroon velvet gown with crème inserts down the full-length sleeves. A six-inch strip of intricate black, gold and cream embroidery ran around the bottom of the gown near the hem. A matching crème shawl was draped over her arms and hung loosely down her back. Her hand rested lightly on what appeared to be the banister of a staircase while a coquettish smile played along her lips.

"She is beautiful, isn't she?" an accented voice asked from just inside the door to the room. Flipping on the light switch, the woman looked at Julia.

Turning toward her hostess she demanded, "Is this some kind of sick joke? Where did you get this portrait?"

"I can assure you it is no joke," the woman answered solemnly. She walked closer to the picture and gazed up at it. "This portrait hung in the main room of this house for more years than anyone can remember. I have looked at this woman's face since I was a small child." Her voice dropped to a low, husky semi-whisper as she continued to look at the portrait. "She is so incredibly beautiful. I fell in love with her image and dreamed of meeting her one day." Dropping her eyes to Julia's, she added, "Now at last I have."

"That's not me!" Julia insisted. *It is me! But there is no way anyone could know that!*

"Do you...do you know who she is?"

"No one knows with any certainty. The portrait was commissioned by a distant relative of mine and is based on her sketches and memory. We believe she hired a local artist to create it."

"What sketches?"

The woman smiled. "I seem to be getting ahead of myself. If you would be so gracious as to follow me to my office we could continue this discussion, *Mademoiselle* Blanchard," she said in an all too familiar accented voice.

"Please...please don't call me that," Julia said.

"My apologies."

"Don't say that either," Julia said more forcefully than she intended.

Clearing her throat, the woman looked down, but continued to smile. Finally she stepped back to the door and opened it. "Allow me to introduce myself. I am Simone Dhuperior, the owner of Montserrat Farms."

Julia turned reluctantly away from the portrait and followed Simone into the hallway, no longer intent on fleeing. She felt Simone's hand against the small of her back and let her hostess guide her back into the main room.

Catching the attention of the boy she had been with earlier, she motioned for him to join her. He smiled as he crossed the room and stood next to Simone. She looked at him affectionately and said, "Dr. Blanchard, this is my stepson, Robert." The French pronunciation. How appropriate, Julia thought. As they shook hands, Simone said, "Robert, would you please go to my room and bring my great aunt's journal to my office?"

"Of course, Simone. If you will excuse me, Dr. Blanchard," Robert bowed as he turned to leave.

"He's a very handsome young man," Julia commented.

"Thank you. He is my partner's son. She passed away a few years ago and left me as his guardian. He has been a handful from time to time," Simone chuckled.

She took Julia by the elbow and led her down a hallway toward another room. Opening the door for her, Simone stepped inside behind her and closed the door. Looking intently at Julia, she asked, "Do you believe in reincarnation, Dr. Blanchard?"

"No."

"Nor do I, but I am certain you are the woman in that portrait who has been haunting my dreams for as long as I can remember." Turning away from Julia and leaning against the edge of her desk, Simone shook her head and said, "I will tell you what I know, but you must agree to hear me out."

Julia glanced around the handsomely decorated office. The walls were lined with trophies and framed awards, all speaking of the obvious successes of Montserrat Farms over the years. Behind the polished walnut desk, Julia saw a glass case holding a single pewter statue. She could barely breathe as she looked at the small statue of the horse, its front legs pawing at the air as it stood on its hind legs.

"Where did you get that statue?" Julia asked in a whisper.

"It has been in my family for generations. If you will have a seat, Dr. Blanchard, I will explain in a moment."

As Simone Dhuperior paused and looked at her, Julia nodded. She leaned back into a maroon velvet-covered wingback chair; Simone sat behind her desk. "The story is this, Dr. Blanchard. Montserrat Farms was established around 1816 by a distant relative, a great-great-great aunt named Simone Moreau. It was rumored she may have been a pirate at one time. Probably nothing more than the ramblings of an old woman nearing the end of her life and then passed down as if a legend. However she arrived here, she founded this farm to breed and train Arabian horses. She never married and, in fact, is buried in the family cemetery on this farm. She is the distant relative who commissioned the portrait of you." Simone held up a hand as Julia opened her mouth to protest. "Or a woman who looks remarkably like you."

Clearing, her throat and staring intently at Julia, Simone continued in a softer voice. "I do not know very much about the woman, but she left behind a journal and that small statue. Over the years, some parts of her journal have been lost or damaged. They lend some credence to the idea she was a pirate. All I know for certain from the journal is that she loved but one person more deeply than anything I could ever imagine. Another woman, whose name was Julia. She never wrote her lover's last name in the journal. The last portion of the journal is a heartbreaking account of losing her lover at sea. Her grief is overwhelming. I would have thought nothing more of what was written in the journal, but your disappearance and survival at sea was covered in depth by the local newspapers. A picture of you accompanied the stories. Quite by accident I also read the articles about the shipwreck you were excavating. When I saw your picture I knew I had to meet and speak with you. *You* excavated the shipwreck, *your* name is Julia, the woman in the portrait could be *you* now. I thought I must surely be imagining it all, but the idea that these things are coincidences or random chance does not sit well with me."

The two women sat in silence for the next several minutes, looking at one another until a knock sounded at the office door. The door cracked open and Robert pushed it open and walked to Simone's desk. "Thank you, Robert," Simone said as she took a small package wrapped in brown, waxed wrapping paper and tied with twine.

"May I see the journal?" Julia asked quietly as Simone carefully unwrapped it.

"Of course," Simone said, rising and carrying it to Julia, who took it gently and ran her fingertips over the worn black cover. Simone waited as Julia went through the pages, scanning each one and periodically smiling as she read.

Tears filled Julia's eyes when she saw the numerous sketches within the pages. *When had Simone drawn them?* she wondered. *Perhaps that's what she was doing when I caught her looking at me.* Julia smiled as she finished the last page and carefully closed the journal, holding it against her chest. Finally looking into Simone's questioning eyes, she spoke softly. "You could be her twin. You look and sound exactly as she did, except with slightly less accent. You have the same mannerisms, same build and height. You're identical to her in virtually every way.

"When I first met her she had an octoroon lover named Esperanza Batista, whose son looked remarkably like Robert. Esperanza was killed in New Orleans in late December of 1814, but I don't know what happened to her son, Joaquin." Pausing to take a shaky breath, Julia stroked the cover of the journal before she went on. "She wrote in this journal every night before going to bed, recording everything to pass the time. Her ship was named *Le Faucon de Mer* and she was not a pirate." She stopped as her voice cracked. Regaining control, she lifted her chin defiantly and said, "She was a privateer and it would be an insult to call her anything else. She was the gentlest, most honorable woman I've ever known."

"And you loved her?" Simone asked, her voice soft.

"More than my own life," Julia answered as a tear escaped and traveled down her cheek. "I was with her in New Orleans in the winter of 1814. I gave her that statue as a Christmas present moments before we were parted. I was later told she was killed in the battle against the British, but refused to leave the city until I saw her body. Of course, as we now know, she was not killed. We left New Orleans a week later sailing back to her home on Martinique."

"And you were lost during that final voyage?"

"During a storm I was swept overboard. When I awakened I was here once again. I thought it was only a hallucination by a dying woman, even though it seemed so real. Sometimes now in my sleep I still see her and feel her touch."

"And the ship you excavated is *Le Faucon de Mer*?"

"It is, but I've found no proof she existed that wouldn't make me look like a lunatic within the scientific community. I had no idea she brought her ship here. We were planning to live together on Martinique. She knew I was from the Savannah area and I suppose it's possible she came here for some reason I can't imagine."

"Perhaps to be closer to you by living where you lived," Simone offered.

"I can only suggest that she sailed to Martinique, transported her horses here and then scuttled her ship before coming ashore, using the old lighthouse on Tybee Island to guide her." Julia leaned her head back on the chair and closed her eyes, letting memories flood through her mind. "Maybe I *am* crazy, but she was real to me."

"She thought she would see you again, in the future," Simone said in a barely audible voice.

"What did you say?"

"Did you tell her you were from the future?"

"I...I tried to, but I don't think she really believed me."

"She believed you," Simone's voice whispered in Julia's ear, sending a shiver down her spine. She opened her eyes and looked into the same eyes that still haunted her. "Come with me, Julia." Taking

Simone's hand, Julia stood and followed her. The night air carried a chill as Simone took a lantern and walked behind the main house and up a small rise. When they reached a large fenced area, Simone held the gate for Julia and led the way until they stopped in front of a weathered headstone. Holding the lantern close to the stone, Julia read the inscription.

Simone Moreau

1782-1847

Je vous attendrai, ma bien-aimée.

"She left instructions in her will to have this carved onto her tombstone," Simone said. "Her brother saw that it was done and apparently never questioned it. I assume he knew of the relationship between you and Simone."

"Yes. Anton knew."

Looking at the inscription, Simone read, "I shall wait for you, my beloved." The sound of her voice sent chills through Julia's body. Stepping back and turning to face her, Simone said, "She waited for you as long as she could. She waited a lifetime."

Spinning away and covering her eyes, Julia sobbed for her loss. She felt strong arms wrap around her from behind and sank into their warmth and comfort. "What am I going to do? I don't think I can live without feeling you beside me."

"I shall hold you in my heart always, *mon amour*" a soft French-accented voice whispered on a light breeze and Julia knew instantly who was speaking.

"And I shall hold you in mine, my love" Julia whispered in return. Moving within the circle of the arms holding her, she looked at the beautiful smiling face she loved so much and drew Simone into a breathless kiss to welcome her home again. She felt soft lips respond to hers, deepening the desire inside her, and didn't want to think about the past or the future, only what existed at that moment as she kissed her lover once again across time.

As Simone brought their kiss to a reluctant end, she held Julia close. Her voice filled with emotion as she tried to make sense of what was happening. "I won't try to explain what I have felt from the moment I saw your picture, but I should like to learn more about you and your dreams, if you would allow it."

Smiling up at Simone, Julia said, "I think I would like that. I would like that very much."

Wrapping an arm securely around Julia, Simone took her hand, turned it over and kissed her palm as they turned to walk away from the cemetery.

More Brenda Adcock titles:

Pipeline

What do you do when the mistakes you made in the past come back to slap you in the face with a vengeance? Joanna Carlisle, a fifty-seven year old photojournalist, has only begun to adjust to retirement on her small ranch outside Kerrville, Texas, when she finds herself unwillingly sucked into an investigation of illegal aliens being smuggled into the United States to fill the ranks of cheap labor needed to increase corporate profits.

Joanna is a woman who has always lived life her way and on her own terms, enjoying a career that had given her everything she thought she ever wanted or needed. An unexpected visit by her former lover, Cate Hammond, and the attempted murder of their son, forces Jo to finally face what she had given up. Although she hasn't seen Cate or their son for fifteen years, she finds that the feelings she had for Cate had only been dormant, but had never died. No matter how much she fights her attraction to Cate, Jo cannot help but wonder whether she had made the right decision when she chose career and independence over love.

Jo comes to understand the true meaning of friendship and love only when her investigation endangers not only her life, but also the lives of the people around her.

ISBN 1-932300-64-3
978-1-932300-64-2

Reiko's Garden

Hatred...like love...knows no boundaries.

How much impact can one person have on a life?

When sixty-five-year old Callie Owen returns to her rural childhood home in Eastern Tennessee to attend the funeral of a woman she hasn't seen in twenty years, she's forced to face the fears, heartache, and turbulent events that scarred both her body and her mind. Drawing strength from Jean, her partner of thirty years, and from their two grown children, Callie stays in the valley longer than she had anticipated and relives the years that changed her life forever.

In 1949, Japanese war bride Reiko Sanders came to Frost Valley, Tennessee with her soldier husband and infant son. Callie Owen was an inquisitive ten-year-old whose curiosity about the stranger drove her to disobey her father for just one peek at the woman who had become the subject of so much speculation. Despite Callie's fears, she soon finds that the exotic-looking woman is kind and caring, and the two forge a tentative, but secret friendship.

When Callie and her five brothers and sisters were left orphaned, Reiko provided emotional support to Callie. The bond between them continued to grow stronger until Callie left Frost Valley as a teenager, emotionally and physically scarred, vowing never to return and never to forgive.

It's not until Callie goes "home" that she allows herself to remember how Reiko influenced her life. Once and for all, can she face the terrible events of her past? Or will they come back to destroy all that she loves?

ISBN 978-1-932300-77-2
1-932300-77-5

Redress of Grievances

In the first of a series of psychological thrillers, Harriett Markham is a defense attorney in Austin, Texas, who lost everything eleven years earlier. She had been an associate with a Dallas firm and involved in an affair with a senior partner, Alexis Dunne. Harriett represented a rape/murder client named Jared Wilkes and got the charges dismissed on a technicality. When Wilkes committed a rape and murder after his release, Harriett was devastated. She resigned and moved to Austin, leaving everything behind, including her lover.

Despite lingering feelings for Alexis, Harriet becomes involved with a sex-offense investigator, Jessie Rains, a woman struggling with secrets of her own. Harriet thinks she might finally be happy, but then Alexis re-enters her life. She refers a case of multiple homicide allegedly committed by Sharon Taggart, a woman with no motive for the crimes. Harriett is creeped out by the brutal murders, but reluctantly agrees to handle the defense.

As Harriett's team prepares for trial, disturbing information comes to light. Sharon denies any involvement in the crimes, but the evidence against her seems overwhelming. Harriett is plunged into a case rife with twisty psychological motives, questionable sanity, and a client with a complex and disturbing life. Is she guilty or not? And will Harriet's legal defense bring about justice — or another Wilkes case?

ISBN 978-1-932300-86-4
1-932300-86-4

Tunnel Vision

Royce Brodie, a 50-year-old homicide detective in the quiet town of Cedar Springs, a bedroom community 30 miles from Austin, Texas, has spent the last seven years coming to grips with the incident that took the life of her partner and narrowly missed taking her own. The peace and quiet she had been enjoying is shattered by two seemingly unrelated murders in the same week: the first, a John Doe, and the second, a janitor at the local university.

As Brodie and her partner, Curtis Nicholls, begin their investigation, the assignment of a new trainee disrupts Brodie's life. Not only is Maggie Weston Brodie's former lover, but her father had been Brodie's commander at the Austin Police Department and nearly destroyed her career.

As the three detectives try to piece together the scattered evidence to solve the two murders, they become convinced the two murders are related. The discovery of a similar murder committed five years earlier at a small university in upstate New York creates a sense of urgency as they realize they are chasing a serial killer.

The already difficult case becomes even more so when a third victim is found. But the case becomes personal for Brodie when Maggie becomes the killer's next target. Unless Brodie finds a way to save Maggie, she could face losing everything a second time.

Coming in July 2009.

Another Yellow Rose title you might enjoy:

Love's Redemption
by Helen Macpherson

Ten years ago talented Lauren Wheatley was on the verge of golf-ing greatness. As the world's number one amateur, she stood on the cusp of entry to the women's professional tour. However in a quirk of fate, she imploded in spectacular fashion, during a tournament that would have signaled her immediate entry into the professional ranks. She walked away and never played golf again.

Jo Ashby is a reporter narrating and producing the "Where Are They Now?" series, a program focusing on well-known people who have left fame behind, instead opting for a different direction in life. Her subject for the final program is the enigmatic Lauren Wheatley who, despite Jo's best efforts, evades her attempts at an interview.

Jo travels to the pristine wilderness of Tasmania to confront Lau-ren. However, instead of confrontation, she is captured by the beauty of the surrounding land and the woman herself. Coupled with this beauty lies a greater story behind the fragile facade of Lauren's life.Can Jo break through the barriers Lauren has shielded herself with, and con-quer the riddle that is Lauren Wheatley? Can Jo reconcile her profes-sional requirements, yet face her own demons and, once and for all, put them to rest?

Set against the backdrop of the Tasmanian wilderness, *Love's Redemption* follows the rocky lives of two headstrong women, affirming that sometimes the phrase "and they lived happily ever after" is often more fairytale than fact.

ISBN 978-1-935053-04-0
1-935053-04-3

OTHER YELLOW ROSE PUBLICATIONS

Sandra Barret	Lavender Secrets	978-1-932300-73-4
Georgia Beers	Thy Neighbor's Wife	1-932300-15-5
Georgia Beers	Turning the Page	978-1-932300-71-0
Carrie Carr	Destiny's Bridge	1-932300-11-2
Carrie Carr	Faith's Crossing	1-932300-12-0
Carrie Carr	Hope's Path	1-932300-40-6
Carrie Carr	Love's Journey	978-1-932300-65-9
Carrie Carr	Strength of the Heart	978-1-932300-81-9
Carrie Carr	The Way Things Should Be	978-1-932300-39-0
Carrie Carr	To Hold Forever	978-1-932300-21-5
Carrie Carr	Something to Be Thankful For	1-932300-04-X
Carrie Carr	Diving Into the Turn	978-1-932300-54-3
Jennifer Fulton	Passion Bay	1-932300-25-2
Jennifer Fulton	Saving Grace	1-932300-26-0
Jennifer Fulton	The Sacred Shore	1-932300-35-X
Jennifer Fulton	A Guarded Heart	1-932300-37-6
Anna Furtado	The Heart's Desire	1-932300-32-5
Anna Furtado	The Heart's Strength	978-1-932300-93-2
Melissa Good	Eye of the Storm	1-932300-13-9
Melissa Good	Hurricane Watch	978-1-935053-00-2
Melissa Good	Red Sky At Morning	978-1-932300-80-2
Melissa Good	Thicker Than Water	1-932300-24-4
Melissa Good	Terrors of the High Seas	1-932300-45-7
Melissa Good	Tropical Storm	978-1-932300-60-4
Lori L. Lake	Different Dress	1-932300-08-2
Lori L. Lake	Ricochet In Time	1-932300-17-1
K. E. Lane	And, Playing the Role of Herself	978-1-932300-72-7
Helen Macpherson	Love's Redemption	978-1-935053-04-0
J. Y Morgan	Learning To Trust	978-1-932300-59-8
J. Y. Morgan	Download	978-1-932300-88-8
A. K. Naten	Turning Tides	978-1-932300-47-5
Lynne Norris	One Promise	978-1-932300-92-5
Paula Offutt	Butch Girls Can Fix Anything	978-1-932300-74-1
Surtees and Dunne	True Colours	978-1-932300-52-9
Surtees and Dunne	Many Roads to Travel	978-1-932300-55-0
Vicki Stevenson	Family Affairs	978-1-932300-97-0
Vicki Stevenson	Family Values	978-1-932300-89-5
Vicki Stevenson	Family Ties	978-1-935053-03-3
Vicki Stevenson	Certain Personal Matters	978-1-935053-06-4
Cate Swannell	Heart's Passage	1-932300-09-0
Cate Swannell	No Ocean Deep	1-932300-36-8

About the Author

Originally from the Appalachian region of Eastern Tennessee, Brenda now lives in Central Texas, near Austin. She began writing in junior high school where she wrote an admittedly hokey western serial to entertain her friends. Completing her graduate studies in Eastern European history in 1971, she worked as a graphic artist, a public relations specialist for the military and a display advertising specialist until she finally had to admit that her mother might have been right and earned her teaching certification. For the last twenty-three years she has taught world history and political science. Brenda and her partner of ten years, Cheryl, are the parents of four grown children, as well as two grandchildren and one on the way. Rounding out their home are three laid-back cats, an occasionally conscious Bassett Hound and a hyperactive poodle-mix. When she is not writing Brenda creates stained glass and shoots pool at her favorite bar. She may be contacted at adcockb10@yahoo.com and welcomes all comments.

VISIT US ONLINE AT

www.regalcrest.biz

At the Regal Crest Website You'll Find

- The latest news about forthcoming titles and new releases

- Our complete backlist of romance, mystery, thriller and adventure titles

- Information about your favorite authors

- Current bestsellers

Regal Crest titles are available from all progressive booksellers and online at StarCrossed Productions, (www.scp-inc.biz), Bella Distribution and many others.

LaVergne, TN USA
14 May 2010
182743LV00004B/91/P